PROLOGUE

Paisley

"Y ou're hurting me, Connor." I whimper as his hand grips my upper arm.

He snarls, his mouth dropping to my ear. "How hard is it to have dinner on the table when I get home from work? The game is on tonight, and I don't want to be eating while I'm watching it."

"I'm s-s-sorry," I stutter. "I got delayed at work."

He pushes me roughly across the kitchen, my side hitting the countertop, and I know instantly I've said the wrong thing. He hates me working. It had taken me weeks to convince him to let me take on a couple of shifts at the coffee shop in town. I'd assured him I could work and keep on top of the chores, especially the cooking, but the coffee machine at work had broken just as I was due to leave, and my boss asked me to stay while he tried to fix it. I thought I could stay and still get home in time to heat up the pasta dish I'd made this morning. I underestimated how long it would take to heat through though, and when I heard the front door open, I knew I was in trouble. I rub my hands over my pounding hip. That'll be another bruise to add to the long list. It'll be hidden though, like they usually are.

"You can tell that asshole at the coffee shop you won't be coming back. How are you going to care for our children as well as me if you're out working all the time?"

I bristle at his words. There is no way I *ever* want children with him. If he treats me this way, I can't even imagine how he'd treat a screaming baby.

"I'll tell him," I lie, saying anything to get him to calm down. I turn my back on him and open the oven, checking on the pasta bake.

I hold my breath as I wait for him to say something. When I'm met with silence, I turn back around to find myself alone in the kitchen. I know he'll be back though, and I try to ignore the pain in my hip as I busy myself getting dinner ready to serve.

My life hasn't always been like this. Connor never used to treat me like shit. We used to be happy. Well, happier than now. It all changed the day his brother died. He was so lost after that, and when he finally came back to me, he wasn't the man he used to be. I begged him to talk to someone, but he refused, instead taking his anger and frustration out on me. I've wanted to leave him for a while, but other than a few hours a week at the coffee shop, I never go out. Connor sees to that. I've got one friend, Taylor. She's never given up on me, even though I hardly see her anymore. I'm pulled from my thoughts as he stalks back into the kitchen.

"Is it still not ready?" he shouts, making me jump.

"Yes... yes, it's ready," I say meekly, my eyes going anywhere but on him. "Sit down and I'll bring it through."

I can feel him staring at me, but I still don't meet his gaze. When he finally turns and heads for the dining table, I breathe a sigh of relief. Picking up the salad, I carry the bowl through the kitchen into the open-plan dining area and place it on the table. I do the same with the pasta bake, the plates already on the table. I'm just about to sit down when he speaks.

"I think you've forgotten something." His voice is low and tinged with annoyance. I quickly look around the table, wondering what I've missed. He pounds his hand on the wood and I let out a squeal. "My beer, Paisley!" He spits my name, and I scurry into the kitchen and open the refrigerator. I was hoping he wouldn't want a drink with dinner. Drinking always makes him meaner than normal. Still, I wouldn't dare say no to him.

We eat in silence, and I'm glad there's a football game on later. I'll be able to stay out of his way and read my Kindle in bed. When he's finished, he gets up from the table with his beer in his hand and goes straight into the living room, leaving me to clear away the dinner dishes. I do so quickly so I can have a bath and get away from him. I'm just loading the last of the dishes into the dishwasher when he shouts from the living room.

"Bring me another Bud!" My blood runs cold as I realize the bottle I gave him with dinner was the last one. I meant to pick some more up after work, but because I stayed late, it slipped my mind.

"I... I just need to go to the grocery store. We've run out," I shout, quickly making my way into the entryway and picking up the keys to his car.

3

"You stupid bitch!" he snarls, meeting me in the entryway and snatching the car keys from my hand. "Why didn't you get them earlier? The game's about to start."

I try to wriggle out of his hold, stilling when my movements seem to annoy him even more. He clenches his jaw, and when I look up and into his eyes, they're dark with anger and not at all the eyes of the man I fell in love with five years ago.

"Answer me!" he booms.

"I… I… I forgot," I say feebly.

"I'll make sure you don't *forget* again," he mumbles before he draws back his arm and punches me in the face. Pain explodes in my cheek and my head hits the wall behind me. Losing my balance, the arm he isn't gripping on to hits the doorframe as I stumble sideways. I fall to the floor and hug my pounding wrist to my chest. Before I can pull my knees into my body to make myself as small as possible, his boot-clad foot swings forward, and I let out a groan as it impacts my stomach. My whole body is crying out in pain, and when his foot connects with my head, black dots dance in my vision and I know I'm going to pass out. Before the darkness takes me, it occurs to me I might not wake up from this beating. I really think he's going to kill me.

CHAPTER ONE

Paisley
Twelve hours later

S omehow, I'm still alive. I'm not sure how. Connor had left me for dead in the entryway and gone back to watching the game. It had fallen dark outside when I'd woken up, and the whole house was silent. The bastard had gone to bed, likely stepping over me to get to the stairs. I'd dragged my tired and broken body up the stairs and into the guest bedroom, not wanting to be anywhere near him. I'd barely slept, terrified Connor would come in and finish what he'd started. He didn't though, and relief flooded my body as I heard the front door open and close ten minutes ago, signaling he'd left for work.

I knew I'd been lucky last night. I'm confident if the football game hadn't been on to distract him, he would have killed me. There's no doubt in my mind it's only a matter of time until he does. Over the last twelve months, the abuse has gotten steadily worse. It started verbally, but soon turned physical. Small things to start with. The odd push, or gripping my arm too tightly. The first time he hit me, he'd been so apologetic, to the point where he'd been in tears. I forgave him. I knew how devastated he was after his brother died, but soon, he was hitting me regularly, and the apologies and tears stopped. I should have left then, but naively, I thought once he was past his grief, he'd be back to the Connor I used to know. The Connor I used to love. Last night's beating had been the worst yet, and I know I have to leave before it's too late.

I stand gingerly from the bed and wince as my ribs cry out in pain. I'm sure I've broken a couple, along with my wrist, which I'm holding awkwardly against me. As I cross the room, I catch my reflection in the vanity mirror. My face is red and swollen where he punched me, and I can't be sure he hasn't broken my cheekbone. I look a mess. I'm still wearing yesterday's clothes, which are crumpled from lying in bed in them, but with my wrist and rib pain, I can't face getting changed.

I brush my teeth as best I can with one hand and grab a few toiletries from the bathroom. Making my way back to the guest room, I reach under the bed for a bag. Inside is a mobile phone Connor knows nothing about. He took my phone from me about twelve months ago, and Taylor had gotten me this one. The contract's in her name and she pays the bill. It's the only way we can stay in touch. I keep it hidden and turned off. I know Connor has no idea about it; he'd have taken it from me if he did.

Pulling up Taylor's number, I hold the phone to my ear as it rings.

"Hey, Paisley," she says when she answers. Hearing her voice makes me break down, and I let out a sob.

Taylor knows Connor and I are having problems, and she knows he's hit me in the past, although I haven't confided in her about how bad it's gotten. She's asked me more than once to leave him, but I've always said no. I don't know why I've never opened up fully to her. Maybe it's because I don't want to admit to myself how bad it is, let alone anyone else. I can't keep it from her any longer though. I need her.

"Are you crying? What's wrong?" I can hear the concern in her voice, and that just makes me love her even more.

"Can you come over?" I ask through my tears. "I need your help."

"Of course I can. Is everything okay?"

"Not really. I'll explain when you get here."

"Okay."

"Taylor," I cry before she ends the call.

"I'm still here, Paisley."

"Can you bring my driver's license?"

"Sure."

"Thanks. See you soon."

I end the call and sit down heavily on the end of the bed. I'd asked Taylor to keep my license a few months ago. Connor had already taken my passport, and I knew my license would be next. I rarely drive anyway, he won't let me, but I knew I might need it if I ever did pluck up the courage to leave him. I told him I'd lost it. I endured a beating that night for being careless, but it was worth it to know I had options if I ever needed to leave.

While I wait for Taylor to arrive, I toss some clothes into a bag. It's not easy with one hand, and I have to keep stopping when the pain becomes unbearable. I've just swallowed down two Tylenol when there's a knock on the door. My heart pounds in my chest, despite knowing it's Taylor. It's not like Connor is going to knock on his own front door.

I make my way downstairs as quickly as I can, wincing with each step as pain shoots through my ribs. Using the peep-hole, I breathe a sigh of relief to see Taylor. Opening the door, she gasps when she sees me.

"Oh my God, Paisley. What the fuck happened?" I reach for her with my good hand and tug her inside, closing the door behind her. "Did Connor…" She trails off, her eyes sweeping all over me. "Did Connor do that?" Her voice is barely a whisper, and I nod. Tears streak down her cheeks, and she pulls me into her arms. I squeal as my wrists gets squashed against her. "Shit! I'm sorry."

"It's okay," I assure her as she drops her arms from around me.

"It's not okay, Paisley. It's not okay at all." She takes my hand and guides me into the living room. "Why didn't you tell me how bad thing had gotten?"

I shrug. "I guess I was ashamed I let him do this to me."

"This isn't your fault. You didn't *let* him."

"It is," I whisper. "I forgot to buy his beer."

"Paisley, your husband shouldn't beat you for *any* reason." She holds her hand out. "Let me see your wrist." I hold it out to her, gasping as she takes it gently in her hand. "I think your wrist might be broken."

"Yeah, I think so too. I think I might have a couple of cracked ribs as well."

"We need to get you to the emergency room."

"No!" She raises her eyebrows at my outburst. "I can't, Taylor. I just need to go."

"Go where?" she asks with a frown.

"Anywhere. He almost killed me last night. I have to get away from him."

"We can go to the police. You can move in with me. You don't have to leave." Her voice sounds desperate, but I can't stay. He isn't just going to let me walk away from him. I have to go somewhere he'll never find me.

"If I stay, I'm never going to be free of him. I want to start over somewhere. I need you to help me, Taylor."

She holds my stare and slowly nods her head.

"I will always help you, Paisley. What do you need?"

"Can you drive me to the airport?"

"That's why you wanted your license?" I nod. "Where are you going?"

I stand up and beckon for her to follow me upstairs. When we reach the guest bedroom, I drop to the floor and pull out the same bag where the phone was hidden. Reaching inside, I take out a wad of cash. "As far away as I can get with this."

Her eyes widen as she looks at the cash in my hand. "How much do you have?"

"About five hundred dollars. That should be enough to get me far away from here."

"And what about when you get wherever you're going? Where will you live? What will you do for money?"

"I'll figure it out. I'll get a job."

"With a broken wrist?"

I close my eyes and drop my head. "I don't have all the answers, Taylor, but I have to do this."

She sighs. "Okay. I have some money I can give you. It's not much, but it should help a bit."

"I don't want your money, Tay."

"I know, but you need it."

"Thank you. I love you."

"I love you too."

"He's going to come to you when he knows I'm gone," I say quietly. "I'm sorry I'm dragging you into this."

She waves off my concern. "He doesn't scare me. I'll tell him exactly what I think of him if he shows up at my place!"

"Taylor, no. He's dangerous!"

"I know, I know," she assures me, as she takes the hand of my non-injured arm and squeezes it gently. "Are you ready to go?"

"Yes, I think so."

Her eyes drop to my arm. "Let me make you a sling for your wrist. Do you promise me you'll get it looked at wherever you end up?"

"I will, I promise."

"Do you have a pillowcase?"

"In the bottom drawer," I tell her, gesturing to the dresser on the back wall. I watch as she pulls one out and tears the material. Coming to stand in front of me, she fixes it so my arm is held and ties it around my neck. "Thank you. That feels so much better."

"Let me do your hair." She picks my hairbrush out of my bag and gently brushes my long dark hair, braiding it down my back. "Ready?"

Taking a deep breath, I nod. She gives me a sad smile as she puts my hairbrush back in my bag and closes it before we head downstairs. I let her lead me outside to her car, and she opens the passenger side door, tossing my bag onto the back seat. I climb in gingerly, wincing as I sit down.

"You okay?"

"Yeah, just a little sore."

"God, I want to kill him, Paisley. He shouldn't be allowed to get away with this."

She closes the car door and jogs around the hood. "I know, but I don't have the energy to fight him, Tay," I say as she gets into the driver's seat. "I'm exhausted with it all. It's taking everything I have to leave him."

She takes my hand again and squeezes encouragingly. "Let's get you out of here. You'll let me know where you end up, won't you?"

"Of course I will. I'm hoping you'll come and visit me when I've settled somewhere."

"I definitely will. If my mom didn't need me, I'd come with you now. I'm going to miss you, Paisley."

"I'll miss you too."

Taylor's mom suffers from dementia, and although she lives in a care home since it became too hard for Taylor to look after her, I know she would never leave her.

It's about a thirty-minute drive to Pittsburgh International Airport, and I'm nervous the whole way. I half expect Connor to pull up alongside us and force Taylor to stop the car. My eyes flick to passing cars as we drive, praying I don't see his truck. I don't, of course. He'll be at his construction job, like he always is. Just before we get there, Taylor stops at a gas station to use the ATM. She's gone for a few minutes, and when she returns, she pushes a wad of cash into my hand, along with my license.

"I'm sorry it's not more."

Tears fill my eyes, and I turn to her. "Thank you, Tay. I don't know what I'm going to do without you."

"I'll come and see you as soon as you're settled. I promise."

All too soon, we reach the airport, and the nerves begin to swarm. I can't believe I'm actually doing this, but I know I can't stay. It's time for a fresh start. I'm not even sure Connor will care that I've left. He doesn't love me. I guess it'll be his ego that hurts the most about me leaving him. It definitely won't be his heart.

After a tearful goodbye with Taylor, I take one last look over my shoulder at her and she gives me a small wave. I know I'm making the right decision in leaving, but it doesn't make it any easier. I hope this isn't the last time I see her.

CHAPTER TWO

Paisley

The airport isn't as busy as I thought it would be, and I'm grateful there isn't a line at the ticket desk. My whole body aches after the car journey, and the pain in my wrist is making me dizzy and nauseous. I approach the desk and the middle-aged woman sitting across from me gives me a sympathetic smile as she takes in my battered appearance.

"Are you okay?" she asks, her eyes dropping from my swollen face to my arm in the sling. "Do you need me to call the EMTs?"

I shake my head. "No. No, thank you. I need to book a ticket," I say quietly.

She holds my gaze before nodding. "Okay. Where would you like to go?"

With my good hand, I reach into my purse and pull out the

cash I'd taken from the box under the guest bed. Placing it on the desk, I push it across to her. "As far away as I can get with this. Inside the U.S. though. I only have my driver's license."

She sighs. "Sweetie, are you sure?" I nod, and she drops her eyes to the computer screen in front of her. "There's a flight leaving in an hour and a half to Phoenix, Arizona. There's one to L.A., but it doesn't leave for four hours."

"Phoenix sounds good." I hand over my license, and her fingers fly over the keyboard as she enters my details. I've never been to Arizona or L.A., but if the flight to Arizona leaves sooner, then that's the one I'm going to be on. I don't want to be hanging around the airport for longer than I need to be. "How much is the seat?"

The woman's eyes meet mine, and she gives me a small smile. "Nothing. I have some air miles, and you need them more than me."

My eyes widen in surprise. "Oh, no. I can't let you do that."

"You can, honey. I've been where you are. Let me do this for you. Please."

I burst into tears and she comes from around the desk and carefully puts her arm around me. "Thank you," I whimper as I sniff and wipe my eyes. She leans over the desk and picks up a box of tissues, holding them out to me. I take one and blow my nose.

"Promise me when you get to Phoenix, you'll get someone to check you over. You're banged up, and I'm betting that wrist is broken," she says, looking inside my sling.

"I will. I don't know how to thank you."

"I don't want thanks. I know it doesn't feel like it now, but you've done the hard part by leaving. No one deserves to be treated that way."

I give her a sad smile. "I was hoping I could say I'd fallen down the stairs."

"You probably could to someone who hasn't been through it. It gets better, I promise."

"I hope so," I whisper.

"When you're strong enough, you should call the cops on the asshole."

"I will," I lie. It's not that I don't want to go to the police. I just don't want to ever have to be near him again. She leans over the desk and passes me a printout with my flight details on it, as well as the cash I handed over to her.

"You can check in now. The desk is open."

"Thank you so much."

"Stay safe, Paisley."

As I walk toward the check-in desk, I'm overwhelmed by a total stranger's kindness. I only hope one day I can pay forward her selfless act. After I've checked in and have my boarding pass, I make it through security and finally feel like I can breathe again. Even if by some stroke of bad luck Connor comes looking for me, I know he'll need a ticket to get into the departure lounge. I'll feel better when I'm on the plane, but it's a relief to be waiting to board.

An hour later, my flight is called. Realizing I haven't eaten today, I grab a sandwich and a Diet Coke to eat in the air and join the line to board. I keep my head down, not wanting to make eye contact with anyone. I don't want pity stares. Despite wanting to tell people I fell down the stairs if anyone asks, I'm not stupid. I know it looks like I've taken a beating. I manage to get on board without having to communicate with anyone other than the flight attendant. When I find my seat, there are already two men in the row, the window seat free. Checking my boarding pass, I realize the window seat is mine.

"Would you mind if I get to my seat?" I ask politely, and the older man on the end stands up.

"Not at all, sweetheart." He moves into the aisle and I bite down on my bottom lip as I see the guy sitting in the middle seat has headphones on and his eyes are closed.

"Excuse me," I say, my voice a little louder. When he still doesn't respond, I lean toward him and tap his arm. His eyes fly open, and I flinch at his movement, pulling my arm back sharply. "Sorry. Could I get to my seat?" His head turns to me, his eyes widening as his gaze falls on my red and swollen face.

"Sure. Sorry, I was miles away."

"That's okay," I say quietly. I step back as he moves into the aisle, and I slip past him, trying not to wince as I maneuver myself along the small space. Sitting in my seat, I place the bag with my sandwich and drink on the floor and attempt to fasten my seat belt.

"Fuck," I mutter after my fifth attempt at trying to fasten it with one hand fails.

"Do you need some help?" the guy to the left of me asks.

"I can't fasten my seat belt with one hand." My cheeks flood with heat and tears fall from my eyes. It's irrational to get upset over something so small, but after everything that's happened over the past twenty-four hours, it's just too much.

What the hell am I doing? How am I going to manage on my own in a new town with no one and no money? I can't even fasten my fucking seat belt.

"Don't cry. I'll help you." He reaches across and effortlessly clips together my seat belt. "Is that tight enough?"

I nod. "I'm sorry. Thank you. I didn't mean to get upset." He must think I'm crazy.

"It's okay. It looks like you've had a tough day."

I give him a sad smile before turning and looking out of

the window. As kind as he's being, I'm not up for small talk. It'll only lead to questions I likely won't want to answer.

I barely notice the plane taking off as I stare out of the window, lost in thought. As much as I hate to admit it, my parents had been right about Connor. They never liked him and thought he wasn't good enough for me, but I loved him and was eager to prove them wrong. So eager, I chose him over them. He assured me he would be all I'd ever need, and he encouraged me to break all contact with them. I've tried to reach out over the past twelve months, but they've never once responded to my letters. I guess I really have burned my bridges with them.

About an hour into the flight, the material supporting my arm begins to bite into my neck, and I slip my arm out of the sling, resting it across my stomach. As I do, my stomach lets out a loud rumble, and the guy in the seat next to me chuckles. I ignore him and bend down to reach for the paper bag with my sandwich inside. I gasp as pain pierces my side. I sit up and take deep breaths, willing the pain to subside and the nausea rolling through my stomach to pass.

"Are you okay?" the guy next to me asks.

I nod, still trying to catch my breath. When the pain ebbs away, I turn to him. "Would you be able to grab my sand-wich?" I gesture to the space under the seat in front of me. I hate having to ask for help, but I don't have much choice. His gaze drops from my eyes to my arm before he bends down and scoops up the bag. He lowers the tray table on the seat in front of me and removes the sandwich and drink, placing them on top.

"Thank you."

"Have you seen a doctor?" he asks, reaching for my bottle of Diet Coke and opening it for me.

I look at him in surprise. I can't help but wonder why a total stranger, despite him being helpful, is concerned about me. "Erm… no. Not yet."

"But you will?" I nod, but I know I probably won't. I don't have the money for hospital visits, and I can't use the insurance and risk Connor finding out where I am. "Look, this is probably me overstepping the line…" He pauses and drags his hand through his hair. "My brother's a doctor. I can ask him to look you over. I think your wrist is broken."

"But you don't know where I'm heading when we land," I say, taken aback by his offer.

"I'm guessing you don't know that either," he says quietly.

"What do you mean?"

"It just seems you were in a rush to leave Pittsburgh. If you weren't, you would have seen a doctor before boarding a six and a half hour flight to the other side of the country." His words are condescending, but his tone isn't.

I'm embarrassed he's calling me out. Despite bursting into tears when I couldn't fasten my seat belt, I thought I was putting on a brave face. Clearly not. Connor's worn me down so much over the past twelve months, I think last night he might finally have broken me, physically and emotionally. Nerves swirl in my stomach, and I don't know how to respond. Instead, I concentrate on the sandwich in front of me, my good hand picking at the cardboard that encases it.

"I'm Nash. Nash Brookes," he says when I stay silent. He holds his hand out, and I cautiously offer him my good one, and he gently shakes it.

"Paisley," I say, not wanting to give him my last name.

"Will you think about letting my brother check you over?"

I'm not sure how to tell him I can't afford to see a doctor, but I nod anyway, hoping by the end of the flight he'll have somehow forgotten.

"You live in Arizona?"

He nods. "In Hope Creek." He pauses to take a mouthful of water from the bottle in his hand. "It's a great town. If you're stuck for somewhere to go, you could do worse than end up there."

Hope Creek seems as good a place as any to head to. "How far from the airport is it?" I ask, knowing I have limited funds to keep me going until I can find some work.

"A couple of hours, but there's a shuttle. That takes a little longer."

I nod, but don't say anything, instead opening the sandwich on the tray table in front of me and taking a bite. It's the first thing I've eaten since dinner last night and I'm starving.

"If you do come to Hope Creek, there's a women's shelter I can get you into." He gives me a sad smile, and my eyes widen.

"I don't need a women's shelter."

"I'm a cop, Paisley. I can recognize when someone's a victim of domestic abuse."

Fear creeps up my spine. A cop? Out of all the seats on the plane, why did I have to sit next to a cop? There's no way I can go to Hope Creek now. I don't want him making it his mission to rescue me.

CHAPTER THREE

Nash

I hadn't planned to involve myself in Paisley's life, but as soon as I'd fixed my eyes on her, I knew she was running from something, or more likely, someone. I might be a cop, but it doesn't take a cop to see some bastard has put his hands on her. Her face is red and swollen, with a dark black bruise forming under her left eye, and her arm looks to be broken and in a hastily made sling. Other than her face and arm, there are no other obvious injuries, but watching her squeeze into her seat, it isn't hard to see how much pain she's in. I'm willing to bet she has some broken ribs too with how gingerly she was moving.

"Have you taken any pain meds?" I ask as she eats her sandwich. She swallows her mouthful before nodding.

"I took some this morning, but they're in my bag in the hold. I'm okay though."

"I have some." I reach down to the space under the seat in front of me and grab my bag. Pulling down the tray table, I place the bag on top. After searching inside, I pull out a bottle of Tylenol and hand it to her. "Help yourself."

"Thanks," she says shyly, taking the bottle from me. She pops out two tablets and then hands me back the bottle. I take it from her and watch as she swallows them down with a mouthful of her drink. I hope they give her some relief. If I can convince her to let my brother, Cade, check her over, he can prescribe something stronger than over-the-counter pain meds.

When she's finished her sandwich, she drops her head back on her seat and closes her eyes. I take that as a sign she's done talking, so I put my headphones back on.

Ten minutes later, I've barely heard a word of the music playing in my ears. I'd seen my fair share of domestic abuse victims, but that wasn't why I chose to reach out to Paisley. Seeing her had transported me back to my childhood. Even as a three-year-old boy, I can still remember how terrified my mother had been every night when my father came home from work. Back then, it had been just me and Cade, and the slightest thing would set my father off. If she cooked something he didn't want that night, or she wore a dress he thought was too short. I remember Cade telling me about a time when she'd had her hair done and he hadn't liked it. Each time, it ended in a beating. Cade was only two years older than me at five, and despite him trying to protect her, he was no match for a grown man. She eventually found the courage to leave, and we packed up only what we could carry and caught a Greyhound bus going anywhere. We ended up in

Hope Creek. With hardly any belongings, we spent just over a year in a women's shelter. Mom worked two jobs to get us out of there, and the day she got the keys to the small two-bed apartment she was able to rent, she cried tears of relief.

A year or so later, a guy moved into the apartment next to ours. He worked hard to gain her trust, and she eventually opened up to him and they fell in love. He put the spark back into her eyes that my deadbeat father had beaten out of her. Henry Brookes showed me what it was to love and respect a woman; something my own father couldn't do. Not only did he treat my mother like a princess, he took Cade and me on as his own. They had three children together, identical twins, Wyatt and Seb, and the baby of the family, the only girl, Ashlyn. Cade and I had taken Henry's last name when the twins were born. I wanted nothing that reminded me of my father. He was nothing to me. Henry taught me you didn't need to be connected by genetics to be a good father.

An hour later, Paisley's asleep. The plane suddenly shakes violently, and she's startled awake, a small yelp leaving her mouth.

"It's turbulence. Do you still have your belt fastened?" I ask her.

She nods and slips her arm back into the sling as the plane continues to be jostled around. The *fasten seat belt* sign illuminates overhead and a voice comes over the speaker.

"Ladies and gentlemen, this is your captain. We're flying through a small pocket of bad weather. I'm afraid it is going to be a little bumpy. Please remain seated and ensure your seat belts are securely fastened. Flight attendants, please take your seats."

Her frightened eyes flick to mine, and she grips the armrest between us with her good hand. "They don't tell the flight attendants to sit down unless it's bad, right?"

She looks terrified, and it's clear she doesn't fly often. "It'll be fine, Paisley. I promise." The lights flicker, and a gasp goes up around the cabin. The plane is still shaking, and I turn to her. Her eyes are squeezed closed, and her head is dropped back on the seat. "So, you know I'm a cop. What do you do for work back in Pittsburgh?"

She opens one eye and looks across at me. I smile encouragingly, hoping chatting to her will take her mind off the turbulence.

"I worked a couple of shifts a week in a coffeehouse."

"Did you like it?"

She lets out a little yelp as the plane is jostled again before levelling out. "Erm... sure. I mean, it's not my dream job, but my boss was nice." Both of her eyes are open now, but she's still gripping the armrest tightly.

"What's the dream?"

"I would have loved to have been a teacher."

"I'm sure you still can."

She shakes her head. "There's no way."

"There's always a way. If you decide to come to Hope Creek, you should speak to my sister. She's a kindergarten teacher. I'm sure she'd be able to point you in the right direction."

Her death grip on the armrest seems to have relaxed a little, and she turns in her seat to face me. "You have a brother who's a doctor, a sister who's a teacher, and you're a cop. Your parents must be so proud."

"Yeah, they are. I've got two other brothers as well."

"There's five of you?"

I nod. "Seb owns a bar in town, and Wyatt plays football."

"Professionally?"

"Yeah. He's a linebacker for the Arizona Cardinals."

"Wow! What are your other brother and sister called?"

"Cade and Ashlyn. Do you have any siblings?"

"No. It's just me. It must have been nice to grow up with all those brothers and sisters."

"Yeah, it was. We're still all really close." I chuckle. "Not sure Ashlyn enjoys having four older brothers, though."

She smiles, and I think I've succeeded in distracting her. "No. I can imagine dating is a little tricky for her."

"We have been known to be slightly overprotective." The turbulence has settled while we've been talking, and her hand has moved off the armrest. "I think we're over the worst now."

"I've only flown once before. I've never experienced anything like that."

"It's always scary the first time. Completely normal though. It's just patches of uneven air."

"You seem to know a lot about it."

"I've got a private pilot's license." Her eyes widen. "I can't fly anything this big, just single-engine planes."

"That's impressive."

I shrug. "My dad bought me a lesson for a birthday one year, and I loved it so much I continued with the lessons."

She's quiet, and I watch as she winces when she repositions herself in the seat.

"Have you thought any more about what I said earlier?" I ask softly. "About my brother looking you over?"

She shakes her head. "I'm never going to want to press charges, if that's why you're offering to help me."

"I'm not a cop right now, Paisley. My concern is for you, not the asshole who did this."

She sighs. "You seem like a nice guy, but honestly I have no idea who I can trust."

"I get that. I don't want to make you uncomfortable. I just want to help."

She frowns. "But why? You don't know me. I'm just someone you were unfortunate to be sitting next to on a flight."

"Unfortunate?" It's my turn to frown. "Why would you say that?" I don't let her answer and carry on talking. "I want to help because I *am* a nice guy..." I trail off, not wanting to tell her about my mom. I'm only guessing it's her husband or boyfriend who's hit her. I could be wrong. My eyes drop to her left hand, and a thin gold band sits on her wedding finger. I guess I'm not wrong.

"I'll get the shuttle to Hope Creek," she whispers, and I smile.

"Cade is picking me up. We could give you a ride?"

"Thanks, but I'd rather get the shuttle." Her guard is up, and I can understand that. I'd go mad if I knew Ashlyn had accepted a ride from two guys she didn't know.

"Okay." I pull out my phone and turn it on, switching it immediately to airplane mode. Searching through my contacts, I find the number for the shelter. "This is Sophie Greene's number. She runs the shelter in Hope Creek. Do you have a phone?"

She eyes me warily before nodding. With her good hand, she reaches into her pocket and pulls out her phone. I wait for her to power it up and switch it to airplane mode. I call out the number and she saves it.

"Thank you," she whispers.

She pushes her phone into her pocket and drops her head against the side of the plane, her eyes closing. She looks exhausted. I'm guessing she didn't get much sleep last night. We're about halfway through the flight, and I could do with catching up on some sleep myself. I hope I've convinced her to give Hope Creek a chance. I know I can't make her get on the shuttle. She could be saying anything to get me off her back, but despite knowing nothing about her, I'm going to worry if I get off this plane and never see her again.

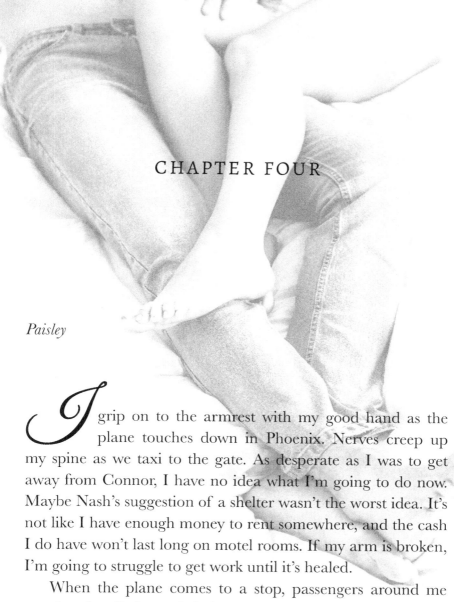

CHAPTER FOUR

Paisley

I grip on to the armrest with my good hand as the plane touches down in Phoenix. Nerves creep up my spine as we taxi to the gate. As desperate as I was to get away from Connor, I have no idea what I'm going to do now. Maybe Nash's suggestion of a shelter wasn't the worst idea. It's not like I have enough money to rent somewhere, and the cash I do have won't last long on motel rooms. If my arm is broken, I'm going to struggle to get work until it's healed.

When the plane comes to a stop, passengers around me stand and pull down their luggage from the overhead bins. I wait in my seat until the initial rush has gone. With a potentially broken wrist, I don't want to get caught in the crush to get off the plane. Nash seems to have the same idea, and as I glance at him, his head is down as he texts on his phone.

"Are you getting off?" I ask when most of the seats around us are empty.

"Sure. Sorry. I was just checking to see if my brother was waiting for me."

"It's fine." He grabs his bag from underneath the seat in front of him and makes his way into the aisle. I check my phone is in my pocket, which is really all I boarded with, and follow. I hang back a little, letting him walk ahead. I don't really know what to say to him. If I decide to head to Hope Creek, then I guess we might see each other again, but to say we're friends after sitting next to each other on a six-hour flight is pushing it.

Once we make it inside the terminal and through security, I head to baggage claim.

"Take care of yourself, Paisley," Nash says, and I turn, offering him a small smile.

"Thanks for all your help."

He waves off my thanks. "Sophie at the shelter has my number if you need anything."

I nod and wave my good hand as he walks away.

Once I've got my bag, I walk through arrivals and pick up a to-go coffee before leaving the airport. The warm April sun hits me as I step out onto the sidewalk, and I sip the hot drink as I tilt my head up, loving the heat on my face. In my rush to leave Pittsburgh, I never considered the weather when choosing somewhere to go. The few clothes I threw into my bag won't be much use if it gets warmer as the months go on, but they'll have to work for now. It's not as if I have spare money to spend on new clothes.

It's busy outside the airport, and I walk along the sidewalk until I come to an empty bench. I sit down and pull out my phone. Holding it to my ear, I call Taylor.

"Paisley! Are you okay? Where are you?" she asks when she answers.

"I'm okay." I pause. I don't want to tell her where I am. I trust her, but I don't want to put her in a position where she has to lie for me any more than she already is. "I'm safe, Tay. Have you heard from Connor?"

"Yeah. He was here about an hour ago. I told him I hadn't seen you in weeks…" She trails off.

"What aren't you telling me, Taylor?" I ask, nerves erupting in my stomach.

She sighs. "He said he was going to report you to the police as a missing person."

"What will the police do? Will they be able to check if I caught a flight? Will they tell him where I've gone?" My words tumble out in a rush, and my body trembles as fear over-whelms me.

"Paisley, take a breath," Taylor says, her voice low and calm. "He's not going to know where you've gone. Not even I know. I doubt he'll go to the police. It's probably an empty threat. He's the reason you left, and he'd be pretty stupid to get the police involved."

"God, I hope not." I bite down on my bottom lip and stand from the bench, pacing up and down the sidewalk.

"You're not going to tell me where you are, are you?"

"No. Not yet. I will, but in a few weeks when Connor calms down. It's better for you if you don't know."

"Okay. Where are you going to stay tonight? Do you have enough money for a motel room?"

"Yeah, I have money. I'll get a room in a cheap motel." I decide not to tell her about meeting Nash. I don't want to have to admit I might need to ask for help. I don't want to go into a women's shelter, but I'm beginning to think I have no choice.

"Are you going to see a doctor about your wrist?"

"Yeah. I'll find an emergency room. I should go. I need to find the shuttle."

"Look after yourself, Paisley, and stay safe. Call me whenever you want."

"Thanks, Taylor. Bye."

I end the call and slip my phone into my pocket. Looking around, I notice a bus terminal across the road, and I head over, enquiring at the desk about the shuttle to Hope Creek. I ignore the sympathetic stare the woman behind the glass is giving me and hand over the thirty-two-dollar fare when she tells me there's a bus leaving in twenty minutes. She directs me to stand twelve, and when I get there, the bus is waiting. Climbing aboard, I take a seat at the back of the empty bus, placing my bag next to me. Pushing down my pride, I reach for my phone and pull up the number Nash gave me for the woman who runs the shelter. Taking a deep breath, I put the phone to my ear.

"Hello," a voice answers.

"Hello… is this Sophie Greene?" I ask quietly.

"Is this Paisley?"

My eyes widen when she knows my name. "How did you know?"

"Nash Brookes called and said he'd given you my number. He was hoping you'd call."

"He said you might be able to help me?" My voice trembles, and I bite my lip to stop the tears that are forming from slipping down my cheeks.

"Yes, Paisley," she says kindly. "I have a vacant room if you need it."

"Yes, please," I whisper, relief washing over me as I realize I have a bed for the night.

"Where are you?"

"I'm just waiting for the shuttle bus to leave the airport. Nash said it would take a few hours to get to Hope Creek."

"I'll meet you from the bus."

"Thank you."

"You're welcome, Paisley. See you soon."

I end the call and drop my head back on the seat. I feel so ashamed I need to ask for help. I hate that Connor has turned me into this person. I'm scared, and physically and emotionally drained. Despite every part of my body aching, I feel like I could sleep for a week.

A WHILE LATER, I'm jolted awake as the bus comes to a stop. Sitting up, I look out of the window to see we've arrived in what I'm assuming is Hope Creek. It's falling dark, and the few people who are on the bus with me stand and make their way to the door. I pick up my bag and follow. My arm is throbbing, and my body screams out in protest as I move slowly down the aisle. Falling asleep in an awkward position has done nothing to help my already aching body.

As I exit the bus, a woman who looks only a couple of years older than me is waiting at the stop.

"Paisley?" she asks, raising her eyebrows in question. I nod. "Hi, I'm Sophie. Welcome to Hope Creek."

"Hi. Thank you for meeting me."

Her eyes track over my swollen face before dropping to my arm. "Let's get you settled in your room. I'll carry your bag." She takes my bag from me before I can protest and gestures up the sidewalk. "The house is just a five-minute walk from here."

We walk in a comfortable silence, and I take in my

surroundings. We're on what I think is the main street, and various shops, bars, and restaurants line the sidewalk. In the distance is a stunning mountain range, and it's simply breathtaking.

"It's beautiful," I say quietly as we walk. "Did you grow up here?"

She nods. "I did. I love it here. I left for a while, but Hope Creek pulled me back. It's where I belong."

We turn off the main street and away from the shops and bars. The area soon turns residential, and the houses are beautiful. Each one is different in style and they are all set back from the road with large front lawns and expensive-looking cars in the driveways. A couple have wraparound porches, and porch swings rock gently in the breeze. I don't know what I imagined a women's shelter looking like, but these houses aren't it.

"We're here," Sophie says as she stops on the sidewalk and points to a house. Turning, my eyes widen in surprise. It's not the biggest house on the street, but it's stunning all the same. A large driveway leads to a two-story white-washed building with a wraparound porch, and wildflowers fill the front yard. It's beautiful.

"This is the shelter?" I ask, my voice not hiding my surprise.

"Not what you were expecting?" she asks.

"I'm not sure what I was expecting, to be honest."

"Come on. I'll show you around."

I follow her down the long driveway and up the steps. She stops outside the front door and punches a code into a small keypad on the door. As the door swings open, she steps aside for me to enter. I walk in and find myself in a small entryway with the stairs to the second floor directly in front of me. The walls are a pale gray, and a vase of pink peonies sits on a small table to the left of the door. The entryway opens out into a large living room, with comfy-looking sofas and a beautiful stone fireplace. As I stand and take everything in, Sophie walks in front of me and beckons for me to follow her. Beyond the living room is a kitchen and a downstairs bathroom, along with a laundry room. Double doors lead off the kitchen into the backyard.

"Do you live here?"

"Yeah. This was my family home. My mom ran it as a shelter when I was a kid. When she died eighteen months ago, I came back to keep it going."

"I'm sorry for your loss. Thank you for helping me." My voice wobbles with emotion, and I blink away the tears that sting my eyes. "I'm not sure what I would have done if I hadn't met Nash on the flight."

She places her hand on my good arm and squeezes gently. "I'm glad I'm able to help you, Paisley, and Nash is a good guy. All the Brookes brothers are."

"You know them?" I assumed she knew Nash because he was a cop and he sent people like me to her. I hadn't thought they were friends, although, thinking about it, in a small town like Hope Creek, I imagine everyone knows everyone.

"I've known the Brookes family all my life. I went to school with Nash, and it's a small town." I nod, and her eyes find mine.

"Talking of Nash's brothers, did he tell you one of them is a doctor? I really think we should ask him to come and check you over."

I nod. "Nash did mention it. I couldn't tell him, but I don't have the money to pay for treatment. I can't see a doctor."

"Paisley, the shelter is a charity, and I have money set aside for medical bills. A lot of the women who come here need medical attention."

"No. I can't possibly let you pay for my treatment. I'll be fine. Things will heal on their own. I'll be fine," I repeat. "I'm sure there are women more in need than I am. Where is everyone anyway?" I ask, hoping to change the subject.

She sighs. "There's only Lyra staying here at the moment, and she's at work right now. You'll meet her later." She pauses, and I know she's going to bring up me seeing a doctor again. "Paisley, I really don't want to push the issue, but I want you to see a doctor. What about a compromise?"

I bite down on my bottom lip. "What compromise?"

"I ask for Cade to come to the house, and if he thinks nothing is broken, we don't have to do a trip to the emergency room."

I groan internally. With the pain in my wrist, I'm pretty sure it's broken. I'm guessing Sophie knows that too, so it's not really a compromise, it's just a way to get me to agree. Knowing I'm not going to convince her, I reluctantly agree.

"Okay."

She smiles. "Come on. I'll show you to your room and then I'll make the call." I follow her upstairs and along the corridor. We pass four closed doors, stopping when we come to the fifth. "This is you. There's a bathroom off your room, and a small countertop refrigerator. You're obviously welcome to use the kitchen downstairs to cook any meals. The fridge in the kitchen is always stocked. Help yourself." She opens the door, and I gasp when I see the room.

It's not overly large, but it's decorated beautifully with white walls and a pale pink comforter on the double bed that sits against one wall. There's a nightstand on either side of the bed, and a matching dresser on the opposite wall. A door leads to what I'm assuming is the bathroom, and a free-standing closet completes the furniture.

"Sophie, this is beautiful." I walk in farther, leaving her at the door. It's not at all how I expected a shelter to be. I imagined it to be an old and tired place full of banged-up women like me with different guys banging on the doors every night, demanding to see their wives. I'd clearly watched too many movies if this place was anything to go by.

"Thank you. I've tried to make it as homely as possible for the women who stay here."

"You've succeeded."

"There's fresh towels in the bathroom, and toiletries. I'll leave you to settle in. If there's anything you need, don't hesitate to ask."

Tears build in my eyes, and before I know it, they're tumbling down my cheeks. Sophie sees and drops my bag on the floor. She's crossed the room in a second and takes my hand, tugging me to sit down on the bed.

"I'm sorry," I mumble through my tears.

"It's okay, Paisley. Everything will be okay."

I want to believe her, I really do, but it's all so overwhelming. I might have a roof over my head, but I'm so far from being able to stand on my own two feet. I've never wanted to rely on anyone for anything, and now I'm having to accept charity from a stranger just to survive. I hate it.

"I'll get a job as soon as I can. I'll pay my way, I swear."

"There's no rush. You're welcome to stay here as long as you want. There's lots of help and support available once you're fit and well. Just concentrate on that right now, okay?"

I nod as I slip my hand from hers and wipe my tears away. "I don't know how I'll ever be able to repay you for helping me."

"There's no need for repayment. You didn't ask for any of this, Paisley. You deserve better. Always remember that." She stands from the bed and makes her way to the door. "I'll let you know when Cade can come."

She leaves the room, closing the door behind her. When she's gone, I kick off my shoes and scoot backwards on the bed, wincing as pain shoots down my side. When my head hits the pillow, I close my eyes, willing myself to fall asleep. I don't though, my mind swirling with everything that's happened in the past twenty-four hours. Despite having somewhere to sleep, my life is still a fucked-up mess. I can't help but feel I made all the wrong choices when I met Connor, and now those choices are going to define me. It's a terrifying thought.

CHAPTER FIVE

Nash

 I stare out of the window as Cade drives us away from the airport. "How was the wedding?" he asks, pulling me from my thoughts.

 I know I shouldn't have gotten involved in Paisley's life, but I did, and now I have to try and stop thinking about her. I'll likely never see her again, and there's nothing I can do to change that.

 "It was… good. Just a wedding. You know me and all that over-the-top shit. Not really my thing."

 "You old romantic!" he exclaims sarcastically.

 I wave my arm. "You know what I mean. Sure, get married, but why do you need a guest list of five hundred?"

 "Fuck! Five hundred?"

I nod. "Who even knows that many people? That's not a wedding, it's a pissing contest."

"Isn't Adam your best friend?"

"Yeah, not that I've seen much of him since he got engaged to Callie. I'm sure if anyone had taken the time to ask him what he wanted, it wouldn't have been the circus I've just attended."

"He did it for Callie, then?"

"I guess so."

"Happy wife, happy life."

"So they say. What about happy husband? I give it five years."

"Nash! You can't bet on your best friend's marriage failing!"

I hold up my hands. "I hope I'm wrong."

We fall silent, and I'm back to staring out of the window. I shouldn't really be commenting on Adam's relationship. He's doing better than I am when it comes to love, and if Callie makes him happy, then I'm pleased for him. I can't help my mind wandering back to Paisley and if she boarded the shuttle bus to Hope Creek.

"You're quiet," Cade says after a few minutes. "Everything okay?"

"Yeah…"

"You don't sound too sure."

"I met a woman on the flight."

His mouth turns up in a smile, and he chuckles. "Didn't the Nash Brookes charm work on her?" He smirks at me.

I roll my eyes. "It wasn't like that, man," I say, irritated he's calling me out. While I might never have had a long-term relationship, I get plenty of attention from women, and I never have to try very hard for that attention. I sigh and drag my hand through my hair. "She was beat up, Cade. I don't know if I did enough to help her."

The smirk falls from his face and he frowns. "Beat up how?"

"Broken arm, I think. Busted face. Maybe broken or cracked ribs by the pain she was in and the way she was moving. I tried to convince her to come to Hope Creek and let you check her over, even offered her a ride, but she was scared. I've no idea if she'll come. I gave her Sophie's number."

His hands tighten on the wheel and his knuckles turn white at the mention of Sophie's name. I don't know why he can't get his head out of his ass and sort things out with her. They were together when he was in med school, but something happened and Sophie left. He had no idea what made her leave, and he was a mess for a long time. She came back to Hope Creek about eighteen months ago when her mom died, and there's been tension between them ever since. I'm still not sure he knows why she left him, but every time I've tried to talk to him about it, he shoots me down.

"Sounds like she needs to see a doctor. She could have internal injuries. How was her breathing?"

"It seemed okay. She wasn't short of breath."

"That's good. If she shows up in Hope Creek, I'm happy to see her."

"Thanks, Cade."

He looks across at me and my eyes meet his. "Did she tell you who hit her?"

"No, but there was a wedding band on her finger, so I'm guessing it was her asshole husband." I turn and look out of the window again. "She was beautiful. Why does someone think they can do that to another person? *No one* deserves to be treated like that. I should have done more to help her."

"You did all you could for her, Nash."

"It doesn't feel that way." I dig out my phone and look up Sophie's number. "I'm going to call Sophie, let her know I've given Paisley her number."

His jaw clenches, and there's a small bob of his head, his eyes focused on the road.

"What happened with you two, Cade? Whatever it was, it was years ago. Can't you let it go?"

"Drop it, Nash. Unless you want to walk home."

I hold up my hands and chuckle. "Fine. Consider it dropped."

Holding the phone to my ear, I wait for the call to connect.

"Hello," Sophie answers.

"Hi, Sophie. It's Nash."

"Hey, Nash."

"Are there any rooms free at the shelter?"

"Yeah. I only have one room occupied at the moment, why?"

"I met a woman on a flight back from Pittsburgh. She was in a bad way. I gave her your number. I don't know if she's going to call, or even if she's going to head to Hope Creek. Her name's Paisley. Can you let me know if you hear from her?"

"Sure."

"If she does show up, I think she'll need to see Cade." The line goes quiet, and I pull the phone from my ear to check the call hasn't dropped.

"Okay," she eventually says. "I'll let you know."

"Thanks, Sophie. Bye."

I end the call and push my phone back in my pocket. "Are you coming to Mom and Dad's for dinner?" Cade asks.

"Yep. I never miss Thursday night dinner unless I'm working."

He nods. "Just thought you might be tired from the flight."

"I am, but not too tired to pass up on Mom's midweek roast."

Every Thursday was dinner at my parents' place. It was always a Sunday roast, even though it wasn't Sunday. It had been the same, even when we all still lived at home. I don't know how it started, but as we grew up, it seemed easier to get everyone together midweek than on a weekend. It was just my parents at home now. Ashlyn had been the last to move out last year, and I knew my mom especially missed us all. It was rare we were all able to make dinner though. Cade and I work shifts and can't always make it, and Wyatt is away half the year playing football. It's the off-season at the moment, but I'm not sure if he's coming. Seb and Ashlyn never miss though, and I often think it's the only home-cooked meal Seb gets in a week. He works day and night at his bar in town, and his downtime is limited.

"Is Wyatt coming tonight?"

Cade shakes his head. "He's at some training camp in Florida."

We're about thirty minutes from Hope Creek, and my phone vibrates with a message. Pulling it from my pocket, I see Sophie's name on the screen.

Sophie: Paisley called. She's waiting on the shuttle. She'll be in Hope Creek in a few hours.

Relief washes over me as my fingers fly over the screen, typing out a reply.

Me: That's great. Thanks for letting me know.

"Paisley's contacted Sophie. She's on her way to Hope Creek."

"I'll bring my bag to Mom and Dad's in case she calls."

"Thanks, man."

"You seem pretty invested in this woman considering you've only just met her." He turns his head to look at me and raises one eyebrow.

"She needs some help, that's all. We both know what Mom went through. I might have been young, but I still remember."

He nods but doesn't say anything. I know he remembers too. It's not something any kid should have to witness, and if I can help Paisley escape the cycle of abuse, then I will.

* * *

A COUPLE OF HOURS LATER, I'm showered, changed, and heading to my parents' place. They live just outside Hope Creek on the edge of town, and it's a short drive from my house. Pulling off the main road, I drive up the track that leads to the house and park next to Cade's Mercedes. Ashlyn's Audi is parked next to Cade's car, and Seb's Harley finishes the lineup. It looks like we've all made it, apart from Wyatt, which isn't unusual.

Pushing open the front door, I make my way to the kitchen, where I can hear the chatter of voices.

"Nash," my mom says as she crosses the room and pulls me into a hug. "How was the wedding?"

"It was great, Mom. They looked really happy."

"I'm pleased for them." She steps out of the embrace and goes back to whatever she was doing before I arrived.

42

"Hey, Ash." I walk the short distance to my sister and lean down to kiss her cheek.

"Cade said you met a girl," she says, my lips still on her cheek.

"You met a girl?" Mom gushes from the other side of the room.

I roll my eyes. "Where is my big-mouthed brother?" I ask, trying to change the subject.

"He's in the den with your dad and Seb. There's some game on. Don't avoid the question. Who's the girl?"

"It's not like that."

"What's it like, then?" Ashlyn asks.

"I wanted to help her. I put her in touch with Sophie. She had nowhere else to go." My mom spins around from the stove, her eyes wide. "I tried to convince her to let Cade look her over."

"Is she okay?" Mom asks, concern evident in her voice.

"I don't know. I think at the very least her arm is broken, possibly some ribs too."

"Did she agree to see Cade?"

I shake my head. "Not yet. I'm hoping Sophie can convince her."

"How old is she?" Ashlyn asks.

"Maybe twenty-five. I'm not good at guessing ages."

"What's her name?"

"Paisley."

"God, that poor girl," my mom whispers. I know she has to be thinking of herself at the same age. It's impossible not to. "I'm glad you tried to help her, Nash. You're a good man."

"I hope I did enough."

She walks toward me and cups my face with her hand.

"You were probably one of only a few people to show her some kindness in a long time, Nash. You did enough."

An uneasy feeling washes over me as I think how sad it sounds that possibly a stranger on a plane was kinder to her than anyone she knows. I wonder if she's made it to Hope Creek yet, and if she's okay.

"I'll go and find the others," I say quietly, not knowing what else to say.

As I make my way to the den, I slip my phone from my pocket, my finger hovering over Sophie's name. Shaking my head, I lock the screen and push away my wayward thoughts. Paisley isn't my concern. If she's with Sophie, then she's safe. I shouldn't get involved.

I push open the door to the den, and my dad, Cade, and Seb are sitting on the worn leather sofa, their eyes fixed on the baseball game on the flat-screen TV that hangs on the wall.

"Who's winning?" I ask as I drop down onto the love seat across from the sofa.

"The Yankees," Seb answers, his eyes never leaving the screen.

I'm not much of a baseball fan. I'll watch a game if it's on, but I'm not as bothered about it as these three are.

I've barely sat down when Ashlyn pokes her head around the door. "Dinner's ready." My dad immediately turns the TV off and Cade and Seb groan.

"There was only five minutes left," Cade moans, and my dad chuckles.

"Yes, but dinner's ready now, and your mom's been cooking all afternoon. That's more important." He stands up and pats me on the shoulder as he passes.

"Good to see you, Nash."

I follow him out of the den and into the formal dining

room, Cade and Seb behind me. The dining room is only used for holidays and Thursday roasts, with a large table to seat ten. My mom's always joking that when we all start to settle down, they'll need a bigger table to accommodate partners, but everyone seems a long way off that. As far as I know, we're all single and have been for a while.

"This smells incredible, Mom," Seb exclaims as we all sit down in the same seats we've always sat in. Wyatt normally sits next to me, but his chair is empty today. I don't think to move up and sit next to Ashlyn though. I've been sitting in this spot since I was six and it would feel weird to sit anywhere else.

It's roast beef today, and I've just loaded my plate up when my phone rings. My mom frowns.

"What happened to the 'no phone at the table' rule?" she asks, flashing me a look.

"Sorry," I say sheepishly. I might be thirty-two and a grown man, but I still respect my mom's rules when I'm in her house. I dig the ringing phone from my pocket, my heart in my throat when I see Sophie's name flashing on the screen. My eyes flick from my phone to Cade. "It's Sophie."

"Take it," my mom says immediately, and I hit the screen, bringing the phone to my ear.

"Hello."

"Hi, Nash. It's Sophie. Is this a good time?"

"It's fine. Is everything okay?"

"I hope it's okay to call you. I don't have Cade's number. Paisley's agreed to let him look her over. She's not too keen on the hospital, so I wondered if he could come here?" She sounds unsure, but I know Cade won't mind.

"Let me check. Hang on."

I cover the phone with my hand and turn to Cade. "Can

you go over to Sophie's place to check on Paisley? She doesn't want to go to the hospital."

He nods. "Sure, but if I think anything's broken, there won't be much I can do."

"She knows that," Sophie says in my ear, obviously overhearing what Cade said. "She's agreed to go to the hospital if anything's broken."

"Okay. We're just finishing up with dinner and we'll be over."

"Okay, thanks."

"Sophie," I say quickly before the call ends.

"Yeah."

"Is she okay?"

"She's tearful and overwhelmed, and she's in pain, even if she won't admit it. I hope Cade can help her."

"Me too. See you soon."

I end the call and drop my phone onto the table, my stomach twisting knowing she's upset and in pain.

"You don't need to come. I'll be fine going on my own," Cade says as he forks a mouthful of food into his mouth.

"I need to know she's okay."

"Why?" he asks when he's swallowed his mouthful of food.

I look around the table to see everyone staring at me. "I just do. I can't explain it. Hurry up and eat," I say, hoping my tone indicates that the conversation is over.

Thankfully, everyone's focus goes back to their food, everyone except my mom's, and I catch her smiling at me. I smile back before averting my gaze and eating what's on my plate. I barely taste it, eager to see Paisley again.

CHAPTER SIX

Paisley

*A*fter a long and painful shower, I emerge from the bathroom with tears running down my face. Trying to wash my body with one arm had been hard. Trying to wash my hair had been almost impossible, and I've no idea if I've managed to get all the shampoo out. I normally condition my hair too, but I just don't have the energy. Shampoo will have to do. With a large white towel wrapped around me, I take a seat on the edge of the bed and take a few deep breaths to try and ward off the pain before I attempt to get dressed.

"Paisley," Sophie calls through the door. "Can I come in?"

"Sure," I shout back, wiping away my tears and standing up. It's her house; she can come in whenever she wants.

"I've spoken to Nash. He and his brother are going to

come over when they've finished dinner," she says as she closes the door behind her.

"Nash is coming too?" I ask, my voice not hiding my surprise.

She nods. "I think he's worried about you."

I bite down on my bottom lip, my fingers fiddling with the edge of the towel that's wrapped around me. "Would you stay with me while they're here?"

"Of course I will. They won't hurt you, though."

"I've made the mistake of trusting the wrong person before," I say quietly.

"I'll stay with you, Paisley," she says, giving me a sad smile. "Do you want some help with your hair? I can only imagine how hard it would be to brush and dry with one hand."

Fresh tears fall down my cheeks, and I nod. "Thank you."

Half an hour later, Sophie's brushed, dried, and even curled my long brown hair in waves down my back. I feel like a different person when I look in the mirror in the bathroom. My face is still swollen, and the bruise under my eye is turning from red to purple. I can open my eye now though, so the swelling must have gone down some. She helps me into a pair of yoga pants and a tank, and I need to sit down once I'm dressed. Pain radiates through my arm, and it's making me feel like I'm going to throw up. My eyes widen as my stomach cramps and I bend over, clutching my good arm around my waist.

"Paisley, what's wrong?" She drops to her knees in front of me, and I lift my scared eyes to hers.

"My stomach," I rasp, inhaling sharply as the pain hits me again.

"Lie down," she says, taking my arm and helping me move

up the bed. When I move backwards, she gasps. "You're bleeding. Are you pregnant?"

"I don't know," I whisper, fear enveloping me.

She pulls her phone from her pocket and calls someone. "Are you nearly here?" she asks into the phone. "I'll come and let you in."

She ends the call and turns to me. "Cade and Nash are just outside. I'll be right back." She rushes out of the room and her words swirl in my mind. Pregnant? If I am, I didn't know. The pain in my stomach has subsided a little, and I try to remember when my last period was. With everything that's happened, I've no idea, and my brain hurts, along with everywhere else as I try to piece everything together. I just catch a glimpse of a man in the doorway before pain explodes in my lower abdomen, and I'm forced to close my eyes, my knees coming up to my stomach so I'm in the fetal position.

"Paisley, I'm Cade," a voice says, and I jump as I feel a hand on my arm. "I'm not going to hurt you. Can you tell me where the pain is?" he asks gently.

"My stomach," I manage to say, tears welling in my eyes.

"Could you be pregnant? When was your last period?"

"I don't... know," I admit.

"Can I feel your stomach?"

I nod and uncurl my legs. He presses gently below my belly button, and I groan, the fingers of my good hand, fisting the comforter.

"Okay," he soothes, removing his hands. His eyes drop to the blood that's on the comforter, and he gives me a small smile. "We need to get you to the hospital, Paisley. I think you're having a miscarriage." The tears that were threatening to fall, now track down my cheeks. "Nash said you'd hurt your arm?"

"Yes, my right one."

"Can I take a look?" I nod and hold my arm out to him. His fingers gently move my wrist, and I cry out. He stops immediately and places my wrist across my chest. "I think it's broken." He reaches down to the side of the bed and picks up a bag I hadn't even noticed. He pulls out a blue foam sling and carefully maneuvers my arm into it, fastening the soft material around my neck. "This will keep it in place while we get you to the hospital. Do you think you can walk?"

Before I can answer, I hear another voice in the room. "I've got her." Stepping around Cade, Nash comes into view. "Hey, Paisley." He moves toward me and kneels down next to Cade. "Can I pick you up?" I'm just about to protest when a wave of pain makes me gasp. As much as I don't want Nash to touch me, I know I can't walk.

"Okay," I whisper. "Please be gentle. My ribs are sore."

"I will be, sweetheart."

Cade moves away from the bed and Nash stands up. He tosses Cade some keys before his arms slip under my legs and around my shoulder, and he picks me up as if I weigh nothing at all. He pulls me against his body and I tense in his arms.

"Relax. It's okay," he says softly.

"Will they be keeping her in?" Sophie asks Cade.

"Yeah, more than likely," he says.

"I'll grab her some stuff." She rushes around the room, throwing clothes back into the bag I've only just unpacked.

"Are you coming with us?" Cade asks her.

"If that's okay?"

He doesn't reply, he just gives a small nod of his head. Pain hits my lower abdomen again, and I grab Nash's shirt with my good hand, fisting the material in my fingers. I close my eyes and try to breathe through the pain.

"We need to go!" Nash exclaims, and I can hear the concern in his voice.

"Ready?" Cade says. Who to, I'm not sure as my eyes are closed, but before I know it, Nash is carrying me down the stairs and outside.

"You drive, Cade. I'll go in the back with Paisley," Nash says, and Sophie reaches around him and opens the door. Effortlessly, he slides into the back seat with me still in his arms.

Thankfully, it's a short drive to the hospital, and I find myself dropping my head onto Nash's shoulder in between cramps. The pain is exhausting, and when it ebbs away for a few minutes, I close my eyes, resting before it crashes over me again.

When we arrive at the hospital, Nash climbs out of the truck and carries me inside.

"Dr. Brookes," the nurse behind the desk says as he walks in ahead of us. "I didn't know you were working tonight."

"Hi, Meghan. I'm not working. I've brought a friend in. Is there a bay free?" She looks past Cade to me and nods.

"Bay three."

"Thanks, Meg. Can you book her in? It's Paisley..." He turns around. "Sorry, Paisley, I don't know your last name."

"It's Prescott," I tell the nurse, and she smiles kindly.

Nash follows Cade through a set of double doors and into a curtained-off bay. There's a bed against one wall and he lowers me gently onto it. My cheeks flush pink when I see there's blood on his clothes.

"God, I'm sorry," I mumble.

He looks down and shakes his head. "It's fine, Paisley. Don't worry about it."

"I'm going to see if I can find the portable sonogram

machine. I don't want to do any X-rays of your wrist until we know what's happening. Come with me, Nash. I'll find you some scrubs."

"You'll be okay?" Nash asks, and I nod, surprised by his concern.

"How's the pain?" Sophie asks once Cade and Nash have gone. She takes a seat in the chair next to the bed and takes my good hand in hers.

"It's eased a little. Is it wrong I wish it hadn't?"

She frowns. "What do you mean?"

"I don't want to be pregnant with Connor's baby," I whisper.

"Is Connor your husband?" I nod. "And he was the one who hurt you?" I nod again.

"This baby wasn't made out of love, and I don't want to have any ties to him."

"I can understand that, Paisley. Let's wait and see what the sonogram shows."

A few minutes later, Cade appears, wheeling a machine into the cubicle. Nash follows him, dressed in blue scrubs.

"Shall we see what's happening?" Cade asks as he sets up the machine.

"I'll wait outside," Nash says, his eyes finding mine before he slips behind the curtain.

"Do you want me to stay?" Sophie asks, and I nod, squeezing her hand.

Cade lifts my top and pulls my yoga pants down a little, exposing my stomach. "This is going to be cold, Paisley. Ready?"

"Yes," I say, taking a deep breath. He squirts some gel on my stomach and gently moves the probe around, spreading the gel. He's silent for a minute or so as he concentrates on the screen.

"It looks like you were pregnant, about nine weeks. I'm so sorry, Paisley, but there's no heartbeat."

Tears of relief track down my cheeks, and I'm sure that makes me the most awful person in the world. Who feels relieved to be miscarrying? I always wanted children when Connor and I got married, but not now. Not with him, and I'm in no position to be bringing a child into the world. I've barely got a roof over my head.

"What happens now?" I ask, wiping my tears.

"As you're under ten weeks, we can let you miscarry naturally. There shouldn't be any need for surgery. The worst of it will be over in a few hours and then it should just be like a heavy period. It's probably best we admit you overnight and we can give you some pain relief."

"Okay," I mutter.

"I'll ask a nurse to find you a hospital gown while I arrange an X-ray for your wrist." Cade passes me some tissue before cleaning off the machine and wheeling it back out.

"Are you all right?" Sophie asks.

"I'm relieved. I know that makes me a terrible person." My voice is barely a whisper, but I know she hears me.

"You're not a terrible person, Paisley. You don't deserve any of this." She helps me wipe the gel from the sonogram off my stomach and tosses the tissue in the trash. "I left your bag in the truck. Will you be okay if I run and grab it?"

"Sure."

"I think Nash is just outside. I can ask him not to come in if you'd prefer not to be alone with him?"

"No, it's okay. He can come in if he wants."

He's been nothing but kind to me. I don't feel threatened by him.

"I won't be long."

"Thank you, Sophie. For everything." She smiles as she leaves the cubicle, and I'm left alone. I drop my head back on the pillow and stare at the stark white ceiling. I must have lost the baby when Connor kicked me in the stomach. I'm surprised it's taken until now to have any pain or bleeding. Part of me thinks it would have been better for everyone if he'd finished me off that night. If he had, all the pain would be over and I'd be free from him for good. Instead, it feels like I'm always going to be looking over my shoulder, waiting for him to show up and ruin whatever life I've made for myself. I'm never going to be happy. He won't let me. Even when I'm on the other side of the country to him, fear keeps me paralyzed and he still has control over me. It feels like I'm never going to be free.

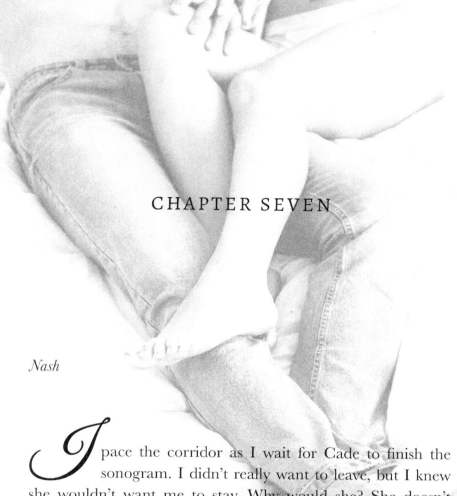

CHAPTER SEVEN

Nash

I pace the corridor as I wait for Cade to finish the sonogram. I didn't really want to leave, but I knew she wouldn't want me to stay. Why would she? She doesn't know me. When the curtain's pulled back and Cade walks out, I catch sight of her crying before he closes the curtain behind him.

"Is she okay? Can I go in?" I ask Cade, my eyes searching his.

"Maybe give her a minute. It's not good news and she's upset. I'm going to fetch her a gown. She's going to need to be admitted overnight."

"She's miscarrying?" I ask, knowing that's what he's saying but needing him to actually say the words.

"I can't tell you, Nash. You know that. It's patient confidentiality."

I drag my hand through my hair. "I'm sorry. I shouldn't have asked."

"It's okay. I'll be back when I've sorted the paperwork out to admit her."

I continue to pace the corridor, not knowing whether I should go in or not. She must be devastated, and despite wanting to see her, I've no idea what I should say. She's lost everything, including her unborn child. I can't even imagine what she's going through. I sit down heavily on one of the hard, plastic chairs a little up from her cubicle. I've only been sitting for a second when Sophie emerges from the bay and I jump up.

"Is she all right?"

She nods. "I'm just going to grab her bag from the truck. Do you have the keys?" Cade gave them back to me earlier, and I dig into my pocket and pull them out, handing them to her. "Thanks. You can go in. She said it was okay."

"She did?" I ask in surprise.

"Yes."

I watch as she walks back through the double doors and out of sight. Taking a deep breath, I slowly pull the curtain back on her cubicle.

"Hey, Paisley. Am I okay to come in?" She gives me a small smile and nods. I step inside and close the curtain behind me. "How are you feeling?"

"I'm okay. I miscarried." Her eyes drop to her lap, where the fingers of her good hand play with the edge of the blanket that covers her.

"I'm so sorry." I want to hold her hand or something, but I don't. That would be inappropriate.

There's a tiny shrug of her shoulder before her eyes find mine. "I didn't even know. I must have lost it when..." She trails off, and tears well in her eyes.

"When what, Paisley?" I prompt.

"When he kicked me in the stomach," she whispers, and the tears that were building fall down her cheeks.

Anger coils in my stomach, and I want nothing more than to punch the asshole who did this to her. "Was it your husband?" I ask quietly, and she nods.

"You're safe now, Paisley. I promise."

"Can I ask you something?" She looks up at me, uncertainty swimming in her beautiful green eyes.

"Sure."

"If he reports me missing, what happens?"

"The police will file a report. They might look at your bank account to see when you last used your card or activate the GPS on your phone. People go missing every day. You're over eighteen and not vulnerable. They're unlikely to do anything more unless they think you've come to harm." I pause. "How do you know he's reported you missing?"

"My friend who helped me get away. I called her earlier and she said he showed up at her place. She didn't tell him anything, but he said he was going to report me missing. I was worried they would somehow find out I'd travelled here and tell him."

"Have you used your bank card since you left?" She shakes her head. "But you've used your phone?" I ask, knowing she has.

"He doesn't know about my phone. It was hidden and in my friend's name."

"That's good. I can do some digging tomorrow and find out if anyone filed a report if you want me to?"

57

"No! If there's no way of anyone knowing I'm here, just leave it, but thanks."

"Okay." She winces, and her hand comes over her stomach. Dropping her head back, she takes deep breaths, and I watch her, feeling helpless. "Should I fetch Cade?" I ask, not knowing what else I can do.

"No, I'm okay."

A few minutes later, a nurse appears with a hospital gown in her hands.

"Hi, Paisley, I'm Lizzie. Dr. Brookes has asked me to help get you changed and then we have a room up on the ward waiting for you."

"I'll wait outside," I say, standing up.

"I feel bad everyone is hanging around here because of me. You don't have to stay," she says, her cheeks flushing pink.

"I want to, Paisley. I'll just be outside."

She gives me a small smile and I slip behind the curtain and into the corridor. Seeing Cade, I walk toward him.

"I've just spoken to Paisley. She told me it was her husband who hurt her and she thinks she lost the baby when he kicked her in the stomach."

"Bastard!"

"What about her wrist?"

"I'm just arranging for her to have an X-ray on the way up to the ward. I'm thinking she might need a CT scan too if she's been kicked in the stomach. I don't want to miss anything. She could have internal injuries."

"God! I want to kill the guy!" I exclaim, my hands fisting at my sides.

He raises his eyebrows. "Is that the cop talking?"

"What?"

"You're concerned about her, and I'm wondering if it's the cop in you that's concerned, or whether it's more than that."

I stare at him. "It's the cop," I say defensively.

"You keep telling yourself that."

I go to protest, but before I can, he's walked off toward the cubicle Paisley's in. I want to follow, but I know that will only confirm what he's been saying. I *am* concerned for her from a cop point of view. I want to call in every favor owed to me and nail the asshole, but maybe he's right, and I'm a little more involved than I should be.

Ten minutes later, I watch as Paisley is wheeled out of the cubicle and into the corridor. She looks up and we lock eyes, her hand lifting in a small wave as the nurse wheels her in the opposite direction and toward radiology. Sophie follows with her bag, and I feel a little like a spare part. I can't really leave since we came in my truck, but I'm not sure she wants me hanging around. She's going through hell and likely doesn't want to have to make small talk with me.

"Should I go?" I ask Cade as he comes to stand next to me.

"I was hoping for a ride back to Mom and Dad's, but if you want to go, I can grab a cab."

"No, it's okay. There's Sophie to get home too. I'll wait."

"If you're sure. Come with us to radiology. Once we've got the X-rays and she's settled in her room, we can go."

Forty-five minutes later, Paisley's had a CT scan and an X-ray on her wrist. I'm waiting outside her room while the nurses get her settled.

"You can come in if you want," Sophie says a few minutes later, poking her head around the door. "Cade's given her something. She's in less pain now."

I follow Sophie into Paisley's room and hang back while

the nurse finishes taking her vitals. She looks exhausted. I hope she manages to get some sleep tonight. Before I can ask her how she's feeling, a knock sounds on the door and Cade walks in.

"I have your scan and X-ray results. Do you want to talk in private, Paisley?" he asks, X-ray films in his hand.

"They can stay. It's okay," she says quietly. Her eyes flick from Sophie to me. I give her a reassuring smile before waiting for Cade to elaborate.

"I'm afraid your wrist is fractured. It's a clean break." He holds up the X-ray film in his hand and points to the obvious break in her wrist. "You'll need a cast for a few weeks, but it'll heal. The CT scan shows you have three broken ribs. I'm afraid there's less we can do for those. You just need to take it easy for about six weeks. There's no internal bleeding, which is good, but the scan does show some old injuries. Several previous broken ribs." He pauses. "Paisley, has this happened before?"

I hold my breath as I wait for her to answer, even though I'm sure I know what she's going to say.

"Yes," she whispers. "But this time was the worst. I thought he was going to kill me." Sophie sits on the edge of her bed and takes her hand.

"Is that why you left?" Sophie asks, and she nods. "You did the right thing, Paisley."

Tears track down her cheeks, and I can't imagine how hard it is for her to open up to us. We're virtual strangers, and I'm sure she's questioning whether she can trust us.

"Do you want to report the attack?" Cade asks gently.

"No! I don't have to, do I?" Her wide eyes land on me, and as much as I want to lock this guy up, I can see she's terrified.

"It's okay, Paisley. You don't have to do anything you don't want to do," I assure her. Relief floods her face, and she drops her head back onto the pillow, her eyes closing.

"How's the pain?" Cade asks.

"Better. Thank you."

"We'll leave you to get some rest. Someone should be in soon to put a cast on your wrist."

"Will she be able to come back to the house tomorrow?" Sophie asks, and Cade nods. "My car's in the shop."

"I'll give her a ride," I offer.

"I hate that everyone is having to run around after me," Paisley says, her cheeks flushing pink.

"It's fine. I'll give you my number and you can call me when you get discharged."

"Are you sure? Maybe I could just walk."

"No," Cade says before I can answer. "You can't walk."

"I'll pick you up, Paisley. It's no problem. Do you have your phone?" Indecision flashes across her face before she reaches into the bag that's on the edge of the bed and pulls out her phone. Unlocking the screen, she hands it to me. I save my number in her contacts and call myself so I have hers.

"Thank you," she mutters as I hand her phone back.

"Will you be okay?" Sophie asks.

"I'll be fine. Thank you for everything you've done today."

"I'll be at the house tomorrow when Nash drops you off. I hope you can get some sleep." Sophie stands from the bed and makes her way to the door.

"I'm working the day shift tomorrow in the ER. I'll come and check on you in the morning," Cade says.

"Bye, Paisley." I offer her a small smile and walk backwards toward the door. Despite wanting to leave earlier, it feels wrong to leave her here alone, but I know I have to.

Once we get outside, we walk in silence to my truck.

There's a definite atmosphere between Cade and Sophie, but I'm too exhausted to try and figure out why. Sophie's only been back in Hope Creek for eighteen months, but the more I think about it, the more I realize Cade's been off ever since she came back.

I pull up outside Sophie's house and she climbs out.

"I'll see you tomorrow, Nash. Thanks for helping her, Cade," she says softly before she closes the door.

"Are you not going to see her inside?"

Cade swings his head around to look at me. "This isn't a date, Nash."

"It doesn't need to be!" I climb out of the car and catch up with Sophie.

When she's safely inside, I head back to the truck. He's staring out of the window when I get behind the wheel, and I don't push him. He'll talk to me when he's ready.

It's late by the time we get back to my parents' place, and the house is in darkness.

"Will you let me know how she is in the morning?" I ask Cade as he gets out of my truck. He gives a swift nod before closing the door and climbing into his car.

I drive home, arriving without really knowing how I got there. My mind is consumed with Paisley. I hope she's managing to sleep and she's not scared to be on her own. Even though she thinks she's falling apart, she's strong. She's already shown that by leaving her asshole husband. I hope she knows how brave she is.

CHAPTER EIGHT

Paisley

When sunlight streaks through the blinds, I'm relieved. It's been a really long night, and it feels like I haven't slept at all. The pain meds Cade gave me wore off around one a.m., and although I was given some more, the pain didn't subside straight away. I hope the worst of the miscarriage is over after a pretty intense night. Despite not wanting a child with Connor, I'd been emotional when I knew the baby was no longer a part of me. One of the nurses had found me sobbing on the bathroom floor, and I'd never felt more alone in that moment.

Needing to use the bathroom, I sit up and swing my legs to the edge of the bed. I'm a little dizzy, so I sit for a few minutes before grabbing my bag and padding across the room to the bathroom. After I've used the toilet and brushed my teeth, I catch sight of my reflection in the vanity mirror and wince. The bruise under my eye is an array of colors, from purple to yellow, and slowly spreading further down my cheek. Thankfully, my hair, washed and curled by Sophie last night, still looks presentable, and I run my fingers through it, realizing I don't have a hairbrush.

As I leave the bathroom, there's a knock on the door, and a nurse walks in with a breakfast tray. My stomach rumbles as the smell of freshly made toast invades my senses.

"Morning, Paisley. How are you feeling?"

"I'm okay. A little tired."

"Your chart said you had some strong stomach cramps during the night. How is it now?"

"Better. Still there, but manageable."

She gestures for me to get back into bed and places my food on the tray over my bed. "Try to eat something and the doctor will be in to see you soon."

"Thank you."

She smiles kindly, and I pick up a slice of toast, taking a bite as she leaves. Hearing my phone vibrate on the nightstand, I reach for it, seeing I have a message from Sophie.

Sophie: Hi, Paisley, it's Sophie. How are you feeling this morning?

I pop the last piece of the toast I'm holding into my mouth and type out a reply.

Me: Hi, Sophie. I'm okay. Looking forward to getting back to the house.

Sophie: Do you know when you can be discharged yet?

Me: Just waiting on the doctor.

Sophie: Okay. Hope you don't have to wait too long. See you later.

Another knock on the door sounds and Cade puts his head around the door.

"Morning, Paisley. Am I okay to come in?"

"Hi, Cade. Yes, come in." He walks in and closes the door behind him.

"How are you feeling?"

"Okay."

"How's the pain?"

"Much better. It was bad in the night, but I think the worst is over." He gives me a sympathetic smile. I'm guessing he's read my chart and knows what happened during the night.

"Have you seen a doctor yet?"

"Only you. Do you think I'll be discharged today?"

"Yeah. I think so. Make sure they give you a shower cover for your wrist. You won't be able to shower without one."

"Okay. I'll remember to ask." I bite down on my lip. "Thank you for everything you did last night."

"You don't need to keep thanking me, Paisley. I'm just glad I could help." He smiles and opens the door. "Don't forget to let Nash know when you're ready."

"I will."

"Take care."

"Bye, Cade."

He closes the door behind him, and I'm alone again. Moving my breakfast tray, I'm suddenly overwhelmed with tiredness. I climb into the bed and drop my head onto the pillow, closing my eyes.

I sleep for about an hour, waking up when the doctor comes in to see me. He asks what feels like a million questions about my broken wrist and cracked ribs, and it feels a little like a police interrogation. He insists on taking pictures to document my injuries, and a nurse comes in with an iPad. When she's taken a load of images, the doctor tries to get me to give over Connor's details, but I refuse, and I'm relieved when he leaves. He hasn't mentioned being discharged, but I want to leave. I get dressed as quickly as I can with a broken wrist and pack what few things I have. Leaving the room, I make my way through the ER and outside. Walking away from the hospital, I slide my phone from my pocket and pull up Nash's number.

"Paisley, hi."

"Hi, Nash," I say quietly. "Are you... are you still okay to come and get me?"

"Sure. Have you been discharged?"

"Not exactly, but I want to leave. I'm waiting outside."

"Is everything okay? What's happened?"

"I just wanted to leave."

There's silence, and I pull the phone from my ear, checking the call hasn't dropped.

"I'm on my way."

"Thank you."

I end the call and sit down on a low wall that edges the parking lot. My wrist is throbbing under the cast, and I reach into my bag, pulling out some Tylenol and a bottle of water. I swallow down two tablets, hoping it takes the edge off.

While I wait for Nash, I call Taylor. As good as Sophie, Cade, and Nash have been, I hardly know them and I miss my best friend. I wish she was here.

"Hello."

"Hey, Tay. It's me."

"Hey, how are you?"

"I'm okay."

"Are you sure?"

"I had a miscarriage," I whisper.

"A miscarriage? When?"

"Last night."

"I'm so sorry, Paisley. Did you know you were pregnant?"

I sigh. "No. I had no idea. I was nine weeks." My voice breaks, and a single tear tracks down my cheek.

"Please don't cry. Where are you now?"

"Outside the hospital. My wrist is in a cast and I have some cracked ribs."

"Fuck, Paisley! I wish I could be there with you. I hate knowing you're on your own."

"I wish you were here too. I'm not on my own though. I've got a room in a women's shelter, and Sophie who runs it has been great; her friends too."

"A shelter?" I can hear the horror in her voice. She must have the same preconceived ideas about a shelter I had.

"It's nice, Tay. I have my own room and bathroom. I'm okay."

"I hope so," she says softly. "I'm glad you're safe from Connor, but I miss you."

"I miss you too." A police car pulls up alongside me, and I raise my hand in a wave to Nash. "I have to go. My ride is here. Can I call you later?"

"Of course. Take care, Paisley."

"You too, Tay. Bye."

I end the call as Nash climbs out. His face is clouded with concern, and I stand from where I'm sitting and make my way to him.

"What's going on, Paisley. Does Cade know you're leaving?" His brow is furrowed as his eyes track from my broken arm to my bruised face.

"I don't think so. The doctor I saw… he made me feel uncomfortable, and I just wanted to get out of there."

"What did he do?"

"Nothing, not really. He was just asking lots of questions. He made me feel like…" I trail off and drop my eyes.

"Made you feel like what, Paisley?"

I sigh. "Like it was my fault."

"What!" he shouts. His voice is laced with anger, and I take a step back. Nash isn't angry with me, but the tone of his voice makes me nervous.

He must see my reaction to his outburst and his face softens. "Fuck," he mutters, dragging his hand through his hair. "I didn't mean to scare you. I would *never* hurt you, Paisley."

"I overreacted," I say quietly.

"You didn't. I didn't think."

"You've been great, Nash. If I hadn't met you on the plane, I don't know where I'd be now."

"I'm glad you decided to come to Hope Creek." His eyes hold mine, and I give him a small smile.

"Me too." He returns my smile, and I yawn, heat flooding my face. "Sorry. I didn't get much sleep last night."

"Let's get you back to Sophie's. Do you have everything?"

I nod, and we walk to his car. He opens the passenger side door, and I get in, dropping my bag in the footwell. He closes the door and I watch as he jogs around the hood and climbs into the driver's seat.

"I've never been in a police car before."

"I think that's probably a good thing." He chuckles as he starts the engine and drives away from the hospital.

"Do you have a partner?" He swings his head around to look at me, and I realize my question has a double meaning.

"A police partner, I mean. I wasn't asking if you have a girl-friend." Heat floods my face again, and I groan internally.

He laughs. "It's a no to both."

I'm surprised he doesn't have a girlfriend. Despite swearing off men after everything that's happened, I can appreciate that he's hot. I slide my eyes across the car and take him in. His dark hair is styled messy, and a couple of days of stubble sits on his face. He's wearing aviator sunglasses, but I know from yesterday his eyes are a piercing blue. His dark blue shirt is pulled tight over his chest, the short sleeves tight around his biceps. He's wearing a utility belt, and I can see a pair of handcuffs and his gun holstered to the belt. He must have his pick of women, his job and uniform only adding to his appeal.

"How's your wrist feeling?" he asks.

"Okay. It's throbbing a little, but I took some Tylenol while I was waiting for you."

He frowns. "You won't have any pain meds if you discharged yourself."

"Shit," I mutter.

"I can ask Cade to prescribe you something, don't worry."

"No, it's not that, but thanks. Cade said I should get a shower cover for my wrist. I can't get the cast wet. I forgot to ask for one."

"I think I might have one. I broke my wrist a few years ago. You can have that."

"Are you sure?"

He nods. "I can drop it over to you after work, if that's okay? Unless you want to shower before then?"

"No. Tonight is fine. I think I'm just going to crash once I get back to the house."

"I'll swing by with it later, then."

"Only if it's not too much trouble. It doesn't have to be tonight if you're tired after work."

"It's not too much trouble. I'll message you before I come."

"Thanks, Nash."

"Here we are," he says as he parks in the driveway of the shelter. He opens his door and climbs out. I follow, grabbing my bag from beside my feet.

"You don't need to see me in. I'm sure you're busy."

"It's fine, Paisley." He walks me up the porch steps and stops outside the front door. "Do you know the code?" he asks, looking at the coded lock.

"No. Sophie hadn't gotten around to telling me." He knocks loudly on the door.

"I don't think she's home," he says when no one answers.

"I'll give her a call. Hopefully she can tell me the code over the phone." I find her number on my phone and bring it to my ear. I bite down on my lip when it goes straight to voicemail. "It's not even ringing." I sit down on the porch swing and drop my bag on the floor. "I'll be fine waiting here. I don't want to take up any more of your time."

"I'm not leaving you here. You're exhausted and we don't know how long Sophie's going to be. I'm guessing she wasn't expecting you back this early."

"I'm fine waiting here," I assure him. "You need to get back to work."

He drags his hand through his hair and paces the small porch. "Try her again. I'm not happy leaving you on the doorstep."

I call her again, but like before, it goes straight to voicemail. "Voicemail again. I'm okay, Nash. Honestly."

"Why don't you come back to my place? I can give you a spare key and you can just sleep."

"What? No! I can't do that." My eyes are wide as I stare at him. I can't invade his personal space like that. He knows nothing about me. "I could steal all your stuff!"

He laughs. "I'm a cop, Paisley. I'm a pretty good judge of character. I'm confident you aren't going to steal my TV!"

"No. I still can't."

"You'd actually be doing me a favor."

"How would me sleeping at your place do you a favor?" I ask, my eyebrows raised in question.

"You can keep Max company."

"Who's Max?"

"My dog. He'd love someone in the house with him." He must see the indecision on my face, and he kneels down in front of me. "Look, you need to sleep, and I'm not happy leaving you here when we have no idea how long Sophie is going to be. You've had a tough forty-eight hours. Please, just come with me."

I sigh and hold his gaze. I *am* exhausted. I was looking forward to crawling into bed and sleeping. The idea of sitting for hours on this wooden porch swing isn't appealing, and my ribs are already hurting. It's not like Nash will be at the house with me. He'll be out at work, and I really do need to sleep.

"Okay," I whisper. "I'll come."

CHAPTER NINE

Nash

*O*nce in the car, Paisley turns to me. "Is there a pharmacy nearby?" she asks, biting down on her lip.

"Yeah. There's one on the main street. What do you need? I have Tylenol."

"It's not Tylenol. I need women's… stuff," she says quietly, her eyes fixed on her lap.

"Oh. Sure. We can stop by the pharmacy on the way." It isn't really on the way. In

fact, it's in the opposite direction, but that doesn't matter.

It's a short drive into town, and I'm able to park right outside the pharmacy. She gives me a small smile and climbs out of the car.

"Be right back," she mumbles before she closes the door.

I hope she has some money. I didn't think to check. I'm

guessing she does. A few minutes later, she's back, a paper bag in her hand.

"All good?"

She nods. "Thanks."

"No worries."

Heading to my place, her head flicks to mine as we drive back past the shelter.

"I thought you said the pharmacy was on the way to your place?"

"It is. In a roundabout way." I laugh. "I live on the next street to Sophie."

"Oh," she mumbles.

She's quiet for the rest of the short drive, and parking on the driveway, I get out and

help her from the car. My house is nowhere near as impressive as Sophie's, but I've done a ton of work on it in the four years I've owned it, and it finally feels like home.

Opening the front door, I gesture for Paisley to go ahead of me. Before we walk in, Max comes flying down the stairs, making straight for Paisley.

"Max, down," I command as he jumps up at her. She drops to her knees in the entryway and fusses over him, letting him lick her face.

"Aren't you just the cutest," she gushes, pulling him into her lap. As she looks over her shoulder and up at me, my stomach flips, and I push down the strange feelings that are stirring inside me as I see her in my house, loving on my dog.

"Come on. I'll show you where you can sleep." I hold my hand out to her and she moves Max off her lap, hesitating before she reaches up and places her hand in mine. I pull her gently up to stand and drop her hand. "The kitchen is straight down there," I tell her, gesturing past the stairway.

"Help yourself to anything you want. My bedroom is upstairs."

"Your bedroom? Don't you have a guest bedroom?"

"Yes, but there's no bed in there. It's my home gym." She bites down on her lip, and I can see she's not happy sleeping in my bed. "Look, I don't want you to feel uncomfortable, so I won't come upstairs with you. It's the second door on the left. The bedding is clean." I reach into the side table in the entryway and pull out the spare key, placing it on top. "The spare key is here. I'll lock the door behind me. Make yourself at home and call me if you want anything." I don't really give her time to argue as I make for the door. "Sleep tight, Paisley," I say quietly, opening the door and closing it silently behind me.

Jumping into the car, I drive away before I change my mind and call in sick so I can stay with her. Heading to the station, I call Cade on the hands-free.

"Hey, Nash," he says when he answers.

"Hey. Do you know the doctor who was looking after Paisley?"

"Yeah, why?"

"He was an asshole to her and she left before she was discharged. She's got no pain meds."

"Fuck," he mutters. "Beckett can be a jerk. I'll bring her a prescription back for some meds. Is she back at Sophie's?"

"No. Actually she's at my house."

"What? Why?"

"When we got back to Sophie's, she wasn't home. Her phone's going straight to voicemail, and Paisley was exhausted."

"So you just took her to your house?"

"What else was I supposed to do? I couldn't leave her on the porch."

"You know nothing about her."

"I know enough."

"What does that mean?"

"It means she's a good person, Cade. She just needs some help."

"Sophie's helping her."

"Well, now I am too." We're both silent for a second and I know he thinks I'm crazy. "I've got to go. I just got to the station."

He sighs. "So do I bring the prescription to your house or Sophie's?"

"Mine. If she's gone back to Sophie's by then, I'll take it to her."

"Okay. See you later."

He ends the call and I see a message from Paisley.

Paisley: I never said thank you, so… thanks.

Me: No need to thank me. Get some rest.

I climb out of the car and make my way inside. I have some paperwork to finish off from a case I was working on before I left for Pittsburgh, and I'm hoping to get it finished today. I head to my desk and spend the next couple of hours tying up loose ends. It's a welcome distraction from wondering how Paisley is.

The last couple of hours of my shift drag as I drive the patrol car around Hope Creek. Not much is happening, and while I'm glad, it does make the time go slowly. When my phone rings, I'm surprised to see Paisley's name flash up.

"Hey, Paisley."

"Hi, Nash."

"How are you feeling?"

"A bit better, thanks."

"Everything okay?"

"Yeah. I finally got hold of Sophie. She'd gone out this morning and forgotten her phone. She thought she'd be back before I was discharged."

"Glad she's okay. Are you back at her place now?"

"Erm, no. I tried to leave yours, but I could hear Max crying as I locked the door."

"Don't worry, he always cries when I leave. He soon calms down."

"I don't want to leave him crying."

"He'll be fine, Paisley, but you're welcome to stay."

"I was wondering if I could take him back to Sophie's, just while you're at work. I can walk him back once you're home. You can say no if you want." Her words tumble out in a rush and she sounds nervous.

I chuckle. "Sure. He'll love all the attention. Are you sure Sophie won't mind?"

"I asked her and she was fine with it."

"Okay. Are you leaving now?"

"Yeah."

"His leash's hanging up in the closet in the entryway."

"Let me know when you're leaving work and I'll walk him back."

"Okay. See you later, Paisley."

"Bye, Nash."

At six p.m. I pull onto the driveway at home and head inside to get changed. It's strange to not have Max come and greet me, and the house is unusually quiet. After a quick shower, I pull on some jeans and a shirt and glance at the bed. The comforter is how I left it this morning, and I'm guessing Paisley slept on the sofa if my bed hasn't been slept in. I hope she was comfortable. Walking into my closet, I search for the waterproof protector for Paisley's cast. Finding it, I jog downstairs just as the doorbell rings.

Swinging the door open, I find Cade on the other side, holding up Paisley's prescription.

"Hey, man. Where's Max?" he asks, knowing I can't normally open the door without having Max jump all over whoever is visiting.

"He's with Paisley at Sophie's. She didn't want to leave him when she woke up. You know how upset he gets when you leave him."

"Are you heading over there now?" I nod. "I'll give you a ride."

"Thanks." I close and lock the door behind me before walking to Cade's car.

"Tell Paisley to take two tablets every four hours as and when she needs them with food," Cade says as he reverses out of the driveway.

"Right. Two tablets, every four hours with food," I repeat. "Got it."

"Are you coming in?" I ask as he pulls up outside Sophie's.

"No." He doesn't elaborate, and I'm guessing it's something to do with Sophie. Not wanting to push it, I don't question him.

"Okay. Well, thanks for the ride." I climb out of the car and close the door, leaning in through the open window.

"I'm working all weekend. See you next Thursday at Mom and Dad's, if not before."

"I think I'm working a night shift on Thursday. I'll check."

"You've remembered it's Ash's birthday next weekend?"

"Fuck. I completely forgot!"

He rolls his eyes. "We're meeting at Eden on Saturday night, then Sunday lunch at Mom and Dad's. I think Wyatt will be back from his training session by then."

"Right, okay. I guess that gives me the week to get her a gift. What are you getting?"

He laughs. "Nice try. I'm not telling you so you can steal my idea again!"

"I only did that once."

He glares at me. "Think of your own gift. I'll see you Thursday." He presses the button to roll the window up, and I step back before he takes off my hand. I guess he's had a bad day. Moody bastard.

Turning around, I jog up the driveway and climb the porch steps. Knocking lightly on the door, I wait for someone to answer. After hearing footsteps inside, the door swings open and Sophie greets me.

"Hey, Nash. Come on in. I'll take you up to Paisley's room. I'm not sure if she's asleep." I follow her up the stairs and along the corridor. Stopping outside a closed door, she knocks quietly on the wood.

"Come in," she calls after a few seconds of silence.

"Nash is here. Is he okay to come in?" She turns to look at me and smiles.

"Yeah."

Sophie opens the door, and my stomach dips as I see her lying on the bed, Max curled up next to her. I frown when her eyes meet mine and they're red and puffy. She's been crying. I hate that she's been crying on her own. I'm glad she's had Max for company at least.

"You should have called me. I'd have walked Max home,"

she says as she sits up and wipes her eyes. Max looks up but doesn't attempt to get off the bed.

"It's okay. I was going to walk over, but Cade brought you a prescription for pain meds and gave me a ride over."

"Are you two okay if I go downstairs? I'm just cooking dinner," Sophie asks. Her eyes are fixed on Paisley, and I know she's asking her if she's okay being alone with me. I'm not offended. Sophie's putting Paisley first, and that's how it should be. Paisley nods, and Sophie turns to me. "You're welcome to stay for dinner, Nash. It's only tomato pasta, but there's plenty."

"Is that okay, Paisley?"

"Of course." She looks surprised I've asked her.

"I'll leave you to it, then. I'll give you a shout when it's ready."

Max finally seems to notice me and jumps off the bed, making his way toward me.

"Hey, boy. Have you been good for Paisley?" I ask, patting him gently.

"He's a great listener," she says quietly. "Thank you for letting me borrow him."

"Anytime. How are you feeling?"

"I'm okay."

"Have you been crying?" I walk farther into the room and sit on the easy chair next to the dresser.

She shrugs. "It's all just a little overwhelming."

"You can talk to me if you ever need to. As good a listener as Max is, I'm guessing you didn't get much conversation back."

She smiles. "No. He wasn't very chatty." She pauses. "Thanks, Nash. You, Sophie, and Cade have restored my faith in people."

"Good. I'm glad. Look, why don't you keep my spare key, and anytime you feel like taking Max for a walk, you can come and get him. It seems he's taken quite a liking to you," I say with a chuckle, seeing he's jumped back on her bed and pressed himself against her.

"I'd like that. I've heard people say dogs know when something's wrong; that they can sense it. I never believed them, but it's true. He hasn't left my side all day." She leans down and kisses his head. He looks up, gazing at her like she's hung the moon.

"I think you're right. They have this sixth sense."

Realizing I'm still holding the waterproof cover for her cast and the prescription Cade gave me, I stand from the chair and take them to her.

"I asked Cade to give you some pain meds since you didn't get any before you left. You can take two, four times a day, but only with food. I can take you to the pharmacy tomorrow if you need me to, and this is the cover for your arm."

"Thank you," she says, taking the prescription and cover from my outstretched hand. "I can walk to the pharmacy now that I know where it is. I need to head into town anyway. I need to find a job."

I frown. "You need to rest."

"I need to earn some money to pay my way. I can work with a broken wrist."

"You can't! What about the cracked ribs?"

"I'll be fine."

"Paisley—"

"I'm grateful for all you've done for me, Nash, but I'm not your concern."

Her words sting, despite them being true. She isn't my

concern, but unfortunately for me, that doesn't stop me *being* concerned.

"I should go." I stand up. "Come on, boy." I pat my leg and Max jumps off the bed. "Hope you're feeling better soon, Paisley."

"Bye, Nash," she whispers, and I sigh as I leave the room, Max behind me.

CHAPTER TEN

Paisley

It's been a week since I last saw Nash. I know I was a bitch the last time we spoke. I didn't mean to be, I just didn't want another man telling me what I could and couldn't do. I know he said what he did because he was concerned. I guess I'm not used to a man being concerned about me. Despite the way things were left between us, I've been to his house every day this week to walk Max. I've made sure his car hasn't been on the driveway. I don't want to invade his downtime.

In between walking Max, I've been searching in the shops and restaurants in Hope Creek for some work. Either no one is hiring or they aren't prepared to hire someone with a black eye and a broken wrist. I can't say I blame them. I'm a mess. I don't really want to work in a bar. With how Connor used to get when he was drunk, I don't want to be around people like that, but with nowhere taking people on, I'm going to have to start enquiring in the bars soon.

It's early afternoon when I make the short walk to Nash's house. His truck isn't parked on the drive, so I let myself in, dropping the spare key on the entryway table. Like every other day this week, Max comes bounding up to me before I've even closed the front door.

"Hey, boy. Did you miss me?" I kneel down on the floor and stroke him, laughing when he's in my face, trying to kiss me. "I love your kisses. Yes, I do," I coo. "Let's find your leash." I stand up and look in the closet in the entryway. I frown when it's not hanging on the usual hook. "Where is it?" I ask, laughing when he barks. "Is it in the kitchen?"

I make my way through the hallway and into the open-plan kitchen. Glancing around, I'm surprised at how tidy everywhere is. For a single guy, he keeps the house cleaner than I could. My eyes flick around the space, but I can't see Max's leash.

"Paisley?" a voice says behind me, and I jump, a squeal leaving my lips.

"Shit! Nash! You scared me."

I spin round and my mouth goes dry as he stands in front of me in just a pair of sleep shorts, his chest bare. His hair is messy from just waking up, and there's a few days' stubble on his jaw.

"Sorry. I didn't mean to scare you."

I drag my eyes off him and focus on the floor. "I thought you were at work or I never would have let myself in. I was coming to take Max for a walk, but I can't find his leash. I'll go. I'm sorry."

I go to walk past him, but he reaches for my hand. "No,

wait." He drags his free hand through his hair and sighs. "I'm sorry if I upset you last week. That wasn't my intention."

"I know," I whisper. "I'm sorry too. I was a bitch."

"You weren't. It was my fault. I shouldn't have tried to tell you what to do."

"It doesn't matter now. Let's forget about it. No work today?" I ask.

"I did the night shift last night."

"Shit! I woke you up. I'm so sorry."

He waves off my apology. "It's fine. I was getting up soon anyway."

"Are you working again tonight?"

"No. I have the weekend off. It's Ashlyn's birthday."

"Your sister, right?"

He nods. "How are you feeling now?"

"Better. My ribs are getting less painful every day, and my wrist only hurts occasionally."

"That's good. Your eye looks like it's healing." He reaches his hand up and gently brushes his fingers over the multicolored skin under my eye. Our eyes lock, and I stare at him for a few seconds before Max barks and pulls me from my daze.

"I can't wait until it isn't noticeable."

"It'll be gone soon. Another week maybe."

"I guess I should go."

"You don't want to walk Max?"

"Well, yeah, if you don't mind?"

"I don't mind. I'll hop in the shower while you're gone. Have you eaten lunch?" I shake my head. "I'll make us something." He opens a drawer and takes out Max's leash. "Come on, boy. You're going out with Paisley."

Max barks, and I laugh. Taking the leash from Nash's hand, I fix it to Max's collar. "I'll see you soon, then."

"See you soon." His eyes drop to Max. "Behave."

"He always does."

I leave Nash in the kitchen and make the short walk to the main street. I hadn't taken much notice of the bars when I'd been looking for work, but as I look up and down, there's at least three I can enquire in. Maybe now isn't the best time. I'm not sure if I can take Max inside. As I walk past one, there's a guy outside changing a poster to advertise a singer they have performing tomorrow night.

"Hi," I say shyly as I come to a stop. "Do you work here?"

He looks up and smiles. "Yeah. I'm the bar manager."

"Are you looking for any staff?" His eyes drop from mine to my broken wrist, and I jump in before he can ask. "It's coming off soon," I lie. "I can still do things with it on."

"We are looking for someone to work the tables. Do you have any experience?"

"Honestly?" I ask with a chuckle.

He laughs. "I'll take that as a no."

"I've worked in a coffee shop, so I'm good with people, and I can carry a tray of drinks."

"Even with a cast?"

"Even with a cast."

He drags in a breath and lets it out slowly. "What's your name?"

"Paisley."

"Hi, Paisley. I'm Ryder. Come by at seven tomorrow and I'll give you a trial. If you can deal with the Saturday night rush, then you're in. Okay?"

I grin. "Okay. Thank you. I won't let you down."

"See you tomorrow, Paisley." He turns and walks back inside, and I look up at the building. It's double fronted with a window on either side of the door, and a black canopy with the name *Eden* written in large white letters juts out from the wall. The door is open, but it's dark inside and I can't see what it's like. I guess I'll find out tomorrow. If I didn't have Max, I'd go in and check it out.

Sitting on a bench directly opposite the bar, I pull out my phone and send a message to Sophie, too excited to wait until I'm back at the house later.

Me: I think I might have found a job!

I can see three little dots flashing on the screen, telling me she's replying.

Sophie: That's great. Where?

Me: A bar in town. I have a trial shift tomorrow night. I hope I can manage with my cast. I told the guy a little white lie that it would be coming off soon!

Sophie: Which bar?

Me: Eden.

The phone rings in my hand, and I answer when I see Sophie's name flash up. "Hi."

"Paisley, you know Eden is Nash's brother's bar, right?"

My eyes widen. "What? No. I had no idea. I thought his brother's name was Seb?"

"It is."

"The guy I spoke to was Ryder."

"He's the manager. Seb's the owner. Nash is going to freak."

When Nash didn't stay for dinner last week, Sophie asked why, and I'd told her about how he'd reacted when I said I was going to look for work.

"He'll be fine. I've just seen him and he apologized for the other night."

"Okay, then, but I don't think he's going to be too happy."

"Tough! It's none of his business. I'm nothing to him."

She laughs down the phone. "Paisley, I think you're a whole lot of something to Nash Brookes."

I frown in confusion. "What does that mean?"

There's silence on the line before she eventually speaks. "Nothing. You're right. It's none of his business."

"Soph—"

"Hey, I gotta go, there's someone at the door. See you later."

She ends the call and I pull the phone from my ear, wondering what the hell she means. Standing up, Max and I walk slowly through town and take the long route back to Nash's. Pushing down Sophie's comments, I think back to meeting Ryder. He seemed like a nice guy. I hope I wasn't lying to him when I said I could manage to carry a tray. The hospital had given me a sling, but I didn't need to wear it all the time. I really hope I can do this. I need a job.

When I get back to Nash's, I decide not to tell him about the trial shift, especially now that I know it's in his brother's bar. I don't want to get into an argument again. We've only just ironed things out. I haven't got many friends and I don't want to lose him. If the trial works out, I can tell him then.

As I stand outside his door, I'm not sure whether I should knock, and Max barks as he waits for me to decide what to do. Suddenly, the door swings open, making me jump. Nash is standing in the entryway, dressed in dark jeans and a Henley.

His feet are bare and his hair is damp from the shower. Despite being sworn off men, I can't help but notice how gorgeous he is.

"Are you okay?"

"Oh, erm… yeah. I didn't know if I should knock or not."

"You don't need to knock, Paisley. Come in."

He takes Max's leash from my hand and walks him into the house. I follow and close the door behind me.

"Something smells good," I say as I walk behind him and into the kitchen. Max is off his leash and jumps around my legs as I walk. "I'm not going anywhere, boy." I reach down to pat him. "I guess he thinks I'm leaving. I normally do when we get back from our walk."

"He's a big softie. Bed, Max." Max immediately stops jumping up and skulks across the kitchen to his bed. "I'm making an omelet, as this is breakfast for me. I hope that's okay."

"An omelet sounds great."

"Take a seat." He gestures to the stools at the breakfast bar, and I slide onto one, watching him as he stands at the stove.

"Can I do anything to help?"

He looks over his shoulder. "I'm good. Do you want a drink?"

"I'll get it. What do you have?"

"There are some sodas in the refrigerator, I think. Unless you want a glass of wine?"

"Soda's fine." I stand, then cross the room and open the refrigerator. "Do you want one?"

"Please." I pull out two cans and set them on the breakfast bar, sitting down just as Nash begins to plate up. When he's done, he pushes my plate across to me.

"This looks great, thanks."

"You're welcome. It's just an omelet."

"I guess I'm not used to anyone cooking for me." He gives me a small smile, and I cut off a slice of omelet and fork it into my mouth. "Yum," I tell him when I've swallowed down my mouthful.

"I love to cook. It helps me unwind after a long day. Maybe I could cook you something a little more exciting than an omelet sometime? As a thank-you for walking Max?"

"Oh… sure," I stutter, wanting to, but knowing I can't. I won't let myself get involved with anyone again. I never want to be tied to someone and out of control like I was with Connor.

"I can see your mind working overtime, Paisley. It's not a date. Just a thank-you."

I eat another forkful of omelet, not knowing how to respond. Taking a pull of my soda, I swallow it down, along with the lump in my throat.

"I know. I didn't think you meant a date," I say softly. "Believe me. I plan on being single forever."

His eyes find mine and he frowns. "Not everyone is going to be like your ex, Paisley."

"I know. I just can't open myself up to anyone like that again. I can't be that vulnerable."

"Paisley—"

"So, what did you get your sister for her birthday?" I ask, cutting him off.

He sighs, and I know he wants to say more. I'm grateful when he doesn't. "Actually, I haven't gotten her anything yet. I've no idea."

"How old is she going to be?"

"Twenty-five."

"Same age as me. Does she wear jewelry?"

"I think so."

"What about a charm bracelet, and then you can add to it for future birthdays or special occasions?"

"That's a great idea!" He eats the last of his omelet and takes a pull of his soda. "Are you free this afternoon? Would you come with me and help me choose one?"

I hesitate before nodding. "Sure. I saw a jewelry store on the main street when I was there earlier in the week. We could try there."

"Great. I'll just clean up and we can go."

"I'll clean up. You cooked."

"You should rest, Paisley. I'll clean up. It won't take me long." Five minutes later, he's loaded the dishwasher and wiped down the counter. "Ready?"

I nod and slip off the stool, following him into the entryway. "Where's your car, by the way?"

"At the station. I was out on a call last night and someone dropped me home this morning. It seemed easier than going back to fetch it. Are you feeling okay to walk into town?"

"I'm good."

Max follows us into the entryway and sits staring at us while Nash pulls his sneakers on. "I won't be long, Max," Nash assures him, and he whines in reply. I kneel in front of him and run my fingers through his silky coat before dropping a kiss on his head. When we get outside and Nash closes the door, I can hear him crying.

"Has he always done that?" I ask as I reluctantly follow Nash down the driveway.

"Yeah. He was a rescue and mistreated. Eventually, the owners abandoned him, and it was a few days before anyone found him. He was in a bad way when they got him to the shelter. I think he worries that when I leave, I won't come back."

"God, that breaks my heart. People suck."

"Yeah, they do," Nash whispers, sliding his eyes to mine. I know he's talking about Connor right now and not Max's previous owners.

"I'm glad he found you."

"I'm glad too. He deserves the best."

His gaze holds mine, and I wonder if he's talking about Max or me.

CHAPTER ELEVEN

Nash

It's Saturday night, and I'm getting dressed for Ashlyn's birthday drinks. I thought about inviting Paisley after she helped me pick out a gift, but I don't want her to think I'm asking her out on a date. She's made it perfectly clear she's not interested, and after everything she's been through, I don't blame her.

When I'm dressed in dark jeans and a pale blue button-down shirt, I push my feet into my black lace-up boots and head downstairs. Ash's actual birthday is tomorrow, so I leave her wrapped gift on the entryway table. I'll give it to her at Mom and Dad's when we all head there tomorrow for lunch.

After saying goodbye to Max, I walk into town. My car's still at the station, but I'm planning on having a few drinks tonight anyway, so I wouldn't be driving. I'm only having a couple of beers. I know what Ashlyn is like on a night out, and I want to keep my eye on her. I can't do that if I'm drunk, plus, it's not a good look if the town cop is smashed.

I walk into the already packed bar, my eyes scanning the room for Ashlyn. I spot her dancing with Ivy, her best friend.

"Nash!" Ashlyn shouts when she sees me, already seeming like she's had too much to drink. Crossing the crowded room, I stop in front of her, dropping a kiss on her cheek.

"Happy birthday, squirt" I whisper in her ear, and she smacks me on the chest.

"Quit calling me that!"

I laugh, my eyes dropping to the drink in her hand. "What are you drinking?"

"Vodka!"

"How about I get you a water and you slow down a little? It's not even nine." She rolls her eyes, and I know my suggestion is falling on deaf ears. "Where's everyone else?"

"Over there." My eyes follow where she's pointing, and I see Seb and Wyatt sitting in one of the booths. "Cade's not here yet."

"Hi, Nash," Ivy says, placing her hand on my arm and going up on her tiptoes to kiss my cheek.

"Nice to see you, Ivy," I say, flashing her a smile. She's like a second sister. She and Ashlyn have been friends forever.

"I'm going to say hi to the others," I say to Ashlyn. "Let me know when you want another drink."

She smiles and kisses me on the cheek.

Moving through the crowd, I raise my hand in a wave when Seb looks up and sees me. Sliding into the booth when I get there, I pull Wyatt into a one-armed hug.

"Hey, man. Good to see you. How've you been?"

"Yeah, good. You?"

I nod and tip my head in acknowledgement to Seb. Looking at both of them sitting side by side, if it weren't for Seb's tattoos, they'd be identical. Wyatt's a little more built than Seb these days, but as kids, even my mom struggled to tell them apart. They loved the fact they were identical though and managed to fool everyone countless times. As they got older, they soon figured out who was good at what subjects academically, and more often than not, they'd pretend to be each other to pass tests in school. The teachers had no idea. If their own mother couldn't tell them apart, their teachers had no chance. I think my parents were actually relieved when Seb got his first tattoo at eighteen; at least they knew who was who then.

"Do you want a drink?" Seb asks, standing and moving out of the booth.

"Just a bottle of Bud, please."

"Wyatt?"

"Same for me. I'm going to enjoy some time off."

"Be right back."

He disappears into the crowd, and I turn to Wyatt. "How was the training camp?"

"Hard work. I'm looking forward to some nights out and some of Mom's cooking."

"Mom will love having you home for a few weeks."

While Wyatt has a place in Phoenix, when he isn't playing or training, he comes back to Hope Creek and stays at Mom and Dad's. He only gets a couple of months a year of complete downtime, but he loves Hope Creek like the rest of us and always comes home. He does make it back at other times during the season, but his visits are shorter, and I know how much my parents miss him.

A few minutes later, Seb comes back to the table empty-handed. "Did you forget our drinks?" I ask with a chuckle, looking down at his empty hands.

"No, jackass. We've got a new server and she's going to bring them over."

"Is that the same server who brought our last round of drinks?" Wyatt asks, and Seb nods. "She was cute. I wouldn't mind getting a piece of that."

"No flirting with my staff!" Seb exclaims. "I don't want her gushing all over the famous football player and dropping any drinks."

"A little flirting never hurt anyone." Wyatt chuckles.

"It'll hurt my profits!"

I'm listening with amusement to Seb and Wyatt's conversation when a tray of drinks is placed on the table. When I look up, my breath catches in my throat as I see it's Paisley who's brought the tray. She hasn't seen me yet, her eyes fixed firmly on the tray. Before she looks up, I take her in. She's stunning. Her subtle makeup completely covers her bruised face, and her hair is curled in loose waves down her back, with small sections pinned up to keep it off her face. She's wearing dark skinny jeans and a tight black t-shirt, the Eden emblem sitting across her chest. When she finally looks up, her eyes widen, and I find myself unable to look away.

"Nash," she gasps. "What are you doing here?"

"Ashlyn's birthday," I say, sliding out of the booth. Standing in front of her, my fingers go to her cast. "What are *you* doing here? Are you sure you should be working?" Her eyes flick from me to Seb, and she nods.

"I'm fine, Nash." She pulls her arm away from my fingers and focuses her attention back on the tray of drinks. "Three bottles of Bud?" she asks Seb and Wyatt.

"One each, sweetheart," Wyatt says with a wink. I glare daggers at him as he flirts with her.

"And the vodka lemonades?" she asks, somehow managing to hold one in each hand.

"Those would be ours," Ashlyn says from behind her. Paisley turns around and smiles before handing one to Ash and the other to Ivy. "Thanks," Ashlyn says as she sips the clear liquid through a straw.

"Can I get anyone anything else?" she asks, loading our empty bottles onto the tray and picking it up.

"Could you bring us another bottle of Bud, Paisley. My other brother will be here soon," Seb asks.

"Is this the Paisley you met on the plane, Nash?" Ashlyn asks from the side of me. Even in the dim light of the bar, I can see Paisley's cheeks color.

"Yes," I mutter, my eyes fixed on Paisley.

"Hi, Ashlyn. Happy birthday," Paisley says. "I'll be right back with that Bud." She turns away from the table and carefully maneuvers through the crowds in the direction of the bar. When she's disappeared from view, I turn to see everyone staring at me.

"You know her?" Wyatt asks, a smile pulling on his lips.

"Yes," I bite out. "Stop fucking flirting with her."

He holds his hands up and chuckles. "Okay. She's off-limits. I hear you."

"That's the girl you and Cade left Mom and Dad's to go and see that time?" Seb asks, and I nod.

"Why the fuck would you hire someone with a broken wrist and cracked ribs? She's not ready to work."

"I didn't take her on, Ryder did. She's just on a trial shift, but she's good, and the cast comes off soon."

"No. It doesn't! She's only had it on a week."

He frowns. "She told Ryder it did. Regardless, it's not stopping her from working. She's managing fine."

"So that's it? You're happy to let her work with a broken wrist and fractured ribs? She should be taking it easy! Cade will agree with me," I say angrily.

"Did I hear my name?" a voice says, and I look behind me to see Cade's arrived.

"Seb's given Paisley a job. She's working the bar. Tell him it's too soon for her to be working!" I sit down and snatch up my bottle of Bud, swallowing down a mouthful.

"Hey, Ash," Cade says, ignoring me and leaning down to kiss her cheek.

"Cade! Tell him!"

"Nash, Paisley's an adult. If she chooses to work, then there's not a lot *anyone* can do about it." He widens his eyes on the word *anyone*.

"So, if Sophie had been beaten to within an inch of her life, you'd be happy for her to be working in a bar less than two weeks later?"

"What the fuck has this got to do with Sophie?" he snaps, his face like thunder. "Paisley isn't your concern. Like I said, she can do what she wants."

I down the rest of my beer and bang the bottle down on the table. "This is bullshit!"

"Hey, Cade," Paisley says as she comes back to the table with a bottle of beer in her hand, thankfully just missing my outburst.

"Thanks, Paisley. How are you?" Cade asks as he takes the beer from her outstretched hand.

"I'm good." She smiles at him, her smile faltering when her eyes go from him to me.

"Paisley, can I have a word?" I ask, standing from the booth.

Her eyes flick to Seb. "No. I'm working." She turns and walks away before I can stop her.

"I like her," Ashlyn says with a giggle. "You should bring her to lunch tomorrow."

"We're not dating, Ash."

"Maybe not, but sure seems like you want to be."

I ignore her and head to the bar. Maybe I'm overreacting, but I need to know she's okay. It's busy, and I fight my way through the crowds. It's about four deep at the bar, and I flick my eyes around the space, trying to find her. I finally spot her at the end of the bar, loading up a tray of drinks. She looks up and her eyes find mine through the crowds. She picks up the tray and walks toward me.

"You're going to get me in trouble, Nash, and I really need this job," she says as she walks past me. I follow her and watch as she serves the drinks to a table full of guys who can't take their eyes off her. I clench my fists at my side as one of the guys reaches out to smack her ass. I'm just about to go over and knock his head off when she grabs his hand and pushes it away.

"Don't touch me," she says before picking the empty tray up and walking away.

I follow her. "Paisley, please. My brother owns the bar. He's not going to fire you for talking to me for a few minutes."

"I don't have the job yet. This is my trial shift," she says over her shoulder.

"He's already impressed," I tell her on a sigh.

She stops and turns around, a wide smile on her face. "Really? He said that?" I can't help but smile back at her.

"Yeah. He did. So will you talk to me now?"

She hesitates and looks around. "Okay. Over here." She gestures with her head to the small corridor that leads to the kitchen and staff room. "Make it quick," she says once we're away from the crush of the bar.

"I just want to check you're okay."

"I'm fine, Nash." She goes to move round me, but I take her good hand in mine. She looks at me before her eyes drop to our joined hands.

"Wait. Are you sure? Didn't Cade say you should rest for a few weeks?"

She sighs. "I don't have that luxury, Nash. I *need* to work. I've got nowhere to live and no money."

"You can stay at Sophie's for as long as you want."

"I know, but I don't want to live in a women's shelter. As nice as Sophie is, I don't want to have to rely on her to put a roof over my head and a meal on the table. Surely you get that."

"I do. I just want to make sure you aren't rushing into working when you still aren't well."

"I'm fine."

"You keep saying that."

"That's because it's the truth."

"I saw how you handled yourself back there with that guy."

She shrugs. "Working in a bar wouldn't have been my first choice for a job, but I've tried everywhere else and no one is hiring, or maybe they're just not hiring me. Either way, I had to look elsewhere. When Ryder offered me a shot, I decided I wasn't going to let a man touch me unless I wanted him to. I don't want to be that weak person again."

"You're letting me hold your hand," I say softly.

She bites down on her bottom lip. "I trust you, Nash. Even if you can be a little annoying." She grins, and I laugh.

"Me? Never!" I joke, loving hearing her say she trusts me.

"I should get back."

"Are you due a break soon?"

"I'm not sure. What time is it?"

I pull out my phone and check the time. "Almost ten."

"I guess so, but Ryder hasn't mentioned it."

"Come and find me if you get a break. I'll introduce you to everyone."

"Okay," she says shyly.

I reluctantly drop her hand and follow her back to the bar. "And, Paisley." I wait until she turns around. "You aren't weak. You're the strongest person I know."

"Thanks, Nash."

I watch her until she's out of sight before going back to Cade and the others.

"Do you feel better now that you've spoken to her?" Seb asks as I slide into the booth.

"Yes. I still think she needs to take more time to recover, but it's her call."

"I'm going to offer her the job. You're not going to have a problem with that, are you?" he asks, raising his eyebrows in question.

"No."

"It's mainly day shifts, maybe one evening shift a week."

Somehow, I feel better knowing she'll be working days in the bar. I don't want her walking home in the early hours of the morning after a night shift. I'll have to see if I can pick her up on the days she does a late. She likely won't like it, but that's tough. She's been through enough. I don't want anything else happening to her.

CHAPTER TWELVE

Paisley

I work for another half hour before Ryder pulls me to one side and tells me to take a break. I've just taken a tray full of drinks to Nash and his siblings, so I know they're all good.

"Can I grab a Diet Coke?" I ask Ryder, and he nods, pouring me a glass.

"How long's my break?"

"A half hour."

"Okay, see you then." He nods and focuses on the crowd of people waiting to be served.

Sipping on my drink, I slowly make my way to Nash. I'm nervous to meet everyone, even though I've been serving them drinks all night. Despite telling Nash earlier I was fine, my feet are killing me and my whole body aches. I'm dying to sit down. I think I underestimated how hard being a server is. I was used to being on my feet when I worked in the coffee shop back home, but my shifts there were only ever three or four hours long. I'd been working since six, and I knew the bar didn't close until two. If I do get the job, I hope I can go the distance.

"Paisley," Nash says as he sees me approaching. Standing up, he makes his way over. "Are you on a break?" I nod. "Come on. I'll introduce you to everyone." He reaches for my hand but has to make do with the fingers poking out from my cast, as my good hand holds my drink. I feel his giant hand wrap around my pinkie as he pulls me toward the booth.

"Guys, this is Paisley," he says when we reach everyone. "This is Wyatt. Seb and Cade you already know, and my sister, Ashlyn, and her friend, Ivy.

He gestures around the table, and I smile at each of them. "Hi," I say shyly. My eyes flick between Wyatt and Seb. If Seb wasn't covered in tattoos, I'm not sure I'd be able to tell them apart. Ashlyn smiles as her eyes meet mine. She's stunning, with long blonde hair that falls midway down her back, and the tiny black dress she's wearing looks incredible on her.

"How are you finding working for my brother? I hear he can be a bit of an asshole," she says with a wink, and I laugh.

"Hey!" Seb exclaims. "I am not an asshole."

"Well, I'm only halfway through my first shift, but no complaints so far," I say with a smile.

"Do you want to sit down?" Nash asks in my ear, and I nod.

"Please. My feet are killing, but don't tell Seb."

He chuckles and guides me into the booth. Following me in, he sits down. I take another mouthful of my drink before putting my glass on the table. I pull my phone from my pocket, smiling as I see a text from Taylor. I'd sent her a message telling her about my trial shift before I started.

Taylor: That's great, Paisley. Hope it goes well! Let me know. Love you.

"Everything okay?" Nash asks from the side of me.

I nod. "Just my friend from back home. I messaged her to tell her about my trial shift. She's just wishing me good luck."

I send her a quick message back, even though it will be late in Pittsburgh.

Me: All good so far! Well, I haven't dropped anything, anyway! Love you too, call you soon.

I slip my phone back into my pocket, not wanting to seem rude by being on my phone. Picking up my drink, I swallow down a mouthful.

"How long are you home for, Wyatt?" Ashlyn asks as she sips on her vodka and lemonade.

"Until August, then training starts again. I've got a few social things I've got to be seen at between now and then, but other than that, I'll be here."

"Anything you need a plus-one for?" Ashlyn asks excitedly. "You can introduce me to all those hot guys you play with."

"No," Wyatt, Nash, Seb, and Cade say in unison, and I can't help letting out a laugh.

She rolls her eyes. "Have you got any brothers, Paisley?" she asks.

"No. No siblings at all."

"You're lucky! I'm going to be single forever if these four don't back off!"

"Trust me, Ash, you don't want to get into a relationship

with any of the guys I play football with. Most of them are assholes."

"Hot assholes though! And who said anything about a relationship! One night would do!"

"Fuck!" Seb exclaims. "That's not something I need to hear my baby sister say."

"I'm twenty-five, despite you four treating me like I'm twelve. Back me up, Paisley."

"Sorry, guys, but I have to agree with Ashlyn. A girl has needs." I wink at her and she grins back. I steal a look at Nash to find him staring at me with a heat in his eyes I've never seen before. His stare makes my stomach dip and leaves me feeling flustered. The conversation between Ashlyn and her brothers continues around us, but I don't hear a word as I gaze at him. When someone clears their throat, I drag my eyes off Nash and reach for my drink, taking a large mouthful. My heart is pounding, and I swear everyone in the bar can hear it.

"What do you say, Paisley? Will you come?" Ashlyn asks, and I've no idea what she said. I was too caught up in Nash to hear.

"Sorry," I say sheepishly. "I missed what you said. Come where?"

"For lunch at my parents' place tomorrow?"

"Oh." I flick my head around to look at Nash, who just smiles. "I don't want to intrude on a family celebration."

"You won't be. Please come. I'm always outnumbered with this bunch. It'll be nice to have another woman there my own age, and one who backs me up." She giggles.

I glance around the table as everyone looks at me as they wait for my answer. "Will your parents mind?" I ask uncertainly.

"Not at all. Mom always makes way more than she needs," Ashlyn assures me.

"Okay, then. I'll come. Thank you."

"I'll pick you up tomorrow," Nash offers.

"You don't have your truck," I remind him.

"I'm going into work in the morning to get it. I'll swing by Sophie's about twelve thirty."

I nod and finish the rest of my drink. I can't help but feel emotional at how this amazing family has taken me under their wing, no questions asked. First Nash and Cade, then Seb with the chance of a job, and now Ashlyn. It's been such a long time since I had anyone other than Taylor in my life. I don't think I realized just how lonely I'd been.

When my half an hour is up, I pick up my glass and stand. "I should get back to work. I don't want to get in trouble with the boss," I joke as I move out of the booth. "Another round?" I ask, gesturing with my head to the empty glasses on the table.

"Same again!" Ashlyn shouts, and I smile.

"Be right back." I walk away, turning to look over my shoulder as I do. Nash is watching me, and I give him a small smile, my stomach dipping again when he winks at me. Letting out a long exhale, I head to the bar. I can't let myself get any closer to him than I already am. It wouldn't be fair on him. I can't offer anything more than friendship, even though my battered heart is aching for more.

An hour later, I'm exhausted. My arm is aching from using it more than I should, and my ribs are screaming in protest at me being on my feet for hours. Maybe Nash is right and I'm really not ready for this yet. Pulling out my phone, I check the time, groaning when it's only just after midnight. There's another two hours until the bar closes, and then time to clean up after everyone's gone, as well as the walk home.

Tears sting my eyes as I realize I've taken on too much. I need to work, but if tonight is anything to go by, I'm not ready.

Telling Ryder I need to use the bathroom, I slip away from the crowds and into the staff restroom. I sit down on the closed toilet seat and drop my head in my hands. The tears that were threatening to fall back in the bar now track down my cheeks, my side throbbing as I cry. I just need to try and get through this shift. I can't let Seb or Ryder down on their busiest night. Wiping my eyes, I open the stall door and tidy myself up as best I can in the vanity mirror. My mascara is waterproof, so at least my eye makeup is intact. I don't look too bad, and it's dark in the bar. No one will know I've been crying.

Opening the door to the restroom, I gasp when I see Nash leaning against the opposite wall, waiting for me.

"What are you doing here?" I ask, lowering my head so he doesn't see I've been crying.

"You've been in there a while. Are you okay?" he asks, not answering my question.

"I'm okay. I should get back."

"Paisley." He takes a step toward me, and I instinctively take a step back.

He stops. "I'm not going to hurt you," he says quietly, and I can hear the hurt in his voice.

I lift my head, hating that I've hurt him. "I know you wouldn't. I'm sorry. It's a force of habit."

"Have you been crying?" His voice is laced with concern, but I shake my head. "Paisley."

I sigh and drop my eyes again. "I don't want to admit you were right."

"Right about what?" He hesitates before moving closer, his

fingers tilting my chin so I'm looking into his beautiful blue eyes.

"That I'm not ready to work." My voice is barely a whisper, but I can tell from the frown that appears on his face that he hears me.

"Are you in pain?" I nod. "Fuck. I'm taking you home." He reaches for my hand, but I pull away.

"No. I only have a couple of hours left. I don't want to let anyone down."

"You aren't letting anyone down. Seb will understand."

"No," I say again. "I'll finish my shift."

"This is ridiculous. Have you taken any pain meds?"

"No. The ones Cade gave me make me sleepy. I'll take some when I get back to Sophie's."

"Nothing I can say is going to change your mind, is it?" She shakes her head. "Fine, but I'm walking you home when you're finished."

"You don't have to do that."

"I'm not going to let you walk back on your own in the early hours of the morning, Paisley. I'll walk you home."

"Thank you."

He follows me down the narrow corridor and back into the packed bar.

"I'll see you later." His face is etched with concern as I nod and leave him watching me as I head to the bar.

An hour later and the pain in my wrist is so bad I can't stop the tears falling as I carry yet another tray full of drinks. In the darkness of the room, no one seems to notice, and I'm grateful they don't. I'm guessing most people don't want their drinks brought to them by a crying server. When Ryder asks me to take more drinks to Seb's table, I groan inwardly. While no one at the other tables has noticed my distress, I know Nash will. Wiping my eyes, I lift the tray up and drag in a shaky breath as I cross the room.

"Drinks," I say as brightly as I can, placing the loaded tray onto the table. I don't look at Nash, knowing I'm likely to burst into tears if I do. I pass the drinks around, everyone thanking me. When everyone has a drink, I collect up the empty glasses and bottles and fill the tray again.

"You can call it a night once you've returned those glasses to the bar, Paisley," Seb says. "I'm impressed. We can chat after lunch tomorrow about a permanent position." My watery eyes fly up to meet his, and he smiles. "I think it's going to be two or three weeks before I can offer you any shifts. I hope that fits in with your timeline for wanting work."

I flick my eyes to Nash, who's looking down at his lap, and swallow the golf ball-sized lump in my throat. "That works perfectly. Thank you," I manage to croak out.

"Come and have a real drink with us now that you've finished," Ashlyn says.

"I'd love to, but to be honest, I'm exhausted and can't wait to crawl into my bed. I'll see you tomorrow though, if the offer of lunch still stands?" I bite down nervously on my lip as I wait for her to reply.

"Of course it does. We'll see you tomorrow," she says kindly.

"I'm going to walk Paisley home," Nash says, standing from his seat. "I'll see you all tomorrow." He brushes a kiss on Ashlyn's cheek as he passes her before making his way to me. "Ready?"

"I'll just drop this tray back." He nods and places his hand on the bottom of my back. Jolts of electricity race up my spine, and I wonder if he feels it too.

"Night, everyone," I say before letting Nash guide me to the bar.

When I've handed in the tray, we head outside. I didn't bring anything with me, just my phone, which is nestled in my back pocket. We walk up the main street in comfortable silence. It's dropped a little cold, but the breeze is a welcome relief after the heat of the bar.

"Thank you," I whisper as we turn off the main street and toward Sophie's place.

"No need to thank me. I was ready to call it a night anyway."

"I'm not talking about walking me home but thank you for that as well."

"What are you thanking me for, then?"

"You spoke to Seb."

He shakes his head. "No. I didn't."

I smile and gently bump my shoulder into his arm. "You did, but it's okay. I'm not mad."

"I'm glad you're not mad, but I don't know what you're talking about." He looks down at me and winks. "How are you feeling?"

"Honestly?" He nods. "Like I've been hit by a truck. You were right, it was too soon. I thought I'd be okay."

"You've been through a lot. It's bound to take some time."

"At least I get a couple more weeks to spend with Max. I'm going to miss him when I'm working."

"You're welcome to come and see Max whenever you want. He's going to miss you too."

"Are you bringing him to your parents' tomorrow?"

"I wasn't going to."

"Will he be okay?"

He smiles. "I'll bring him."

Before I know it, we're back at the house. "I'll see you tomorrow, then?" I ask uncertainly as he follows me up the driveway and onto the porch.

"I'll pick you up about twelve thirty."

"Can I ask you a favor? Another one!"

He chuckles. "You can ask me anything, Paisley."

"Could we stop on the way to your parents' place so I can get Ashlyn a birthday card? I can't show up with nothing for her."

"You could, but yes, we can stop on the way. I'll come a little earlier, then."

"Thank you. For everything."

"Stop thanking me. I'm not doing anything."

"You're doing more than you know." I hesitate for a second before surprising myself and going up on my tiptoes, pressing a kiss to his cheek. He looks as surprised as I am.

"Sleep tight, Paisley. I'll see you tomorrow."

"Bye."

He makes no attempt to leave, a small smile pulling on his lips. "Paisley, I'm not going until you go inside. I'm not leaving you standing on the porch at two in the morning."

"Oh," I gasp, my cheeks heating. Turning around, I key in the code to open the door and step inside. He's chuckling as I close the door and drop my head back on the wood. The more time I spend with him, the more he's making me want things I know I can't have. We're friends, and that's all we can ever be. I'm just not sure my heart got the memo.

CHAPTER THIRTEEN

Nash

$\mathcal{D}$riving from the station to Sophie's place, I replay last night in my head. After I'd seen Paisley upset, I knew I had to speak to Seb. I was worried I'd overstepped the line of friendship, but seeing her in pain wasn't something I could handle. Her body needs time to heal, and Seb's a great guy. Once I explained, he was more than happy to wait for her to recover. He handled it well when he spoke to her, managing to make it look like it was him who was delaying her starting. I should have known she'd see right through him, but as long as she isn't mad, I'm happy. Even if she had been mad, I know I did the right thing.

"Are you looking forward to seeing Paisley, boy?" I ask Max, who's sitting in the back seat of my truck. He barks in reply, and I laugh. "Yeah, me too, boy. Me too."

I pull up outside Sophie's, jump out, and jog up the drive-way. Knocking on the door, I smile when Sophie answers.

"Hi, Sophie."

"Hey, Nash. Come in. I think she's almost ready."

I walk in and she closes the door behind me. Going to the foot of the stairs, she shouts up.

"Paisley, Nash is here."

"I'll be right down," Paisley shouts back, and I smile.

"How is she this morning?" I ask quietly. "I know she was struggling at the bar last night."

"She's in some pain, even if she won't admit it. I think yesterday was a bit of a wake-up call for her that her body needs time to heal properly."

"I'm glad she's got you looking out for her."

"She's got you too, Nash, and the whole Brookes clan, by the looks of it."

Before I can respond, there's movement on the stairs, and all the air rushes from my lungs as I look up and see Paisley on the top step. She's wearing a pale yellow sundress that falls mid-thigh, and her dark hair is curled in waves over her shoul-ders. She's carrying a denim jacket over her arm and a small black purse. She looks stunning. Her makeup's been done to hide the fading bruise on her face, and whatever she has on her eyes makes them pop. I can't tear my gaze off her as I watch her walk down the stairs. When she reaches the bottom step, she smiles.

"Hi," she whispers.

"Hi." We're both staring at each other, and after a minute or so of silence, Sophie clears her throat, snapping me out of my haze. "You look beautiful, Paisley." Her cheeks flush pink and she drops her eyes.

"Thank you. Sophie lent me a dress."

"You two should go," Sophie says with a chuckle. "Otherwise you're going to be late."

"Right. Yes, we should. Are you ready?" I ask, and she nods.

"Did you bring Max?"

I smile. "He's in the truck and excited to see you."

"How do you know he's excited to see me?"

"I asked him."

She laughs. "I'm excited to see him too." She turns to Sophie. "Thank you for helping me this morning."

"Have a great time. I'll see you later."

"Bye, Sophie," I say, my eyes still fixed on Paisley.

"Bye, Nash."

We walk in silence to the car, and I hold open the passenger side door for her. My truck is high, and I take her hand, helping her up. Max barks as she gets in, and I laugh.

"Told you he was excited to see you."

I close the door, leaving her turning in her seat to greet him. I walk slowly around to the driver's side, giving myself a minute. I'm beginning to feel things for Paisley, things I know she wouldn't want me to be feeling, but I'm powerless to stop them. I know I can't act on them. Not yet, anyway. I can wait though. She's worth it.

After stopping at a store in town for a birthday card and some flowers, we head to my parents' place.

"How are you feeling after your shift last night?"

"Sore, but I'm okay. I've taken Tylenol, and I'll take a stronger one later. I don't want to fall asleep at your parents' dinner table." She laughs nervously and twists her hands in her lap.

"Don't be nervous. You've already met everyone," I assure her.

"Not your parents. I'm just glad my makeup covers my eye. It's bad enough with the cast. I can't imagine what they'll think of me if I show up with a black eye."

"They won't think anything, Paisley. My mom knows better than anyone what it's like to be in your position." I park the truck outside the house and she turns her head sharply.

"What do you mean?"

I'm just about to explain when the front door flies open and Ashlyn rushes down the porch steps, swinging open Paisley's door.

"Thank God you're here!" she exclaims dramatically. "Seb and Wyatt are driving me crazy!"

"Happy birthday, Ashlyn," Paisley says as she unclips her seat belt.

"Thanks. Are you coming inside?"

"We've just pulled up, Ash. Give us a minute."

She looks between us and smiles. "Oh... I'm interrupting something! I'm so sorry. I'll see you inside." She backs away from the car, a huge smile on her face.

"No!" Paisley shouts. "You're not interrupting anything. We were just talking." She looks at me before climbing out of the car, the card and flowers in her hand. Crossing the driveway, she catches up with Ashlyn. I quickly follow, bringing Max with me. I catch them up just as they're heading inside. Ashlyn leads Paisley into the kitchen, where my mom is standing in front of the stove.

"Mom, Paisley's here," Ash says, and I try not to feel annoyed. It's ridiculous, but I wanted to be the one to introduce her to my mom.

"Paisley, it's lovely to meet you," my mom says with a smile.

"It's lovely to meet you too, Mrs. Brookes. Thank you for having me for lunch."

"Please call me Tessa, sweetheart," she says, waving her arm. "And you're welcome. The more the merrier." She smiles before looking past her to me. "Hi, Nash. What's Max doing here?" she asks, crossing the room to kiss me on the cheek before stroking Max.

"I think that might be my fault," Paisley admits. "I'm a bit of a softy and hate to know he's at Nash's crying."

She laughs. "There's nothing wrong with being a softy. It just shows you care. lunch won't be ready for about a half hour. Now that everyone's here, Ashlyn can open her gifts."

"Are they in the den?" I ask, letting Max off his leash. He goes straight to Paisley, who leans down to pet him.

She nods, and we follow her through the house and into the den, where my dad, Cade, Seb, and Wyatt sit, watching a rerun of one of Wyatt's games. Paisley looks over her shoulder at me and I give her a reassuring smile.

"Turn that off now," my mom says. "Nash and Paisley are here, and Ashlyn can open her gifts."

"Dad, this is Paisley. Paisley, my dad, Henry," I say before anyone else gets a chance to introduce her.

"Hi, Mr. Brookes," Paisley says shyly.

"Hi, darlin'. Call me Henry." He smiles at her and she smiles back. "Sit down," he says, gesturing to a free seat next to Wyatt.

After a round of hellos, Paisley takes a seat next to Wyatt. There aren't enough seats for everyone, and I sit on the floor with Max. Looking across at Wyatt, he catches my eye before whispering something in Paisley's ear, making her blush. I've no idea what he's said to her, but I've never wanted to punch my brother in the face more than I do now. He must see the look on my face, and he grins. Bastard.

Cade hands Ashlyn a card and drops a kiss on her cheek. "Happy birthday, Ash."

"Thanks, Cade." She opens the card and squeals. "Concert tickets for Brett Young! Oh my God!" She stands and throws her arms around him. Chuckling, he hugs her back. "Thank you!"

"You're welcome. It's in Phoenix, and I've booked the weekend off work. I'll drive you and whoever you want to take."

I shake my head. No wonder he didn't want to tell me what he got her. She's adored Brett Young forever. I don't think anyone's gift is going to top that. Both Wyatt and Seb go with gift cards, which is always a safe choice. None of us would be any good at picking out clothes for her. Paisley hands her the card we stopped for and the bunch of flowers.

"Sorry it's not more," Paisley says quietly.

"I wasn't expecting anything. They're beautiful, thank you," Ash says, giving her a smile.

"This is from me," I tell Ash, handing her the small gift bag containing the charm bracelet. While it isn't concert tickets, I'm confident she'll love it.

"Thanks, Nash."

She unties the small red bow that closes the gift bag and reaches inside, pulling out the box. Her eyes widen as she recognizes the name of the jewelry store. Lifting the lid off, she gasps.

"Nash, this is beautiful," she says as she pulls the delicate silver charm bracelet out. Paisley and I chose two charms: a daisy, which is her favorite flower, and a book, knowing how much she loves to read. She stands from the sofa and leans down to kiss my cheek. "Thank you."

"You're welcome. I have to admit, I had some help." I look across to Paisley, who's smiling.

"I hope you'll stick around to help him with presents every year." Ashlyn laughs. "You have great taste."

Paisley's cheeks color, and I smile when her eyes find mine. I hope she sticks around too.

CHAPTER FOURTEEN

Paisley

"I hope you'll stick around to help him with presents every year." Ashlyn laughs. "You have great taste."

I feel my face heat at her words, and I look across to Nash, who sits on the floor with Max. He smiles when our eyes meet, and my heart races. I want nothing more than to stay. I've just no idea if I can. Watching Ashlyn and seeing how close this whole family is makes me realize I've never had anything close to this. Even before I met Connor, my relationship with my parents wasn't great. I craved that stability and family unit, and I thought Connor could give me that. It didn't turn out that way though, and now I've lost everything.

"I'll go and check on lunch," Tessa says, standing from the sofa.

"Do you need any help?" I ask.

"Sure, honey. I could always use another pair of hands in the kitchen."

I stand and follow her out of the den. "You have a beautiful house."

"Thank you. We'll have been here twenty-six years in August."

When we reach the kitchen, she gestures for me to sit at the breakfast bar. "Take a seat, sweetheart. Do you want a drink? How about a glass of wine?" She must see the indecision on my face. "I'm having one," she says, pulling a bottle of white wine from the refrigerator.

"Okay, then. Just a small one." She nods as she sets down two wineglasses and fills them half full. Handing me one, I'm surprised when she sits down next to me.

"I used the food as an excuse to get you alone for five minutes," she says sheepishly. "Nash told me what happened to you, Paisley. I just wanted to let you know that I've been exactly where you are."

"You have?" I whisper. She nods, and I frown. "Henry?" I ask in confusion.

"No. Cade and Nash's dad. I left him when they were little, with only what we could carry. A Greyhound bus brought us here, and it was the best decision I've ever made. In fact, it probably saved my life."

"I had no idea. I'm so sorry. I can't imagine how hard it must have been with two children. I only had myself to worry about, which was hard enough."

"If it wasn't for the support of the people in Hope Creek, I'm not sure how I'd have managed. It was Sophie's mom who ran the shelter back then. I stayed there for over a year."

"Everyone's been so kind. Especially Nash and Cade."

Before I know it, tears are falling down my face. She reaches for a box of tissues and hands me them.

"I promise you things will get better." Her arm slips around my shoulders. "You've been through a lot, Paisley. If you want to talk about anything, then you can always come and talk to me."

"Thank you."

"I'm proof that life can be good again."

"Paisley? Are you okay?" a voice asks from the door, and I quickly wipe my eyes, knowing it's Nash.

"She's okay. A good cry is sometimes all we need," Tessa says. "I'll go and get the table ready." She pats my shoulder as she leaves the kitchen.

"Are you really okay?" he asks as he comes to stand next to me. I nod, and he takes my hand, pulling me gently to my feet. "You can talk to me, you know? About anything."

"I know. Thank you. Your mom said the same."

He reaches his hand up and wipes a stray tear from my cheek. "Can I hold you?" he whispers.

A million butterflies take flight in my stomach and my heart pounds in my chest. He's still holding my hand, and he squeezes gently.

"You can say no. I won't be offended."

"I don't want to say no," I say quietly.

"Then don't."

"Okay."

"Is that a yes?"

I nod.

He drops my hand and wraps his arms around my shoulders, pulling me gently against him. My arms go around his waist, and I rest my head on his chest. His heart races under my ear, and I'm sure it matches my own. It's been so long since anyone has held me like this, and as nervous as I am to be this close to him, I can't deny how good it feels.

"Are you okay?" he asks after a couple of minutes.

I lift my head to look at him. "It's been so long I'd almost forgotten what it feels like." He gives me a sad smile.

"I'm happy to provide hugs whenever you need them."

"I might have to hold you to that." He takes a deep breath and drops a kiss on my head before dropping his arms and stepping back.

"I see Mom has you on the wine already. I'm surprised Ash hasn't got a glass in her hand yet!"

I laugh. "I hope you're up for carrying me home. I haven't had a drink in quite a while."

"Not a big drinker?"

"Not in the last year... I never wanted to let myself be that vulnerable."

"Fuck," he mutters, and before I know it, I'm back in his arms. I go willingly. "I'm sorry, Paisley."

"It's not your fault," I whisper into his chest.

He smells so good, and I inhale deeply, my senses overwhelmed by him. His strong arms hold me tightly, and I find myself wishing he'd never let go. When someone clears their throat behind us, I step out of his embrace.

"Sorry to interrupt," Tessa says, smiling as she passes us and takes a piece of meat out of the oven.

"Do you need any help?" I ask, willing my cheeks not to color.

"No, sweetheart. I'm good. Why don't you go with Nash and let everyone know to take a seat in the dining room?"

Nash takes my hand and tugs me gently into the hallway. "Are you sure you're okay?" His eyes search mine, and I nod.

"I'm okay, Nash. I promise. My makeup isn't streaked all

down my face, is it?" I ask, reaching my hand up and touching my cheeks.

He shakes his head. "No. You look beautiful." His words cause my heart to jump, but I push down my growing feelings for him. They're dangerous. I trusted Connor, and he betrayed me in the cruelest possible way. I know Nash is nothing like Connor, but I'm damaged and I don't know if I'll ever be able to let anyone in again. I was nothing to him, just someone to take his temper out on and a warm body when he needed it. Connor took what he wanted from me, even when I didn't want to give it. I don't know how to move on from that, or even if I can.

"We should tell everyone lunch's ready," I say quietly, slipping my hand from his. I try not to see the disappointment that flashes across his face as I turn and walk away from him. It's better to end whatever this is between us now, before anything starts and things get complicated. Nash is gorgeous; he can do so much better than me.

After we've eaten, we move to the living room, where there's more space for everyone to sit. It's still a tight squeeze though with the eight of us, and I'm sitting between Ashlyn and Nash. Max sits at my feet, and I lean forward to stroke his head, wincing as my ribs scream out in protest.

"How do you feel about last night, Paisley?" Seb asks from across the room. "Saturday nights are always the busiest, but it looked like you were a natural."

"A natural at what?" Tessa asks, and her eyes go wide. "You didn't make her do a shift at Eden, did you, Sebastian?"

"I didn't make her do anything!" Seb exclaims.

"It wasn't Seb's fault," I say quickly, not wanting him to get into trouble with his mom. "I need a job, and I thought I'd be able to manage, but it was a struggle, and I'm paying for it today. I should have listened to Nash and Cade."

"There'll be some shifts for you in a couple of weeks, when you're feeling up to it," Seb says.

"Thank you, Seb."

Max begins to whine, and I look at Nash. "I think he wants to go out," Nash says as he begins to stand.

"I'll take him. I could do with a walk after sitting for so long." I stand and walk to the living room door, Max following me. "He won't run off, will he?" I ask, never having taken him outside without his leash.

"No, he shouldn't. Do you want me to come with you?" he asks.

"No. I'll be fine." He nods, and I can feel his eyes on my back as I walk out of the room.

Once we're outside, Max runs off, and I follow him around the side of the house where the space opens out into an enormous backyard. There's a large tree set a little way from the house with a wooden tree house and a swing hanging from one of the branches. I can't help but smile as I look up and imagine all of the Brookes children having hours of fun out here as kids. They must have had an incredible childhood, although I had no idea Nash and Cade had such a rough start until Tessa told me what she did. She was so brave to leave everything she knew with two small children. She must have been so scared. At least when I left, I only had myself to think about. I can't even imagine how hard it must have been for her with two young children.

Walking toward the swing, I turn and hold on to the rope, sitting down gingerly. I'm guessing it's been hanging from the tree for quite a few years, and I've no idea if it will hold my weight. I breathe a sigh of relief when I don't crash to the floor, and I gently push my feet off the floor and let myself swing. Despite vowing to never fall in love again, I look around at what Tessa has achieved. She endured something no one should ever have to face and came out the other side. It gives me hope that maybe one day I might get to be happy again too.

CHAPTER FIFTEEN

Nash

I watch as Paisley leaves the room with Max, sighing loudly as I flop backwards onto the sofa when she's gone.

"You really like her, don't you?" Seb asks.

I shrug. "I'm trying to hold back. I know she's not ready for anything yet, but…"

"But what?" he prompts.

"God, when I see her upset…" I trail off and drag my fingers through my hair. "I just want to wrap her in my arms and make her forget her asshole husband."

"Give her some time, Nash. Another relationship won't even be on her radar at the moment. She's likely thinking there's no way she can ever give herself to someone again, not after being so badly betrayed the first time."

"Is that how you felt, Mom?" Ashlyn asks.

"Yes, honey. For a long time, but then your dad came along and he never gave up on me. I pushed him away so many times, but he pushed back, and eventually, I realized he was nothing like the man who had hurt me."

Dad stands from where he's sitting and walks to where my mom is, pulling her to her feet.

"I knew as soon as I saw her she was the one for me. Slowly, she opened up, but I always knew I'd wait as long as it took for her to be ready," my dad says, wrapping his arms around her in a hug. "Don't give up on her, son. Just be there for her."

"I'm not going to give up on her."

"Why don't you go and see if she's okay?" my mom suggests, and I nod.

Making my way outside, I go around the house and into the backyard. I stop and smile when I see her on the swing attached to the old oak tree. Max is sitting on the ground next to her, and her hair blows in the breeze as she swings. I watch her for a few minutes before she lifts her head and sees me. A smile appears on her face, and she stops swinging and raises her hand in a wave. I wave back and cross the lawn.

"You look like you're having fun," I say with a smile.

"I don't know what it is about swings, but they make me feel like a little girl again."

"Do you want a push?"

"Sure."

I walk around the back of her and softly place my hand on her back, pushing her gently.

"Did your dad build the tree house?"

"Yeah, not long after we moved here. Mom was pregnant with Seb and Wyatt, and Dad spent the whole summer building it. Cade and I had hours of fun playing in it, and then Seb, Wyatt, and Ashlyn when they were old enough."

"I would have loved a tree house when I was a kid."

"Are you close to your parents?"

She sighs. "No. Not anymore. I was young when I met Connor, and they didn't approve."

"Your husband?"

She nods. "When I told them we were getting married, they made me choose. I chose wrong," she says sadly. "I've tried to reach out to them, but they've never responded to any of my letters."

"I'm sorry, Paisley."

"Maybe one day they'll come around."

My heart breaks for this beautiful woman in front of me. As if she hasn't had to endure enough, she doesn't even have the support of her family. I figured as much when I first met her on the flight. If she had a good support network around her, she wouldn't have needed to run. Well, now she has me and the rest of my family. Whatever happens, she'll always have that.

"Do you want to go in the tree house?" I ask, coming around the front of the swing and gently pulling on the rope to stop her swinging. Her face lights up in a smile and she nods. "Come on, then." I hold my hand out to her and she slips her small hand in mine. Pulling her out of the seat, I lead her to the steps of the tree house.

"How long has it been since you've been up there?" she asks, looking up at the huge wooden structure.

"Actually, not as long ago as you might think. Ashlyn decided it was a good idea to bring her prom date up here. I didn't!"

She pulls back on my hand, and when I look over my shoulder, her eyes are wide. "What did you do?"

I swear I can see fear swirling in her eyes, and I turn around, reaching for her other hand.

"Not what you're thinking, Paisley. I didn't hit him." She lets out a breath and relief flashes across her face. "I've never hit anyone. Well, apart from Cade, but I'm hoping sibling arguments don't count. I think I was ten."

I'm surprised when she drops her forehead on my chest. "I'm sorry," she whispers.

"There's no need to apologize."

She lifts her head and takes a step back as if she's just realized what she's done. "What did you do, then?"

"I took him for a drive in my patrol car."

"You didn't!" she exclaims.

"We just had a friendly chat."

"About what?"

"About how he should treat a woman, especially if that woman was my sister."

"What did Ashlyn say?"

"She didn't speak to me for about a month. It was a quiet month," I say with a chuckle.

She laughs, and I can't take my eyes off her. I'm still holding her hands, and I want to kiss her, but I know she's not ready for that. My mom's words from earlier swirl in my mind, and I squeeze her hands gently before dropping them.

"You know she's going to meet a guy one day, and probably soon. She's stunning. You can't arrest every guy she meets."

"I can try," I mumble.

"Nash!"

"I'm joking. Kind of. If he's one of the good guys, then he

won't be intimidated by me or my brothers. He'll fight for her, and then I'll know he's worthy of her."

"Ash is lucky to have you all. I wish I'd had an older brother to look out for me."

"I wish that too, Paisley." Dragging my eyes off her, I turn back to the tree house. "I'll go up first to make sure the ladder holds."

The ladder's as solid as it was when my dad made it twenty-five years ago, and when I reach the top, I climb inside. It looks like prom might have been the last time anyone was up here, and it's a little dirty. Peering back through the opening, Paisley is staring up at me.

"Is it good?" she asks, her foot on the bottom step.

"Yeah. It's a little dirty up here. I think there might be the odd spider lurking in the corners."

"I don't care about that." She climbs the ladder slowly with one hand, and I help her inside when she reaches the top. "Wow! It's bigger inside than it looks. Even you can stand up. You could live in here!"

"We used to sleep out here all the time in the summer months. Mom and Dad barely saw us."

"It sounds like great fun."

"It was."

There's a small balcony that overlooks the yard, and she steps out onto it, holding on to the railing my dad installed to stop us falling over the edge.

"It's beautiful here. You can see for miles."

I stand behind her and follow her gaze. "I guess I never really appreciated it as a kid, but it is beautiful."

We're silent for a couple of minutes, and I'm just about to suggest we head inside when she starts to talk.

"Your mom told me a bit about what happened to her. I'm

sorry you and Cade had to go through that."

"I don't remember much. Cade remembers more, but it was worse for my mom."

"She was so brave."

"You were brave too, Paisley."

"Not like that. I only had to worry about myself. I don't think I'd have had the strength to leave if there had been children."

"You would, Paisley. You're stronger than you think." I watch her shoulders fall as she exhales deeply. "How are you feeling after the miscarriage?" I haven't mentioned her losing the baby since that day at the hospital. I didn't know if it was my place to ask. I still don't. She doesn't answer straight away, and I wonder if I've upset her.

"I'm relieved," she whispers. She turns around to face me, her tortured eyes meeting mine. "Do you think I'm a terrible person?"

"No, Paisley. I don't."

"I cried when I knew the baby was gone, but I was relieved too. I'm ashamed to admit it. It was my baby and a part of me, but I don't want to be tied to him in any way."

"You have nothing to be ashamed of. Nothing you're feeling is wrong."

"It seems it."

I take a step toward her and pull her into my arms. I know I shouldn't, but I can't stop myself. "It's time for a new chapter. One where you get to be happy."

"I hope so… one day." I want to tell her that day can be now, with me, but I don't. I know she's not ready to hear it. Max barks below us, and Paisley steps out of my arms, turning to look over the rail. "I think someone is feeling a little left out."

"He's so needy." I chuckle. We walk back into the tree house, and I help Paisley onto the ladder, watching as she climbs down. I do the same, and when I reach the ground, she's kneeling down with Max pretty much on her lap.

"Off, Max," I say, holding my hand out to pull Paisley up when he's moved off her. She winces, and I frown. "Are you still in pain?"

"A little. I'm okay."

We head around the front of the house, just in time to say goodbye to Seb and Cade. Seb needs to get back to the bar, and Cade is working tonight.

"Stop by the bar in the next few days, Paisley. We'll talk about those shifts," Seb says, before pulling on his helmet and climbing onto his bike.

"Okay, will do," she says from the side of me. He raises his hand in a wave as he starts the engine and drives away from the house. Cade also offers a wave as he climbs into his car and drives away.

"Are you ready to head back?" I ask Paisley, conscious she's in pain.

"Yeah, if you are. I want to thank your parents for having me over."

"Sure. Let's go and say bye."

Max bounds into the house, and Paisley and I follow. Everyone else is still in the living room, talking and laughing.

"We're going to head out. Happy birthday, squirt," I say, ruffling Ashlyn's hair.

"God, you're annoying!" Ashlyn exclaims, standing up and punching me on the arm.

"Stop it, you two! We've got a guest," my mom says, stepping between us.

"Thank you for inviting me. Lunch was delicious," Paisley

says, and my mom goes to her, pulling her into a hug.

"You're welcome anytime, sweetheart. I hope you'll come again soon."

"I hope so too." She pulls out of the hug and turns to Ashlyn. "Happy birthday, Ashlyn."

"Thanks, Paisley. I'll get your number from Nash and we can arrange a girls' night when you're feeling up to it."

"I'd love that."

After saying goodbye to Wyatt and my dad, we head to my truck. I put Max in the back and help Paisley inside. As I pull off the driveway and onto the main road, she turns to me.

"Your family is great, Nash. Everyone's so close."

"Yeah, they are pretty amazing, when they're not being annoying." She laughs, and I don't want today to be over. I want to spend some more time with her. "Do you want to come back to my place and watch a movie?" Her wide eyes and raised eyebrows tell me she's surprised by my question. "If you'd rather go back to Sophie's, that's fine too," I add quickly, not wanting her to feel like she has to say yes. I can see the indecision in her eyes, and I almost hold my breath as I wait for her to answer.

"I really want to say yes, Nash, but I can't. I'm sorry." She looks as gutted as I feel.

"It's okay, Paisley. I understand."

She's pushing me away, and after speaking to Mom and Dad earlier, I understand. It doesn't mean I like it though. I really hoped after she'd started to open up to me today, she might feel differently. She needs time, and I can definitely give her that. I always want to be there for her, and having her in my arms today just cemented my increasing feelings for her. I would never push her into something she's not ready for, but I hope one day she's able to see how good we could be together.

CHAPTER SIXTEEN

Paisley

I really want to say yes when Nash asks me to watch a movie with him. I almost do, but fear holds me back. I trust him. He's been nothing but incredible since we first met, but spending time with him is only going to give him the wrong idea. I just can't let anyone in right now. We're quiet on the short drive back, and I don't know if I've upset him. I hope not.

When we pull up outside Sophie's house, he goes to climb out of the truck, but I stop him, putting my hand on his arm.

"Nash, wait." His eyes drop to my hand on his arm before he looks up. "Will you ask me again in a few weeks?" I say quietly, and he smiles.

"I was planning on it, sweetheart." My cheeks flush at

hearing him call me *sweetheart,* and I smile. "Come on. I'll walk you inside."

I remove my fingers from his arm and open the truck door. Before I can climb out, he's there, holding his hand out for me to take. I slip my hand in his, and he helps me down. I expect him to release my hand when he's closed the truck door, but he doesn't, not until we're on the porch outside the front door.

"Are you working next week?"

He nods. "I'm on nights Monday, Tuesday, and Wednesday."

"I won't come and walk Max, then. I don't want to wake you."

"No, come. If you still want to, I mean. Just come late afternoon. I'll be awake by then."

"Okay."

"I guess I should go."

"Thank you for today. I had a great time."

"Me too, Paisley. I'll see you soon." He leans down and brushes his lips against my cheek, my skin tingling where he's kissed me. I turn and key in the code for the door, pushing it open with my good hand.

"Bye, Nash."

I watch as he jogs to his truck, raising his hand in a wave as he climbs in and drives away. I stand with the door open until he's out of sight before sighing and closing the door.

"I thought I heard the door. How was Sunday lunch?"

"Hi, Sophie," I say, turning around. "Sunday lunch was great. Nash's family is something else."

She smiles, a hint of sadness in her eyes. "They really are. I was just going to watch a movie with Lyra. Do you want to join us?" I can't help but smile. "What?" she asks, seeing my face.

"You're the second person to ask me that today."

"I am? Who else has asked you?"

"Nash."

"But you said no?" I nod. "He's a great guy, Paisley."

"I know. I just can't right now. I want to, but I can't."

She smiles sympathetically. "Well, you're welcome to join us."

"I think I'm just going to lie down. I need to take a painkiller."

"Okay. Well, if you change your mind, you know where we are."

"Thanks, Sophie."

I leave her in the entryway and head to the kitchen. I grab a banana from the fruit bowl and head upstairs. I'm not really hungry after lunch, but I need to take the painkillers Cade prescribed with food. Changing into a pair of yoga pants and a tank, I eat the banana and swallow down two tablets before climbing into bed. It might only be four in the afternoon, but I'm exhausted.

IT'S THURSDAY LUNCHTIME, and the past few days seem to have flown by. I've walked Max late afternoon on each day, briefly seeing Nash when I pick him up and drop him off. I know from speaking to him that today and Friday are his rest days after working three night shifts, and I'm not planning on stopping by. He's home, so he doesn't need me to walk Max. Instead, I'm heading to Eden to speak to Seb about some potential shifts. He doesn't know I'm coming. I could have asked Nash for his number, but it's not an issue if I walk into town and he's not there. I'll just come back another day. It's not like I have anything else to do.

Pushing open the door to Eden, I'm surprised to find it's bright and airy inside. The complete opposite to how it feels at night. There are a few customers scattered around the tables, some drinking and some eating lunch. I didn't realize they served food during the day. Walking farther inside, I head to the bar, where Ryder is serving a customer.

"Hi, Paisley. How are you?"

"I'm good, thanks. Is Seb around?"

"Sure. Just give me a minute to finish up here and I'll grab him for you." I nod, watching while he finishes serving the guy at the bar. "Okay," he says when he's done. "I'll just go and see if he's free."

He disappears into the back, and I pick up a menu on the bar, seeing what sort of food they serve. It looks like the usual bar food. Burgers, nachos, hot dogs. Simple stuff, but food people want. A few minutes later, Ryder returns.

"He's just finishing something off. If you take a seat, he'll be right with you. Do you want a drink? On the house, of course."

"Thanks. Just a Diet Coke, please."

"I'll bring it over."

I smile in thanks and head to a table just across from the bar. Ryder brings my drink and I sip the fizzy liquid.

"Hi, Paisley," Seb says as he appears at the side of the table a few minutes later.

"Hi."

He slides into the booth and gestures to the bar for Ryder to bring him a drink. "How are you feeling? How's the wrist?" he asks, his eyes going to my cast.

"It's not too bad, thanks. I'm getting used to doing things one-handed."

He smiles, turning to Ryder and thanking him as he puts a glass of Coke in front of him. "When is the cast due to come off?" he asks when Ryder has gone.

"In about four weeks, I think."

"Do you want to wait for the cast to come off, or do you want to start before? I'm easy either way. The server I was looking to replace has decided to stay on for a few more weeks, so I won't be short-staffed if we wait."

Despite needing to start earning money, I had struggled to carry the trays and serve the drinks with the cast on. It would be better if I could wait until it came off. I still had the money I hadn't had to use on the flight, so I was able to buy food and toiletries.

"If you're sure you're happy to wait for the cast to come off, I think that might be better," I say.

"Sure. It's going to be three daytime shifts and one night shift. Does that sound okay?"

"That sounds great."

"There might be some more shifts available once I've worked the schedule, but you'll never have less than what I've said each week. I know you're looking to get your own place, so I'm happy to give you extra shifts if I have them."

"Thank you, Seb. I appreciate that."

He shrugs. "You're important to Nash, so you're important to me."

My eyes widen in surprise, and I pull my eyebrows together in question. "Important to Nash?"

He laughs. "Yeah, Paisley. Do you know how many women Nash has introduced to our parents?" I shake my head. "None."

"Ashlyn invited me."

"But you came with Nash." He pauses. "Maybe I've said too much. He's a good guy though, Paisley. In fact, he's one of the best."

"I know," I whisper.

"Okay. I've definitely said too much. Nash is going to kill me. Maybe don't tell him I said any of that."

"I'm not sure I know what you're saying anyway," I admit, chuckling nervously.

"So, we'll work on you starting in another four weeks, but maybe next time you see Cade, double-check about the cast coming off?"

"Okay," I say, trying to ignore what he's just said about Nash. I don't know quite what to make of it. Has Nash said something to Seb? Or is it just his opinion? He doesn't need to worry about me saying anything to Nash, though. It's not like I'm going to ask if I'm important to him. I'd be too nervous to hear his answer.

CHAPTER SEVENTEEN

Nash

It's been almost three weeks since I've spent any time with Paisley. I've seen her occasionally when she comes to walk Max, but never for longer than five minutes. She's quick to pick him up and even quicker to drop him off, and on the days I'm working, I don't see her at all. She's put up a wall, and despite being desperate to knock it down, I have no idea if she wants me to.

It's Saturday night, and although I'm tired after working the day shift, I'm heading to Eden to meet Wyatt and Cade. I haven't had much chance to spend any time with Wyatt since he's been back. I've been working a lot, so I'm looking forward to catching up with him.

Pushing open the door to Eden, I cross the crowded room,

spotting Wyatt sitting in one of the booths. It doesn't look like Cade's here yet.

"Hey, man," I say as I stand at the table. "Do you need a drink?"

"Another beer, please."

"Is Cade on his way?" He nods. "I'll grab him one too."

After fighting my way to the bar, I order three bottles of Bud, and by the time I get back to the table, Cade's arrived. Handing the drinks out, I slide into the booth and clink my bottle with Cade's and Wyatt's.

"How was work?" Wyatt asks Cade.

"Busy. It always is." Cade looks at me but doesn't say anything.

"What?" I ask.

"Nothing." He shakes his head and takes a pull of his beer.

I frown at him, having no idea why he's being weird. "What have you done all day, Wyatt?"

"Not a lot. I went to the gym."

"I wish I had your life!" Cade exclaims. "I've just done a twelve-hour shift."

"You chose to be a doctor. Plus, you were shitty at football. I might be able to get you a job as the team mascot," Wyatt says, his voice deadpan.

Cade rolls his eyes. "I think I'll pass."

Two women walk up to the table, their eyes fixed on Wyatt. "You're Wyatt Brookes, right?" one of them asks, and Wyatt nods, a wide smile on his face.

"I am, and who are you?"

"I'm Zoey, and this is Cora."

"Nice to meet you. Would you like to join me and my brothers?"

They smile and nod, and I groan inwardly. I hadn't

planned on spending my night with two of Wyatt's groupies. Glancing at Cade, I can see he looks equally annoyed. Most people in the town know Wyatt and have ever since we were kids. They don't see him as anything special and don't treat him any differently to anyone else, but there's always new people in town, and I guess these two girls don't know he grew up here.

"Can I get you both a drink?" Wyatt asks, standing from the booth.

"White wines, please," Zoey says with a wink. It's clear Zoey is more outgoing than her friend, who looks terrified.

"I'll go!" I say, jumping up. I don't want to be left making small talk with them while Wyatt gets their drinks. I walk off and fight my way to the bar. I catch Seb's eye, and he beckons me over.

"Hey, Nash. What can I get you?"

"Three buds and two white wines."

He frowns. "Who's drinking wine?"

I roll my eyes. "Wyatt's attracted some *fans*."

He laughs. "I'll bring the drinks over. I want to see him in action!"

"God, you're as bad as him!" I leave him chuckling behind me as I head back to the table. Cade's not there when I get back, and I sit down, finding myself next to one of the girls.

"Hi, I'm Cora," she says shyly. I look at her and smile. She's pretty but young. Her friend is practically on Wyatt's lap, and I can see she looks a little uncomfortable sitting on her own.

"Nash," I tell her, picking up my Bud and swallowing down the last of the beer.

"Do you play football too?" she asks, and I laugh.

"No, that's all Wyatt. I'm a cop."

141

Silence descends, and I wonder where the hell Cade has gone. I breathe a sigh of relief when I see Seb with the drinks.

"Having fun?" Seb asks, amusement in his tone. I flash him a look, and he laughs as he hands the drinks out.

"Oh my God! Are you twins?" Zoey asks, looking between Wyatt and Seb.

"Yeah, but I'm the better-looking one," Seb answers, winking at her. I groan and take a pull of my beer.

"You're not from around here, are you?" I ask, and Cora shakes her head.

"No. We live in Florida. We're on a tour of the U.S. We're only in Hope Creek for a couple of nights."

"Where are you off to next?"

"Vegas!" Zoey shouts before Cora can answer. "Hey! You should come!" she says to Wyatt, who laughs.

"I'm not sure I can fit a trip to Vegas into my busy schedule."

"Busy doing fuck all," Cade says as he appears at the table.

"Where did you go?" I ask, moving farther into the booth so he can sit down.

"The bathroom. I wasn't aware I needed your permission."

"You're such a moody bastard lately. What's going on with you?"

He sighs and shakes his head. "Nothing's going on. I'm fine."

"That's bullshit, but I'm here when you're ready to talk about it."

He doesn't really acknowledge me, and I wish he'd open up. I'm not an idiot. I know something's going on with him, and I know it's something to do with Sophie. I remember how hurt he was when she left him. I can't force him to talk to me though, but I'll keep offering to listen.

Cade and I make small talk with Cora for the next half an hour, while her friend makes out with Wyatt. So much for spending some time with him. I'm pretty sure we've lost him for the night. Seb keeps the drinks flowing, and when he brings the latest round, he looks out into the crowd before turning back to me.

"Isn't that Paisley?" he asks, gesturing with his head to the middle of the room. I look past him, my eyes finding her through the crowds. She looks beautiful. She's wearing black skinny jeans and a cream cami. Her dark hair falls over her shoulders, and I watch her as she laughs at something Sophie says. I can't tear my eyes off her.

"Yeah, she's with Sophie," I say, and I notice Cade sit up a little taller next to me.

She must sense me staring at her, and she turns, her eyes finding mine. She smiles when she sees me, the smile faltering when she looks at Cora. She gives me a small wave before going back to talking to Sophie. I wonder if she thinks I'm here with Cora. I'm not interested in Cora and don't want her thinking I am. I stand, and Cade moves out of the booth to let me past.

"Where are you going?" he asks.

"To Paisley."

"Of course you are," he says with a chuckle. Ignoring him, I disappear into the crowds.

* * *

Paisley

. . .

143

"Please come, Paisley. It'll be fun," Sophie says as she stands in my bedroom doorway.

"I don't have anything to wear."

"I can lend you something. I have the perfect top to wear with your black jeans."

Excitement swirls in my stomach at the thought of a girls' night out. I haven't been out with friends in years. I have some of the money I brought with me from Pittsburgh left, and I'm due to start working at Eden next week, so I can afford to buy a couple of drinks.

"Okay, then," I say excitedly, and she smiles.

"Great! Come and choose something to wear." I follow her along the hallway and into her bedroom. There's a large walk-in closet, and she waves her hand as she walks inside. "Help yourself."

"Are you sure?" I ask over my shoulder.

"Yes, I'm sure. I was thinking this." She pulls down a cream silk cami. "But you can choose anything."

"No, this is beautiful. Thank you."

"How's your wrist feeling?"

I gingerly move my wrist around, glad to be free of the cast. Sophie had taken me to the hospital earlier, and after an X-ray, the doctor had decided the cast could come off. My wrist ached a little but felt fine.

"It feels good. I'm looking forward to washing my hair with two hands," I say with a chuckle.

"Let's get ready and we can head into town."

"Where are we going?"

"I was thinking Eden. It's the best bar in town."

"Do you think Nash will be there?" I ask quietly.

"I'm not sure. Maybe. He meets his brothers in there quite often, I think. Why?"

I shrug. "I just wondered." She smiles knowingly but doesn't say anything.

I leave her in her bedroom and go back to mine to get ready. I haven't seen much of Nash over the past few weeks, other than when he's been on a night shift and he's home when I go to walk Max. I've wanted to text him more than once, but after pushing him away when he asked me to watch a movie, I didn't know if I should.

An hour later, Sophie and I walk into Eden. It's busy, and we head straight to the bar. With a glass of wine in our hands, we search for a vacant table. I think if possible, it's busier tonight than it was when I did my trial shift, and all the tables are full.

"My feet are going to be killing me if I've got to stand all night," Sophie says, and I laugh.

"This is the first time I've worn heels on a night out in about two years! I think you'll be carrying me home."

She laughs too, and I turn around, my eyes landing on Nash, who's looking right at me. My breath catches in my throat, and I smile when I see him. The smile slips from my face as my eyes go to the beautiful woman sitting next to him, and I wonder if he's on a date. I raise my hand in a small wave and drag my eyes off him. Why wouldn't he be on a date? He's gorgeous, and it's not like anything is happening between us. Despite that, waves of jealousy crash through me. I want to look back at him, but I don't. Spotting a table that's about to become free, I tap Sophie's arm and point to where a couple is just leaving. It's on the opposite side of the bar to Nash, and that suits me. As much as I pushed him away, I don't want to watch him on a date.

Just as we're making for the table, I hear my name being

called. Turning around, Nash is pushing his way through the crowd toward us.

"Looks like he's here," Sophie whispers in my ear, and my cheeks flush.

"Hi, Nash," I say softly when he reaches us.

"Hi, Paisley." His eyes sweep over me, and my cheeks heat further. "You look great."

"Thank you."

His eyes go from me to Sophie. "You too, Sophie." She smiles at him before taking a sip of her wine. I feel his fingers on my wrist. "When did you get your cast off?"

"Today. Didn't Cade say? I saw him when I went for my appointment."

"No, he didn't. How is it feeling? I would have taken you for your appointment."

"That's okay. I know you're busy. Sophie took me. It's good. It aches a little, but I'm relieved to have the cast off."

"That's great, Paisley." His hand is still on my wrist, and his fingers stroke over my skin, sending tiny electric shocks up my arm. "Come and sit with us."

"Oh, we don't want to interrupt your date," I say.

He frowns. "I'm not on a date."

I'm surprised to feel a wave of relief wash over me. "Oh, I just thought… never mind."

"They're Wyatt's friends. Come and sit with us." I turn to Sophie, who nods.

"Okay, if you're sure?"

"I'm sure." He snakes his hand into mine and guides me across the room to his table. I look over my shoulder to make sure Sophie's following. She grins at me, and I smile back.

When we've all squeezed into the small booth, I find myself sandwiched between Nash and Sophie. I'm so close to

Nash, my senses are overwhelmed by the smell of his cologne. He's worn the same cologne every time I've seen him. The first couple of times, I hadn't noticed, but now I do. As crazy as it sounds, the smell makes me feel safe. He makes me feel safe.

Shaking away my wayward thoughts, I reach for my glass and finish the last of my wine. I haven't had a drink in a while, and despite only having one glass, my head already feels a little fuzzy.

"Do you want another one?" Nash whispers in my ear, his breath hot on my skin.

"Maybe in a minute. That's gone straight to my head."

He chuckles. "Are you starting work soon if your cast is off?"

"Yes. Next week. I can't wait."

"Are you doing any of the evening shifts?"

"Yeah, one a week, I think. Not sure yet which night though, why?"

"I don't want you walking home after a shift. I'll come and pick you up. Just let me know what night."

I raise my eyebrows in surprise and turn to look at him. We're sitting so close, when I turn my head, his face is only inches from mine. "Nash, you don't have to do that. It's not going to be until late. You might have work the next day, or even be working the night shift yourself."

"I want to. I'd worry if I thought you were walking home on your own."

"Why?"

"Why what?"

"Why would you worry?" I ask quietly.

He stares at me, and I find myself holding my breath as I wait for him to answer. "I don't think you're ready to hear why."

147

"Oh," I mumble, not really knowing what he's saying.

He chuckles when he sees the confusion on my face. "I don't really want to talk about it here. Take a walk with me?"

"Okay."

After making everyone move so we can get out of the booth, I leave Sophie talking to Seb. I feel bad abandoning her on a girls' night, but she's deep in conversation. I don't think she'll miss me. I let Nash tangle his fingers with mine and we head outside. Nerves swirl in my stomach, and I wonder if I really am ready to hear what he's going to say.

CHAPTER EIGHTEEN

Nash

I'm nervous as I lead Paisley through the bar and out onto the sidewalk. I've given her some time, but I'm not ashamed to say I've missed her these past few weeks. Seeing her for ten minutes when she's picked up and dropped off Max hasn't been enough, and I want to spend some real time together, just the two of us. I know last time I asked her, she said no, but I'm hoping she's in a better place now. If she's not, then I'll wait, but I want to try.

Her hand is still nestled in mine, and I make no attempt to release it as we walk away from Eden.

"How are your parents?"

"They're good. They want me to bring you over for lunch again."

"They do?" she asks, her voice laced with surprise.

"Yeah. You made quite the impression, and not just with them."

"With who else?"

I chuckle. "Me, Paisley." I stop walking and turn to face her. "I can't stop thinking about you," I admit quietly.

"Oh." Her eyes widen, and it's as though she's surprised anyone would want her.

I smile and brush my thumb over the back of her hand. "Are you free tomorrow?" She nods. "Can I take you to the lake for a picnic?" She bites down on her bottom lip, and I really want her to say yes.

"I'd like that." I let out a breath I didn't realize I was holding and pull her into a hug. She wraps her arms around my neck, and I try not to think how perfectly she fits against me.

"Just so I know I'm not reading this wrong, tell me why you're going to worry about me walking home?" she asks into my chest, and I lean back slightly so I can see her face.

"Because I like you, Paisley. A lot. Is that so hard to believe?"

She shrugs in my arms. "Kind of. You're..." She trails off, and I move a hand off her waist to brush my fingers across her cheek.

"I'm what?"

She drops her head onto my chest. "Gorgeous, and I'm a mess." Her voice is barely a whisper, but I hear her.

"Look at me," I say softly, and she slowly lifts her head.

"I think you're beautiful, Paisley, and strong, and so brave. You amaze me." She's clearly not used to being complimented as she drops her eyes from mine. I'm desperate to kiss her, but

I don't want to rush her into anything. Instead, I drop a kiss on her forehead and pull her closer against my chest. "Shall we go back inside?"

She nods. "I like you too, just so you know." I grin. "I was so jealous when I saw you sitting with that girl. I thought you were on a date." I lean my head back and look down at her. She widens her eyes. "Not that I could stop you going out on a date. It's not like we're together or anything," she rushes out. "If you wanted to go out with her——"

"I don't," I say, cutting her off. "I wanted a night out with my brothers, and Wyatt asked them to join us. I was only talking to her because her friend was ignoring her."

"You don't have to explain."

"I do. I want you to be able to trust me."

"I do trust you, Nash." My heart jumps in my chest. I know trusting a man is a massive thing for her, and I always want her to feel comfortable with me.

Reluctantly, I drop my arms from around her and reach for her hand. "You don't mind me holding your hand, do you?" I ask, acutely aware I've already held it tonight and didn't ask her if it was okay.

"I love it when you hold my hand," she whispers, and I wonder if her jackass husband *ever* showed her any sort of affection. I guess not.

"I always want to hold your hand," I tell her as we walk back to Eden. Pushing open the door, I keep her close as we make our way back to the booth. I breathe a sigh of relief when we reach the table and Wyatt's groupies are gone.

"Finally came up for air, then?" I ask Wyatt, who gives me the finger before taking a pull of his beer. "Charming!"

"Where's Sophie?" Paisley asks from the side of me.

"She went to the bar with Cade. You should go and find them if you want a drink."

"Do you want another wine?" I ask Paisley.

She nods. "Just one more." She goes up on her tiptoes and whispers in my ear. "I don't want to be hungover for our date." I grin stupidly at her, and keeping hold of her hand, I guide her to the bar.

"I don't see them, do you?" My eyes scan the bar area, and although it's busy, Cade is tall and I don't think I'd have any trouble spotting him if he were here.

"No. Oh, hang on. Oh my God! Is that them?" I look to where she's pointing and see Cade has Sophie pushed against the wall and is kissing her. It's an area blocked off for staff, and I wonder if they realize they aren't hidden from view.

"Thank God for that!"

"What?"

"He's been like a bear with a sore head ever since Sophie came back to Hope Creek eighteen months ago. They were together while Cade was in medical school and then something happened and she left. Cade won't talk about it, but I hope this means they're sorting things out."

"I had no idea. She hasn't said anything, but then, why would she? I've not known her very long."

"I doubt it's you, Paisley. If she's anything like Cade, she won't have opened up to anyone."

"I think they make a great couple."

"Everyone thought they'd get married and have kids, but then Sophie just left. Mom was devastated. She was really close to her." They still haven't come up for air and I squeeze Paisley's hand. "I guess it's my round, then." I chuckle.

"I'll get them," she says, reaching for her purse.

"No, I've got it." I walk to the end of the bar and get Seb's attention. I turn to Paisley. "Being related to the owner has its perks. No waiting in line!" She laughs, and I drop her hand, slipping my arm around her waist and pulling her against me. I can't help it; I need her as close as possible.

After ordering the drinks, I take hold of Paisley's hand again while carrying two bottles of Bud in my other one. She's carrying her wine, and I decide against getting Cade and Sophie a drink. I figure they'll head to the bar once they're finished. I pass a bottle to Wyatt before sliding into the booth with Paisley.

"Where's Cade and Sophie?" Wyatt asks as we sit down.

I shrug. "No idea." I wink at Paisley, who smiles. "How did you manage to get rid of your fans? Or did they find someone even more famous to make out with?"

"You're an asshole, Nash Brookes!" He's laughing, so I know he's joking. "I think I had a lucky escape, actually. She kept trying to get me to agree to go to Vegas with her. Thankfully, they have a flight first thing in the morning and had to leave. I think I might call it a night after this." He holds his half-empty bottle in the air. "Are you coming for lunch tomorrow at Mom and Dad's?"

"No. I have plans with Paisley." I turn to smile at her. "I'll be there on Thursday, though." He drinks down what's left of his beer before placing the empty bottle on the table and standing up.

"I'll see you Thursday, then. Have a good time tomorrow, you two."

After a quick goodbye, he leaves, and we're suddenly alone. "You okay?" I ask, bumping her shoulder gently with mine. She nods. "Are you sure? You look a little nervous." She's quiet and holding her wineglass as if it's her lifeline, her eyes fixed on the liquid inside.

"I guess I am nervous. I'm sorry."

I reach for her free hand. "Don't ever apologize, Paisley. It's okay to be nervous. I'm nervous too."

"You are?" she asks in surprise, and I nod.

"I like you. I don't want to do the wrong thing or say something that might upset you. I know you're probably nervous for different reasons, but however this plays out, we go at your pace. Okay?"

"Okay," she whispers. "Thank you." She swallows down a mouthful of wine and turns her body to face me. "What made you want to be a cop?"

"I've wanted to be a cop for as long as I can remember. I guess it goes back to what happened to my mom."

"That makes sense."

"What about you? What happened to wanting to be a teacher?"

She sighs. "I started a bachelor's degree in early childhood education, but then I met Connor and dropped out. Another bad decision."

I take her hand and lace her fingers with mine. "It's never too late, you know."

"I think it probably is, but I'm okay with that."

"You can do whatever you want, Paisley."

"I like your enthusiasm. I only wish it were true."

I don't push her. I know she doesn't believe me right now, but she just needs to build her confidence up after her bastard ex beat it out of her.

We're still talking when Sophie turns up at the table. She's alone, and it looks like she's been crying.

"Are you okay?" Paisley asks, standing from the booth and going to her. "Where's Cade?"

"I'm okay. He left. I think I'm going to go home." She looks past Paisley to me. "Will you walk Paisley back, Nash?"

"I'll come with you," Paisley says before I can answer.

"I don't want to ruin your night."

"You're not."

"I'll walk you both home," I interject, picking up my beer and draining the bottle.

"Thanks, Nash," Sophie says before she heads away from the table toward the exit.

"I couldn't let her go home on her own," Paisley says, her worried eyes flicking to mine. "I hope you don't mind."

"Of course I don't mind. There's no way I'd let her walk home on her own anyway. Cade is an asshole for leaving her here." I take her hand and we head outside. Sophie doesn't say a word on the short walk back to the house, and after thanking me for walking her home, she goes inside.

"I'll go and see if she's okay. I'm not sure she's going to be up for much talking though. Thank you for walking us back."

I wrap my arms around her, and she rests her head on my shoulder. "I hope she's okay. I'll speak to Cade in the morning." I hold her for a few minutes before dropping my arms and taking a step back. "I'll pick you up at twelve tomorrow. Night, Paisley."

"Night, Nash."

I lean down and press a kiss to her cheek. She smiles before turning and going inside. I wait until the door closes before I turn and walk slowly home. I can't wait to spend some more time with her tomorrow. I'm so glad she's taken the leap of faith and decided to give us a shot. The more time I spend with her, the more I want to know everything about her, even the bad bits, although I know hearing them will kill me.

Not wanting to think of her being hurt, I reach for my phone and try to call Cade, but it goes straight to voicemail. I'll be having words with him tomorrow for leaving Sophie on her own at the bar. He didn't know Paisley and I hadn't left. It's so unlike him. I wish I knew what was going on with him. I think it's about time I made him tell me.

CHAPTER NINETEEN

Paisley

*N*ervous excitement swirls in my stomach as I wait in the entryway for Nash. I hardly slept last night. As much as I was looking forward to spending some time with him, I was apprehensive. After what he'd said last night, it was obvious he wants to be more than friends. I'm attracted to him, but after Connor crushed me, I don't know if I have anything left to give.

"What time is Nash coming?" Sophie asks as she emerges from the kitchen.

"Any minute now."

"You look great, Paisley."

I smooth my hands down the dark blue maxi dress she's lent me. "Thank you for letting me raid your closet again."

She waves her hand dismissively. "It's fine."

"I know I said it last night, but if you ever want to talk to me about anything, I'm here for you. You've helped me so much. I'd like to be there for you too."

"Thanks, Paisley." I sigh when she doesn't say anything else. I know we haven't known each other long, but I'd like to think we're friends. I hope she feels like she can open up to me one day. I jump when a knock sounds on the door, and she smiles. "Have a great time." She turns and heads back into the kitchen, leaving me alone in the entryway. Smoothing down the soft material of my dress, I take a deep breath before gripping the door handle tightly.

As I swing the door open, all the air rushes from my lungs as my eyes fall on Nash. He's wearing dark jean shorts and a blue t-shirt that's pulled tight across his chest. There's more stubble than last night on his jaw, and he's wearing aviator sunglasses. He looks gorgeous.

"Hi," I say shyly, and he smiles.

"Hi, Paisley. You look beautiful."

I feel my cheeks heat from his compliment, and I drop my eyes. "Thank you. You look good too."

He pulls down his sunglasses and his eyes meet mine. "Are you ready to go?"

"Yes." He holds his hand out, and I place mine in his, our fingers entwining. He leads me to his truck and opens the passenger door, helping me inside. Max barks from the back seat, and surprised to see him, I turn around to say hello.

"You brought Max?" I say as Nash climbs into the driver's seat.

He nods. "I figured you'd only worry about him if we were out for a while. We've had words though. I've warned him he has to share you today."

I laugh and reach back to stroke Max, who licks my hand. "Did he agree?"

"I didn't get a reply, so we'll have to see."

"You're crazy!"

He reverses off the drive and heads toward town.

"I thought we'd go to Lynx Lake. It's about a ten-minute drive from here."

"Sounds good. I had no idea Hope Creek even had a lake."

"There's actually a few to choose from that aren't too far from here. Lynx is my favorite though."

"I can't wait."

"How was Sophie last night?" he asks as we head away from the town.

"Okay, but she wouldn't talk to me. I didn't tell her we'd seen them kissing. Did you speak to Cade?"

He shakes his head. "No. I tried a few times to call him. His phone either rings out or goes to voicemail."

"Hopefully they'll sort whatever it is out between themselves. Sophie knows she can talk to me when she's ready."

"How did you sleep?" he asks as we merge onto the highway.

"Okay, what about you?"

"Yeah, not bad…" He trails off. "Actually, I slept like shit."

"Really? Why?"

"I guess I was excited for today." He smiles at me and my stomach dips.

"I hope I don't disappoint. I'm not that exciting," I tell him with a nervous laugh.

"I won't be disappointed, Paisley." He reaches his hand across the cab and tangles his fingers with mine. "This okay?" He lifts up our joined hands, and I nod. He turns off the highway and onto a dirt track. The truck bounces along, and it's clear not many vehicles come down here.

We drive for a few more minutes in silence, his thumb stroking circles on the back of my hand. Tiny sparks of electricity shoot up my arm, and I love having his hand in mine. Connor never held my hand, not even when things were okay between us. He'd never been one for public displays of affection. He was my first and only boyfriend, and I just thought that was how it was meant to be. Spending time with Nash makes me realize maybe it wasn't.

"Wow. This is beautiful," I exclaim, when the dirt track opens up and a secluded section of the lake comes into view. There are trees lining either side of the space, and when I look to the lake, a small wooden jetty juts out into the water. "It looks like this is our own private bit of the lake," I say, both excited and nervous to be completely alone with him.

"It is. We used to come here as kids all the time. My parents stumbled across it when Dad took a wrong turn one time. Once we found it, we always came to this spot. Occasionally, there were other people here, but more often than not, it was just us."

He parks the truck and climbs out, running around the hood to open my door. Taking my hand, he helps me down before opening the back door to let Max out. Max tears off toward the water, and I giggle as he flies off the end of the jetty and into the water.

"I'm guessing Max likes the lake?"

"He does. We haven't been here for a while, though. Work's been a little crazy." He drops my hand and reaches into the back of the truck for a blanket and the picnic basket. "I hope you're hungry. I didn't know what you liked, so I brought lots."

"I'm starving, and I'm sure I'll love it, Nash." I take the blanket off him, and he slips his free hand back into mine, leading me to the edge of the lake. I lay out the blanket, and we sit down. "You must have had a great time out here as kids with your brothers and Ashlyn."

"We did. We'd bring canoes and paddleboards down here. We pretty much lived in the water the whole time. We camped here a couple of times too. Not Mom and Ash, but the rest of us."

"Ash not a keen camper?"

"Nah. Nowhere to plug her hairdryer in."

I laugh. "I think I'd probably have to agree!"

He reaches for the picnic basket and begins to pull out sandwiches, pasta salads, chips, and drinks.

"This looks great, Nash."

As if knowing the food is ready, Max comes hurtling toward us, dripping wet.

"Max! No!" Nash shouts, scrambling to his feet in an attempt to stop him launching himself on me. He just grabs his collar in time to stop him ending up on my lap. "I've got a towel in the truck."

I laugh as I watch him take Max to the truck and dry him off. When they both come back to the blanket, Max drops down next to me, his head on my lap.

"Do you want me to move him while we eat?" Nash asks.

"No, he's fine."

After eating far too much of the delicious food, I flop backwards onto the blanket. Max has moved off me and is lying on the grass, fast asleep.

"Thank you for lunch. It was great."

"You're welcome."

Nash lies down next to me, and I turn my head to find him looking at me.

"Hi," I whisper, my eyes locked with his.

"Hi." He smiles and reaches his hand up to tuck a stray piece of my hair behind my ear. "How's your wrist?"

"It's okay."

"Good." His eyes drop to my lips, and my heart pounds in my chest. As much as I want to feel his lips on mine, I don't know if I'm ready. He takes a deep breath, as if reading my mind. "How are you feeling about starting work?"

"I'm nervous but looking forward to having something to fill my days. I'll miss walking Max though."

"You're welcome to come and walk Max anytime you want. Do you still have my key?"

"Yes. I'll grab it when we get back to Sophie's and you can have it back."

"I didn't mean for you to give it back. Keep it and come and see Max whenever you want."

"Thank you. I'm hoping I can find somewhere to rent now that I've got a job."

"You want to leave Sophie's?"

"Yeah, if I can find somewhere I can afford. I don't need anything big. A studio apartment would be fine."

"I'll keep a lookout for anything that comes available."

"Thanks."

We lie in silence for a few minutes until Nash rolls on his side, propping himself up on his elbow.

"Tell me about you, Paisley."

"What do you want to know?" I ask, looking up at him.

"Everything."

I smile. "Everything?" He nods. "I'm not sure there's much to tell. It was just me and my parents growing up. I would have loved a brother or sister, but I think they struggled to have me, and a sibling just never happened. They were pretty strict about letting me go out when I was a teenager. I guess I was a bit of a nerd because of that. I wasn't allowed to go to parties, or to date boys." His eyes widen, and I laugh. "What?"

He shakes his head. "Nothing. I just figured you would have been popular in school."

"Why?"

"Because you're beautiful. You must have had guys interested."

I screw up my nose. "No. Not really. I wanted to be popular. Who doesn't? I wanted to try out for the cheerleader squad, but my parents wouldn't let me. I guess that's why when I went to college and met Connor, I rebelled. I was nineteen, but I didn't feel like I was able to make any of my own decisions. I was still living at home, and Connor was older, with his own place. He persuaded me to leave. He promised me the world, and naively, I believed him."

"I'm sorry, Paisley." His fingers stroke up and down my arm, goose bumps erupting on my skin where he's touching me.

"Me too." We're silent for a few seconds as he stares at me. "Tell me what you were like in school." I smile. "I'm guessing you were popular. Prom king?"

He laughs. "Am I that obvious?"

I roll onto my back and stare at the perfect blue sky. There's not a cloud in sight, and the warm May sun beats down on my face. "No, just a lucky guess. I have a feeling all of the Brookes brothers were popular at school."

He moves closer to me, and I tilt my head to look at him. "Why do you say that?"

"You've looked at your brothers recently, right?" I ask, raising my eyebrows.

"Are you saying you think my brothers are good-looking? I'm not sure how I feel about that." His voice is laced with humor, so I know he's joking.

"Yes, but there's only one Brookes brother who makes my heart race. Even if admitting that terrifies me," I say quietly.

His eyes widen, and I think I've shocked him. I've definitely shocked myself.

"Paisley," he whispers as his hand cups my face. I lean into his touch and he gently strokes my cheek with his thumb. He stands up and reaches for my hand, pulling me up and into his arms. I wind my hands around his neck and drop my head on his shoulder.

"You make my heart race too, Paisley," he whispers into my hair before pressing a kiss on my hair. "Can I kiss you?"

Lifting my head, I lean back slightly so I can see his face. His eyes search mine, and I know if I said no, he'd understand, but I don't want to say no. I'm terrified to put myself out there again, but I can't keep denying my attraction to him.

"Okay," I whisper. Both of his arms are around my waist, and he removes one arm and snakes his hand around the side of my neck and into my hair.

"You are so beautiful, Paisley," he mutters, his eyes dropping to my lips. A million butterflies take flight in my stomach as he drops his head. I close my eyes as I feel his lips on mine. It's gentle at first, and I melt into him, winding my hands into the hair at the nape of his neck. When his tongue swipes against my bottom lip, I open up to him, moaning into his mouth as our tongues collide. My heart pounds in my chest, and I tug on his hair as he consumes me. His kiss is everything, and it feels like fireworks are exploding in my chest. When he pulls away, he kisses me softly once more before dropping his forehead on mine.

No one has ever kissed me like that. I've never been so consumed by someone and felt like I couldn't get close enough to them. Despite feeling apprehensive about putting my heart on the line again, now that he's kissed me, I can't wait to feel his lips on mine again.

CHAPTER TWENTY

Nash

I've never wanted to kiss anyone as much as I want to kiss Paisley. I hope I'm not pushing her before she's ready, but when she said I made her heart race, I took a chance. She's always made my heart race, and it's racing now as I wait for her to answer whether I can kiss her or not. When she agrees, I slide my hand around her neck and drop my lips to hers. My stomach dips as she opens her mouth to me, her tongue sliding against mine. I nearly lose it when she lets out a moan, and my cock jumps in my shorts. She tugs on the hair at the base of my neck, and I pull out of the kiss, kissing her once more before dropping my forehead to hers. It's never felt like that for me, with anyone. I saw fucking stars when I kissed her.

"Fuck, Paisley," I mutter.

"You felt it too?" she asks quietly.

"Yeah, baby. I did." Before she can say anything, Max barks loudly from the side of us. I hadn't even noticed he was standing there. I lift my head and look down at him, Paisley still in my arms. "I told you you have to share today," I say to Max.

Paisley laughs as he barks again. "I'm not sure he got the message." She steps out of my embrace and kneels down to stroke him. "I still love you, boy. Yes, I do," she tells him, and I smile down at her. She's perfect.

"Shall we go for a walk? There's a path through the trees that leads to a busier part of the lake. We could get an ice cream."

"That sounds great. Should we take his leash?"

"Yeah. I'll get it from the truck." Leaving her fussing over Max, I run to the truck and grab it from the back seat. When I get back to where I left her, she stands up and reaches for my hand. As our fingers lace together, I can't help but smile. That's the first time she's initiated holding hands. It's always been me that's reached for her. While holding hands isn't a huge deal for most people, I know for her, it is.

We walk together through the path in the trees I'd walked hundreds of times with my family. I'm sure we haven't been the only ones to walk this way, but it feels like that after years of visiting and only seeing a handful of people. Max runs on ahead, going so far and then running back to check we're still following him. Although, he's likely to be checking Paisley's following. He doesn't seem at all bothered about me when she's around. I can't say I blame him.

"Are you okay?" I ask, squeezing her hand.

"Yeah, I'm good. You?"

I nod. "I'm really good. Kind of hoping I get to kiss you again soon," I admit with a smile.

"I'm hoping that happens too," she says shyly.

"Will you come to dinner at my parents' house on Thursday night? It's Thursday roast."

"Thursday roast?"

"Yeah. It's a bit of a family tradition. When we were growing up, Mom could never get us all together on a Sunday, so she opted for a midweek roast. A Thursday stuck, even when we all started to move out. I try to go as often as I can when I'm not working. Same goes for the others."

"I love that tradition. I just need to check Seb doesn't want me to work that night, but if he doesn't, then I'll come. Thank you for asking me."

As the path comes to an end, the trees open up and the lake comes into view again. This part of the lake is much more commercialized than where we've just come from, and there are food trucks serving every sort of food you can imagine. Designated picnic areas are full of couples and families enjoying the warm weather, and chatter and laughter fills the air. At the water's edge you can hire canoes, rowboats, and in recent years, jet skis. The lake is full of people swimming, and there is a handful of boats out too, some with people fishing from them.

"You can rent jet skis! I've always wanted to do that," Paisley exclaims as her gaze falls on the lake.

"We can rent a jet ski sometime."

"Really?" she asks, excitement lacing her voice.

"Sure. Maybe when your ribs are fully healed. It can get a little bumpy."

"You've been on one?"

"Yeah, a couple of months ago. When we met on the plane from Pittsburgh, I'd been to my friend's wedding. His bachelor party was in Key West in Florida a few weeks before. We rented jet skis for a couple of hours in the ocean."

"Sounds like great fun."

Keeping hold of her hand, we walk to the ice cream cart. After getting a strawberry cone each, we find an empty picnic table and sit down.

"I can see why you'd come here all the time, Nash. It's beautiful."

"I've always loved Hope Creek. A lot of the guys I went to school with couldn't wait to leave, but it's home to me. I'm glad my family think the same and we've all ended up staying. Even Wyatt comes back whenever he can."

"I love how close you all are."

As we eat our ice cream, various people pass by the table and say hello. After the fifth person stops to say hi, Paisley chuckles.

"Does everyone know you?"

I smile. "Not everyone, but a lot of people. It's a small town."

"I guess."

"Nash!" a voice shouts, and I look up to see Leo, one of my few friends from school who decided to stay in Hope Creek. His young daughter, Scarlet, is with him.

"Leo. Good to see you," I say, standing up and pulling him into a one-armed hug when he reaches us. Scarlet is by his side, an ice cream in her hand. "That looks nice," I tell her with a smile. She winds her free arm around Leo's leg and looks up at him with a worried expression on her face.

"She's a bit shy," Leo explains.

"Leo, this is Paisley. Paisley, this is Leo, a friend from school."

"Nice to meet you, Leo."

"You too, Paisley."

"How are Bree and Oliver?" I turn to Paisley. "Leo and his wife had a baby a few weeks ago."

"Congratulations," Paisley says with a smile.

"Thanks. They're good. They're over there," he says, gesturing behind him. "Come and say hi."

I look over to Paisley. who smiles and nods. "Sure." I reach for Max and slip on his leash, not wanting him jumping all over Bree and the baby. Paisley stands and I go to her, winding my arm around her waist and pulling her into my side. Her arm snakes around my back, and I press a kiss on her hair. Leo and Scarlet have gone on ahead, and we follow them, arm in arm.

"Are you okay meeting my friends?" I whisper in her ear as we walk. She nods, and I can tell she's nervous. "We'll just say hi and then head back."

"Don't rush. I'm happy to spend some time with your friends." I look down at her and she smiles back at me. I drop a kiss on her forehead and my hand squeezes her waist.

"Leo and Bree are great. I think you'll like them."

"Their little girl is beautiful."

"Nash Brookes!" Bree exclaims as we reach where they're sitting. "It's so good to see you." She stands up with a tiny baby in her arms and pulls me into a hug. I bring my arm from around Paisley and hug her back, careful not to squash the baby. It's been a while since I last saw them. They moved to a place just outside of Hope Creek a few months before the baby was due.

170

"It's good to see you too, Bree. You look great!"

"Thanks, so do you." Her eyes flick past me to Paisley and she smiles. "Hi, I'm Bree," she says to Paisley.

"Bree, this is Paisley." I reach my arm back and lace her fingers with mine.

"Hi, Bree. Congratulations. He's beautiful," Paisley says, her eyes dropping to Oliver.

"Nice to meet you, Paisley, and thanks. Come and sit with us."

After spending half an hour chatting with Leo and his family, they invite us to a barbecue at their place in a couple of weeks. We both need to check our shifts, and we say goodbye, promising to let them know if we're free. I want to make sure Paisley is happy to go before I say yes, so using our shifts as an excuse works well. I know she's been through a lot, and I want her to always feel comfortable.

"Your friends seem great, Nash," Paisley says as we walk back through the trees to where we picnicked. I let Max off his leash, and he rushes through the trees ahead of us.

"Yeah, they are. They met at school and have been together ever since."

"They seem really happy."

"Do you want to go to the barbecue?"

"Sure, if I'm not working. Don't you?"

"Yeah, I do. I just want to check with you. We don't have to."

"No. I want to."

I squeeze her hand. "Good. I think you and Bree will get along great."

The trees open up and the clearing comes into view. It's still deserted, and we head back to the picnic blanket we left laid out on the grass. Paisley lies down and closes her eyes. I lie next to her and gaze up at the sky.

"I'd love to take you flying one day," I say, tracking a light aircraft across the cloudless sky. She laughs, and I smile, turning onto my side and propping myself up on my elbow. "What's funny?"

She turns her head and opens her eyes. "You do remember my meltdown on the flight from Pittsburgh?"

I smile. "Yes. I remember." How could I forget? I'm pretty sure meeting her on that flight has the potential to change my life. I don't tell her that though. I don't want to come on too strong, too soon. "A small aircraft is different, and I'd only take you up if the weather is good."

"I think I might need a couple of glasses of wine first." She giggles, and I love hearing her laugh.

"I didn't know you needed to be drunk to spend time with me," I tease, my voice tinged with amusement.

She grins. "I don't if my feet are planted firmly on the ground."

"I'd keep you safe."

"I know you would," she whispers, her eyes fixed on mine.

"Can I kiss you again?"

She nods, and I lower my head, watching as her eyes flutter closed seconds before my lips brush hers. One of her hands comes up and fists the material of my t-shirt, holding me to her. Kissing her again feels as amazing as the first time, and as she opens up to me, our tongues slide together. Her grip on my t-shirt increases, and it's like she can't get close enough to me. I know how she feels. I feel exactly the same. I pull away and pepper kisses around her jaw and down her neck.

"God, Nash," she moans as she rolls her head to one side, giving me better access. I drag my tongue over the pulse point on her neck, noticing her heart is racing and her breathing is labored. I love how affected she is by my touch. I kiss her mouth gently before reluctantly pulling my lips from hers. My heart's pounding in my chest, and I want to do so much more than kiss her, but I know she's not ready for that. I can wait. I'll wait forever for her.

CHAPTER TWENTY-ONE

Paisley

*A*s we pack away the picnic basket and fold up the blanket, I can't stop thinking how I felt when Nash kissed me. I thought the first time he kissed me was incredible, but the second time, I never wanted him to stop. It scares the hell out of me how much I want him. I honestly never thought I'd want to be in a relationship again, and I'm still finding it hard to believe someone like Nash would be interested in me. I guess it will take me a while to truly believe he is.

We load everything into the truck, and Nash drives away from the lake. I've had the best day, and I don't want it to end. Nash is quiet though, and he's hardly said a word since we kissed. I hope nothing's wrong. Despite his hand being tangled with mine, the longer the silence stretches out, the more worried I get.

"Are you okay?" I ask eventually. "You're quiet."

He squeezes my hand. "I'm good. Just thinking I don't want our date to be over."

My stomach dips knowing he feels the same. "I don't want it to be over either," I admit quietly.

He looks across the cab. "Do you want to come back to my place?" I bite down on my bottom lip. I *really* want to spend some more time with him. I'm just worried about what he's going to expect from me. "I know you're not ready to take things further than we have today, Paisley, and I'm good with that."

"How is it you know exactly what I'm thinking?"

"Lucky guess." He winks, and I smile. "Is that a yes?"

"Okay."

It's a short drive back to Nash's place, and when he parks on the drive, I climb out and open the back door for Max. He jumps crazily around my legs as we walk to the front door.

"Down, Max!" Nash exclaims. "She's coming inside with us." I laugh as Max takes no notice of him.

"You'd think he'd be worn out after an afternoon at the lake."

"Nothing wears him out."

He unlocks the door and places his hand on the small of my back as he guides me inside. Once Max sees I'm staying, he disappears into the living room.

"Do you want a drink?"

"A soda, please, if you have one?"

"Sure. I've got wine too."

"Just a soda for now. Maybe some wine later."

He nods and presses a kiss to my cheek. "Make yourself at home, baby. I'll be right back." He gestures to the living room before heading into the kitchen to get the drinks. I watch him go, butterflies exploding in my stomach when he calls me *baby*.

Grinning like an idiot, I go into the living room and flop down on the comfy sofa. I know it's comfy after sleeping on it a few weeks ago when I'd been discharged from the hospital. Despite Nash offering me his bed, it didn't feel right to sleep there, and instead, I'd chosen the sofa.

It's a cozy room, with a dark gray sofa and a gray checkered love seat. Directly opposite the sofa is a beautiful open fireplace. The wooden mantel over the fireplace holds a handful of picture frames I'd been too tired to notice last time. Standing up, I cross the space and smile as my eyes flick over the photographs. All of them are of Nash and his family, and although I've seen it for myself, these pictures just cement how important his family is to him. One of the frames shows two young boys sitting outside, each with a baby in their arms. I'm guessing it's him and Cade just after Seb and Wyatt were born. They're both smiling widely, and they look like the proudest brothers.

"What're you looking at?" Nash asks from behind me, his arms snaking around my waist as he pulls me back against his chest.

"Your photographs. I love this one," I tell him, picking up the frame and leaning back against him. "Is that you?" I point to the smaller of the two boys and turn my head to look at him.

"Yeah, that's me."

"You were cute."

"Were?" he asks, tickling my side.

Giggling, I push his hands away. "Okay. You're still cute! Who are you holding? Seb or Wyatt?"

He snorts. "No idea! They looked exactly the same. None

of us knew who was who most of the time. Not even Mom! It was only when Seb got his first tattoo we could tell them apart!"

I laugh and put the frame back. "I bet they had great fun tricking everyone."

"They did!" He drops his arms and reaches for my hand, turning me to face him. "Do you want to watch a movie?"

"Sure." He leads me to the sofa, and we sit down.

"What sort of movies do you like?" he asks, turning the TV on.

"Oh… anything."

He looks and me and frowns. "When was the last time you watched a movie, Paisley?"

"It's been so long I'm not sure I can remember."

"How about a classic?" He searches through the films he can download with his satellite package, stopping when he gets to *Forrest Gump*.

"*Forrest Gump?*" I ask with a giggle.

"Have you seen it?"

"Yeah, but ages ago. We can watch it again."

"*Forrest Gump* it is." He leans forward and picks up a can of soda from the table in front of us and hands it to me.

"Thanks." I open it and take a mouthful before placing it back on the table. Sitting back into the plush sofa, Nash opens his arms to me. I hesitate for half a second before moving into his embrace. His arm slips around my shoulder, and I rest my head on his chest. The movie starts, but I can't concentrate on it, consumed by how it feels to be held by him. He makes me feel safe and wanted, and like I'm important to him. I haven't felt any of those things in a really long time.

As the movie goes on, we somehow end up lying on the

sofa, my body pressed against his. The sofa's deep enough for us to lie side by side, and my head still rests on his chest.

"You okay, baby?" he asks, and my stomach flips.

Looking up at him, I smile and nod. He lowers his head and brushes his lips with mine. The kiss starts off softly and soon becomes heated. His tongue pushes against mine, and I moan into his mouth. Before I know what's happening, he's flipped me onto my back, his body pressing me into the sofa. He's still kissing me, and despite knowing it's Nash on top of me, I can't help but feel like I'm out of control. His weight pressing down on me feels like I'm being suffocated, and images of Connor pinning me down and taking whatever he wanted from me flashes through my mind. Panicking, I drag my mouth from his and claw at his t-shirt, pushing him off me.

"No! Stop," I whimper. Immediately, the weight pressing down on me is gone.

"Shit! I'm so sorry, Paisley." He sounds distraught, and I open my eyes, looking anywhere but at him. My whole body is shaking, and I sit up, wrapping my arms around myself.

"What happened?" He's moved off the sofa and is kneeling on the floor in front of me.

I shake my head. "I'm sor-sorry," I choke out, feeling like I want the ground to open up and swallow me.

"Paisley, look at me." I shake my head again. "Please."

Taking a deep breath, I finally look up, my heart breaking when I see the guilt in his eyes. "You don't ever have to apologize. It's my fault. I went too fast."

"No. It's not your fault. It's me. I'm fucked up." I uncurl my legs from underneath me and stand. "I should go."

"Please don't. Not like this." He's almost begging, and as much as I want to stay to make him feel better, I can barely deal with my emotions right now, let alone his. I wish I was

178

stronger, but I'm not. "Talk to me, Paisley. I want to be here for you."

He stands up and reaches for my hand, but I instinctively pull away, regretting it the second I do. The look on his face just about kills me. I thought I could do this. I thought I was ready. Maybe I was wrong.

"Nash," I whisper, tears welling in my eyes.

"It's okay, baby. It's okay."

"You deserve better than me." My voice is barely audible, but he hears me and shakes his head.

"No, Paisley. You deserve better than your asshole husband. We can go back to holding hands. We can take this as slowly as you need. Please don't push me away."

"Can you hold me?" I ask, surprising myself with my request. I'm desperate to feel how I felt before the kiss.

Nash looks confused. "Are you sure?"

I nod. "I'm not going to freak out. I promise."

He takes a step toward me and opens his arms. I go to him, pressing my body against his. His strong arms envelop me, and I drop my head on his shoulder. I melt into him, feeling even more embarrassed about my breakdown.

"I'm sorry," I say into his shoulder.

"Will you quit apologizing. You have nothing to be sorry for."

"Connor used to hold me down," I admit softly. "I know that's not what you were doing, but I guess I panicked."

His hold on me tightens, and I feel him drop a kiss on my head. "Fuck, Paisley. I'm sorry." His fingers track up and down my back, and I feel a tension in his body. I wonder if it's because of what I've just told him. "Did he do… things you didn't want him to?" His voice is low, and I close my eyes tightly, pressing myself closer into him. I know he's asking if Connor raped me without saying the words.

"Yes."

He breathes in sharply, and if possible, holds me even tighter. "Was he always rough with you?" he asks softly.

I sigh and step out of his arms, wiping my eyes. "No. His brother, Aaron, died suddenly about a year ago and things were never the same after that…" I trail off. "He said it was my fault he died." I drop my head onto his chest. I've never told anyone that before, and I can't help but hope Nash doesn't think the same when he knows what happened.

"What? Why would he say that?"

He guides me to the sofa and pulls me to sit down with him. I keep my head down, not wanting to look him in the eye.

"Aaron called him late one night. He was drunk and wanted Connor to go and pick him up from a bar in town. I'd been sick all day. Stomach flu, I think. I'd been throwing up and spiking a fever. I asked him not to leave me, and he told Aaron he couldn't give him a ride." I pause, taking a deep breath. "He was knocked over in a hit-and-run accident when he tried to walk home. He died on the side of the road."

"God, I'm sorry, Paisley." He pulls me against his side, and I bury my face into his chest. "So he decided because you'd asked him to stay with you while you were sick, his brother's death was your fault?"

I lift my head, my eyes finding his. "Yes," I whisper. "Do you think he was right?"

He frowns and shakes his head. "No, Paisley! It was an accident, and no matter what happened, it doesn't justify your husband beating you for a year."

"It started off with a shove, or holding my arm too tightly. I should have left then, but I knew he was grieving and I thought it was the grief that had turned him into this man I barely recognized. It soon turned into more though, and by the time it got really bad, it was too hard to leave. I was isolated from all my friends, and he made me believe I deserved it."

"No, Paisley," he whispers, his arms increasing their hold on me. "You *never* deserved any of it."

"I know that now." He holds me, and I love being in his arms. Despite that, he's silent, and my insecurities bubble to the surface. Is he going to look at me differently now that he knows everything? I'm not only broken physically, but emotionally too. He could have anyone he wants, someone who isn't messed up and doesn't freak out when he touches her. I wouldn't blame him if he ran from me and never looked back.

CHAPTER TWENTY-TWO

Nash

My alarm sounds from the nightstand, and I groan as I roll over and reach out to turn it off. I've tossed and turned all night, and it feels like I've only just fallen asleep when the alarm screams out. The room fills with silence, and I stare at the stark white ceiling, Paisley's words from last night playing in a loop in my mind. After she'd opened up to me, I'd wanted to kill her deadbeat husband with my bare hands. It broke my heart when she told me the abuse had been going on for a year. I can't comprehend how scared she must have been, living like that. I wanted to hold her against me all night and show her just how much she means to me, but I knew if I asked her to stay, she'd have said no. It's too soon.

Climbing off the bed, I pad to the bathroom and turn on

the shower. After using the toilet and brushing my teeth, I stand under the hot spray, letting the water wash over me. I dropped her back at Sophie's last night, and I hated how quiet she was. Maybe I was quiet too. I could see her mind working overtime. I just wish I knew what she was thinking. She was fighting so many demons. I wanted more than anything to take her pain away.

Half an hour later, I'm ready for work. Max has been fed, and I'm sitting at the breakfast bar with a piece of toast. I'm not hungry, but I force myself to eat it anyway, knowing if it's a busy shift, I might not have time to stop for food. I'm hoping for a quiet day. My head's definitely not in the game today. Picking up my phone, I send a message to Paisley. She likely won't be up yet, but it's her first lunch shift at Eden today, and I know how nervous she is.

Me: Morning, baby. How did you sleep? Just wanted to wish you good luck for today even though you won't need it. I'll call you later. Nx

Slipping my phone in my pocket, I put my plate in the dishwasher, and after saying goodbye to Max, head to work. When I get to the station, I sit staring at my computer screen. I've typed Paisley's husband's name into the police database, and my finger hovers over the return key. Knowing what she told me last night, I want to find out as much as I can about him. I know Paisley won't want me to, and that's what's holding me back. I want to respect her wishes, but I can't comprehend him getting away with what he's done to her. Taking a breath, I close my eyes and hit the key. To my surprise, there's nothing on him other than a couple of speeding tickets. I don't know what I was expecting, but I was expecting *something*.

Before I can rationalize what I'm doing, I start typing, filing a report noting down the timeline of the attacks and logging Paisley's injuries from when she first arrived in Hope Creek, as well as the miscarriage and the sexual assaults. I know it's not what she wants, but I'm not going after the guy, just logging everything in case he's ever arrested for something similar. Knowing there's nothing more I can do, I put an alert on his name, meaning if he gets taken into any station, I'll know about it.

My hope for a quiet shift doesn't quite go to plan after the local bakery on the main street reports a break-in just after I've finished looking up Paisley's ex. Break-ins are unusual in Hope Creek, but unfortunately, they do happen occasionally.

Arriving at the bakery, I interview a distraught Mrs. Stone, who's owned the store since I was a kid. It seems the door's been forced at the back. There's no CCTV at the back of the building, but the forensic guy that's with me manages to pull a print off the door. Thankfully, there was no cash on-site, so other than gaining access to the bakery, nothing's been taken. It was probably kids, but I'll run the print when I get back to the station and see what comes up. It's almost lunchtime when I'm finished speaking to everyone and helping Mrs. Stone secure the back door. It's not really part of my job, but since her husband died last year, there's no one else to do it, and the insurance company can't come out until tomorrow. I don't mind, and it doesn't take long.

When I head out onto the sidewalk, my eyes go across the street to Eden, and I wonder if Paisley's started her shift yet. Pulling my phone from my pocket, I check the time, noticing a message from her. Smiling, I open it.

Paisley: Hi, Nash. Thanks, I'm nervous. Hope I don't drop anything. Px

Deciding I should check Seb's CCTV footage from the cameras that face the sidewalk, I jog across the empty road, pushing open the door the Eden. I'm not expecting to see anything on the cameras, but it's a good excuse to say hi to Paisley. My eyes flick around the room, but I don't see her.

"Hey, Nash. What are you doing here? Or is that a stupid question?" Seb shouts from behind the bar. Laughing, I cross the room to him.

"I'm here as a cop, actually. Mrs. Stone's bakery had a break-in overnight. I was hoping I could check out your camera that faces the sidewalk?"

"Oh. Sure. You don't want to see Paisley, then?"

"Well, if she's here, I'll say hi."

He smiles. "Thought so. I think she's in the kitchen. I'll show you the footage first and then fix you up with some lunch."

"Thanks, man."

I follow him out the back and into his office. "Is Mrs. Stone okay? They get anything?"

"She's shaken up. There was no cash in the building, so they just made a mess. It's likely kids."

After watching the footage from Seb's camera, I'm no closer to knowing who broke into the bakery. Not that I expected to be.

"Nothing," I say to Seb, who's sorting through some paper-work. "Hopefully the print we lifted will be in the system and we get the bastards that way."

"I hope so. You want some lunch?"

"Burger and fries?"

"Coming right up."

"Thanks, Seb."

I follow him out of his office, and he heads to the kitchen

to give my order over. I go in the opposite direction in search of Paisley. When the bar comes into view, I see her waiting on a drink order at the bar. Walking up behind her, I slide my arms around her waist and pull her gently against my chest. She tenses in my arms, relaxing when she hears my voice. "Did you drop anything yet?" I whisper into her ear.

She turns in my arms, a smile lighting up her face. "What are you doing here?"

I lean down and brush my lips against hers. "I came in for lunch, and to see you."

She smiles. "You're going to get me fired on my first day. I don't think I'm supposed to flirt with the customers."

"I'm pretty sure you're only supposed to flirt with me," I tease, my heart stuttering as I look down at her and kiss her nose.

"I didn't know if I'd see you today after my meltdown yesterday," she admits, her eyes dropping from mine.

I frown and lift her chin with my fingers so she's looking at me. "Why?"

She shrugs. "I don't know why you want to be with me. I'm such a mess." Her voice is barely a whisper, but I can still hear the dejection in her tone.

"You aren't a mess, Paisley. I want to be with you because you're beautiful, and kind, and brave. I think you're incredible."

"You do?" Her voice is laced with surprise, and I smile.

"Yes. I do. I thought you knew that."

"I guess I just can't quite believe it's true."

"You don't ever have to question whether I want you, Paisley. I'm always going to want you." I lower my head and kiss her.

"Put my staff down, Nash!" Seb shouts from across the

bar, and Paisley tenses against my lips, pushing me away. Turning to the bar, she picks up the tray full of drinks.

"He's joking, baby," I assure her, placing my hand on her arm.

"I am joking, Paisley," Seb says as he comes to stand next to us. "I couldn't be happier for you both." He smiles at her, and she smiles back shyly.

"I'll take these drinks over."

I wink at her as she passes me before turning back to Seb. "I won't come in and distract her too often," I lie, and he laughs.

"That's bullshit, but okay. Are you two together now, then?"

"I think so."

He raises his eyebrows in question. "You think so?"

"We haven't exactly had the conversation, but for me we are. I'm all in, man."

"I figured as much. I hope it works out for you both." He pulls me into a one-armed hug and slaps me on the back. "Grab a seat. Your food won't be long. I'll ask Paisley to bring you over a soda. I'm sure she won't mind."

I chuckle as I leave him at the bar and take a seat in one of the booths. My eyes follow Paisley as she delivers food and drink orders to the tables around me. She knows I'm watching her, her eyes flicking to mine as she passes where I sit. I wish she could see how I see her. I meant every word of what I said, and I'll tell her every day until she believes it. When she brings me my soda, I pull her into the booth to sit next to me. "What time do you get off?" I ask, slipping my arm around her waist.

"Six."

"I'll come and pick you up."

"You don't have to. I can walk."

"I want to. I finish at six too."

"Okay. Thank you."

"Do you know if you're working Thursday night yet?"

"I'm not. My evening shift this week is Friday."

"You can come for dinner, then?" She nods and smiles. "I'll let Mom know."

"Thank you for not giving up on me," she whispers.

"I'll never give up on you, Paisley. I promise." She kisses me softly on the cheek.

"I'll go and see if your lunch is ready."

I watch her cross the room, and I know without a shadow of a doubt I'm falling in love with her. She's my very first thought when I wake up, and my last thought before I go to sleep. I want to spend every second with her, and seeing her cry just about kills me. Knowing what that bastard of a husband did to her makes me so angry I can't see straight. I want to make him suffer the way Paisley has, which as a cop should go against everything I believe, but I'd do anything to protect her. The intensity of my feelings should scare the hell out of me, but they don't. It just feels right, and when she's in my arms, I know that's where she belongs. I just have to convince her of that.

CHAPTER TWENTY-THREE

Paisley

*I*t's been three weeks since I started working at Eden, and I love it. Seb and the rest of the staff are great to work with, and everyone's been so friendly. I do one evening shift a week, and Nash insists on meeting me when I finish, even if he's working. We've spent every spare minute together during the past three weeks, and I feel like I've known him forever. Thankfully, I haven't had any more meltdowns with him, but that might be because we've done nothing more than kiss, and never like we did on the sofa when I panicked. He's so patient with me, and while I know he won't wait forever, he seems happy with how things are at the moment.

It's Saturday lunchtime, and I'm waiting for Nash to pick me up. We're going to Leo and Bree's for the barbecue they invited us to when we met them at the lake. For the first time since I arrived in Hope Creek, I'm going out with Nash in clothes I haven't either brought with me from Pittsburgh or borrowed from Sophie. I'd used a little money from my first paycheck to buy some new things. There's a small clothing store just down the block from Eden that Ashlyn told me about, and they have some beautiful dresses. I'd been careful with the rest of my pay, saving it for a deposit on somewhere to live. There's nothing suitable to rent right now, but I'm hoping something will become available soon.

"Nash is here," Sophie shouts up the stairs. I take one last look at my reflection in the mirror, smoothing down the black and white polka-dot sundress I'm wearing before flicking my curled hair over my shoulder. As nervous as I am to spend the afternoon with Nash's friends, I can't wait to see him. Despite only seeing him yesterday, I want to spend all my time with him.

Walking to the top of the stairs, I stand and watch Nash talking to Sophie. My heart stutters in my chest when I see him, and it terrifies me how quickly I'm falling for him. He's gorgeous inside and out, and I still struggle to see why he's chosen to be with me when he could have anyone. As if sensing me watching him, he looks up, his face lighting up with a breathtaking smile.

"Hi, baby. You look beautiful."

I walk down the stairs toward him, stopping on the bottom step, putting me almost face to face with him.

"Thank you." I wrap my arms around his neck and press a kiss to his cheek.

"Have fun, you two. See you later, Paisley," Sophie says, smiling at me as she walks backwards and into the kitchen.

"Did you bring your swimsuit?" he asks, his arms still around me.

"No. I don't have one. Why?"

"Leo and Bree have a pool. Don't worry, maybe next time."

"You can still go in the pool. I wouldn't mind seeing you in a pair of swim trunks," I say with a chuckle.

His eyes widen in surprise. "Is that right?" he whispers, and I nod, my mind flicking to a few weeks ago, when I'd woken him up after a night shift and he'd come into his kitchen wearing only his sleep shorts. He'd look incredible in a pair of swim trunks, his bare chest wet from the pool. "If it means you're going to look at me like that again, I'll definitely be getting into the pool."

"Like what?" I ask, my cheeks heating.

"You know." He holds my gaze before his eyes drop to my lips. He kisses me softly before reaching for my hand. "Come on. Let's go before I need a cold shower!"

It's about a fifteen-minute drive to Leo and Bree's place, and I gasp when Nash pulls off the highway and their house comes into view.

"This is incredible, Nash."

"It is, isn't it? I haven't been here before, but it's easy to see why they bought this place."

As Nash parks, I gaze up at the impressive two-story house in front of me. It's enormous, with large windows on either side of the door and sleek modern lines. It looks like something from a design magazine. There's a small front lawn with topiary trees lining the edges, and a detached double garage sits to the left of the house, with a convertible car parked outside.

"What does Leo do for work?" I ask, in awe of their gorgeous house.

"He's a dentist. He owns a practice in town." I screw up my nose and Nash laughs. "What's that look for?"

"I hate going to the dentist."

"I don't think he's going to give you a cleaning while he's got the grill going, babe."

"Ha ha!" I roll my eyes at him and reach for the door handle.

"Wait." I turn to look at him and he beckons me closer with his index finger. "Kiss me before we go inside."

I smile and let go of the door handle, moving across the cab to him. His hand reaches up and tangles in my hair, pulling my mouth to his. His lips press against mine, and he bites down on my bottom lip, seeking entrance. I open up to him, and he pushes his tongue into my mouth. I moan against his lips. Every time he kisses me, my body ignites, and I want to crawl onto his lap and get as close to him as possible. I've never felt like this before, not even when I first met Connor. I can't help but think, with how intense my feelings are becoming for him, if things don't work out between us, I'll be devastated, and that makes me nervous.

He pulls out of the kiss and drops his forehead to mine. "I don't think I'll ever tire of kissing you, Paisley."

"I hope you always kiss me like that," I tell him shyly.

"I promise I will." He leans back and presses a kiss to my forehead. "You deserve to be kissed every hour of every day, Paisley."

"Are you two coming in? Or are you going to sit in the driveway and make out?" a voice shouts. I turn and look at the house, seeing Leo standing on the porch. My eyes widen, and Nash chuckles.

"Asshole," he mutters, flashing Leo the finger through the windshield. "Ready, baby?" he asks, and I nod.

He climbs out and jogs around the hood, opening my door before I've even grabbed my purse from the footwell. Reaching for my hand, he helps me down. His fingers lace with mine, and we walk hand in hand to where Leo is waiting for us.

"Come on in, guys. Bree and the kids are out back." He leads us through a large entryway, the walls full of family pictures. "Do you want a drink before we go outside?"

"A beer for me if you've got one," Nash says.

"Sure. Paisley, do you want a beer? Or there's wine?"

"Do you have a soda?"

"Yep."

We follow him into the biggest kitchen I've ever seen. White cabinets with dark wood countertops fill the space, and a large island sits in the middle of the room. Leo opens the refrigerator and hands Nash a beer.

"Your house is beautiful," I tell him as he reaches back inside and pulls out a can of soda.

"Thanks." He gestures to the kitchen. "This room sold the place to Bree. This and the master bedroom. I'm sure she'll want to give you a guided tour before you leave." He smiles and hands me the soda.

Leading us through bifold doors at the other end of the kitchen, we step outside into the backyard. It's a beautiful space with a large pool off to the left. A patio area sits opposite the pool, and Bree waves from the outdoor sofa she's sitting on, beckoning us over.

"I'd get up," she calls. "But someone's hungry."

My eyes drop to Oliver, who's snuggled against her chest, discreetly being breastfed. Scarlet sits on the floor by her feet, feeding a doll with a bottle. I smile as I look at her copying Bree.

"Come and sit down. Leo's got the grill on," Bree says.

Walking across the lawn, I smile at Bree before kneeling down in front of Scarlet. "Hi."

"Hi," she says shyly.

"What's your baby's name?"

"Joey."

"You're doing a great job feeding him. Do you help Mommy with your new brother?"

"I help with his diapers, but I can't feed him because I haven't got any milk in my boobies."

"Is that right?" I hide a smile as she nods.

"Do you want to feed Joey?" She holds the doll out to me, and I take him from her outstretched hands.

"Can I sit up here, next to Mommy?" I point to the outdoor sofa, and she nods. "Come and sit with me in case I do it wrong." Turning around, I catch Nash watching me, a smile on his face. I smile back and sit down, Scarlet climbing onto the seat next to me. "Am I doing it right?" I ask.

"Yes. Can I feed him now?"

"Of course. A baby needs his mommy." I hand the doll back and watch as she carries on feeding him.

"Would you like to hold Oliver, Paisley?" Bree asks, and I look up to see she's finished feeding him.

"Sure." Standing up, she places him in my arms. He's fast asleep after his feed, and I look down at him, his long, dark eyelashes resting on his cheeks. His skin is flawless, and I reach a finger up to stroke his cheek. "He's beautiful."

"Thank you. I think so, but I'm biased," she says with a laugh. She turns to Nash. "So how did you two meet? You're not from Hope Creek, are you?"

I pull my eyes off Oliver and shake my head. "No. I'm from Pittsburgh. I actually met Nash on the flight here."

"The old Nash Brookes charm swept you off your feet?" She laughs, and I smile.

"Something like that."

"What brings you to Hope Creek? Do you have family here?"

Nash reaches his hand to my knee and squeezes gently. "No, no family here. I needed to get away from Pittsburgh, and the first flight leaving from there was going to Phoenix. Nash told me about Hope Creek, and here I am."

She smiles sadly at me. "I'm sorry, Paisley. I didn't mean to pry."

"It's okay. I'm starting to think boarding that flight was the best decision I ever made." I look across to Nash, who leans down and kisses me softly.

"You two are cute. I've been waiting for someone to come and knock Nash on his ass."

"Hey! I'm right here, you know," Nash says, his voice full of humor.

Bree laughs and stands up. "Are you okay with Oliver while I see what Leo's doing with the grill? I want to check he isn't burning anything!"

"I can hear you, Bree!" Leo shouts from across the yard. "*Nothing* is burning."

"I'm still going to check," she whispers. "If you're okay with Oliver."

"He's fine," I assure her, and she grins before heading over to Leo, Scarlet following her.

My eyes drop back to Oliver, and I place my finger in his hand. Despite him being asleep, he grasps my finger tightly, and a wave of emotion crashes over me. Tears fill my eyes as I gaze down at him.

"Are you all right?" Nash asks, and I nod. "If it's too hard, I can take him."

"I can't help but wonder if I would have had a boy or a girl…" I trail off, knowing I'll never know. "I didn't think holding him would make me feel like this. I haven't really let myself think about the miscarriage since the hospital, but seeing him brings everything back. I can't really explain it. I guess I don't really understand it myself."

"It's okay to feel confused, baby. You've been through more than any one person should have to endure." He slips his arm around my waist and presses a kiss to the side of my head. "You can talk to me, you know. About anything. Even the miscarriage."

"How are you so amazing? Most guys would have run a mile by now."

"I'm not going anywhere, Paisley."

"Food's ready," Leo shouts from across the yard.

"We should head over. Thank you for understanding and being so patient with me."

I lean over and kiss him. Meeting him that day on the plane really did change my life. I was at rock bottom and had no idea how I was going to crawl out of the hole I'd been thrown into. Because of him, I had a place to live, a job, and a real chance at a new life. I can only dare to dream that Nash Brookes gets to play a starring role in that new life.

CHAPTER TWENTY-FOUR

Nash

I watch as Paisley disappears inside the house with Bree and Scarlet for the guided tour Leo said would happen. I've literally been left holding the baby while Leo grabs me a soda from the kitchen. Glancing down at Oliver, I can't help but think about how emotional Paisley had been when she held him. It hadn't occurred to me she might get upset. I should have realized. She's never mentioned the miscarriage, and I guess I thought she was over it. Seeing her today makes me think she isn't.

"Do you want me to take him?" Leo asks as he comes back, placing my soda on the small table at the side of the sofa.

"I'm good. If he starts crying, he's all yours."

He laughs. "Okay." He takes a pull of the beer in his hand. "So, Bree was right?"

"Right about what?"

"Paisley knocking you on your ass. I've never seen you like this with anyone before."

I smile. "She's the one, Leo. I think I knew it as soon as I saw her. She's had a rough time though, so we're taking things slowly."

"I'm happy for you, man. I hope it works out."

"Me too." My eyes drop to Oliver, who stirs in my arms. His eyelids flutter open and piercing blue eyes find mine. A smile pulls on his lips, and I look up at Leo. "He's smiling at me."

"It's likely gas," he says with a chuckle.

"No, it was a smile for his uncle Nash."

"If you say so."

I look up to see Paisley and Bree watching me from the bifold doors. Bree says something to Paisley, and she laughs. I can't help but wonder what she's saying to her.

"It suits you, Nash," Bree says as she and Paisley make their way across the lawn to where we're sitting. Her eyes drop to Oliver, and she smiles. "Someone's awake."

"He just smiled at me," I tell her.

"I told him it was gas," Leo says, and Bree laughs.

We spend the next couple of hours or so talking and laughing, and I hear Paisley and Bree arranging a girls' night out. I'm glad they've hit it off. Ashlyn and Bree are friends, so I'm sure Ash will want to get in on the night too.

When Scarlet and Oliver both begin to get cranky, we take that as our cue to leave, and after a round of goodbyes, we head back to my place.

"When are you going out with Bree, baby? I heard you

talking about a girls' night out," I ask as I drive us back through Hope Creek.

"Next Saturday. Is that okay?"

I look across the cab at her and frown. "Of course it is. You don't have to ask me if you can go out with your friends, Paisley."

Her hands are clasped together in her lap, and she wrings them together nervously. "Sorry. Force of habit."

I reach across and pry her hands apart, entwining her fingers with mine. "I'm happy you got along well with Bree. You know Bree and Ashlyn are friends?"

She nods. "Bree said she was going to ask her if she wanted to come."

"If I know Ash, she'll want to come."

I park on the driveway and jump out, jogging around the hood to help her from the truck. I take her hand, and we walk inside. Max goes crazy when we get in the entryway, and Paisley releases my hand to stroke him.

"Do you want a drink?"

"Can I have some wine?"

"Sure."

I kiss her before heading into the kitchen. Opening the refrigerator, I take out the open bottle of wine and pour two glasses. I want to ask her to stay the night. I don't want her to do anything she isn't ready for, but I want to sleep with her in my arms. I don't want to drop her off at Sophie's and come back to an empty house. Taking a deep breath, I leave the kitchen and find her in the living room on the sofa with Max.

"Down, Max."

Max jumps off the sofa and settles on the floor. Sitting down, I hand Paisley her drink. She takes a mouthful before putting her glass on the side table. She folds her legs underneath her and presses her body to mine. I put down my glass and wrap my arms around her, holding her close.

"Can I ask you something?"

"Of course." She lifts her head and looks at me.

"You can say no."

"What is it?"

"Do you want to stay over tonight? We don't have to do anything you aren't ready for. I just want to fall asleep with you."

I hold my breath as I wait for her to answer. She's quiet for a long time and I think she's going to say no.

"Okay. I'd like that," she says quietly.

"Really?"

She nods and kneels up next to me. She hesitates for half a second before leaning in and kissing me, her tongue pushing into my mouth. I pull her onto my lap and reach a hand up, tangling my fingers into her hair. My other hand stays on her waist as her palms fall onto my chest, and she fists my t-shirt as the kiss intensifies. My cock hardens underneath her, and I know she must be able to feel it. I don't want to freak her out, but I can't stop my body's reaction to her. I want her, even though she's not ready for that. She rolls her hips, and I moan into her mouth, pulling gently on her hair.

"Fuck, Paisley," I whisper, pulling out of the kiss. She drops her forehead onto mine, and my eyes fall to where her dress had ridden up her legs, her toned thighs exposed. My fingers itch to touch her, and I move my hand from her hair and gently stroke the skin of her leg. "You're so beautiful, baby."

"I'm really falling for you, Nash," she whispers. "It scares me."

She lifts her head, and her uncertain eyes find mine. My

heart squeezes in my chest as I gaze at her. "Don't be scared. I won't *ever* hurt you, I promise."

"I want to believe that. You've done nothing to make me doubt you, it's just..." She trails off and drops her eyes.

"I know, sweetheart." I know she's referring to her asshole ex. "I'm falling for you too, Paisley."

Her eyes flick to mine, surprised. "You are?"

I nod. "I'm pretty sure I've already fallen."

Her eyes widen. "What?"

"I'm falling in love with you, Paisley." I didn't plan on telling her I loved her today, and I know telling her how I feel is a risky move when she's scared, but I want her to know exactly what she means to me.

She shakes her head. "You can't be..."

"Why?"

"Because... I'm not... and you're..."

Her cheeks are pink and she's flustered. She looks adorable. I wrap my arms around her and tug her against my chest. It's clear she doesn't think she deserves to be loved, but that's just bullshit. She's amazing, and if I have my way, I'll never let her go.

"I know you're scared, but I'll wait as long as it takes for you to realize I mean every word I say. I plan on showing you every day how important you are to me."

I can see she doesn't know how to respond, so I kiss her, pouring everything I feel for her into the kiss. Her fingers go to the hair at the nape of my neck, and she tugs gently when my tongue seeks entrance to her mouth. She opens up to me, and our tongues dance together. With her body pressed against mine, I can feel her nipples harden through the thin material of her dress, and I know she's as turned on as I am. My cock strains against my pants, and she moans into my mouth as she grinds against me. My hands grip onto her waist, and I move her harder over my erection. She gasps, and I pull out of the kiss, pressing my lips around her jaw and down her neck.

"That feels so good," she mutters. "Don't stop."

"Are you sure?" I ask against the skin of her neck.

"Yes."

Her voice is breathless, and it turns me on even more to hear her turned on. I continue to kiss her neck while my hands move her over my hard cock. The thin material of her dress and panties isn't much of a barrier against my jean-clad erection, and when she starts to move faster against me, I know she's close.

"Oh, God, Nash," she cries as she drops her head onto my shoulder, her body shuddering in my arms. I hold her close while she comes down from her orgasm and her breathing evens out. When she doesn't lift her head, I reach a hand up and stroke her hair.

"Are you okay?" She nods but stays silent. "Are you sure?"

She finally sits up, her eyes focused on my t-shirt. "I've only ever been with one man, and it was never like that. You were hardly touching me, but it felt like my body was on fire."

"It's never been like this for me either."

Her eyes fly up to mine. "Really?"

"Really, baby."

"But you didn't… erm… finish."

"No, but that doesn't matter. It still felt incredible, and I want it to be good for you."

She bites down on her bottom lip. "It was."

"Good, and when I use my fingers and mouth, it'll be even better."

"Nash!" she exclaims, dropping her head back onto my shoulder. I chuckle and squeeze her waist gently.

"Maybe I can repay the favor later," she whispers into my neck, and my eyes widen in surprise.

"You don't have to, Paisley."

She lifts her head from my neck, her cheeks flushed pink. "I want to, and I'm hoping maybe you want to do that again?"

I smile. "I definitely want to. I can't keep my hands off you, but you hold all the cards, sweetheart. We go at your pace."

"I've never wanted anyone like I want you, Nash, and I don't know how to deal with that. Sex was never that important, and in the end, it was just used as a way to hurt me. There was no love, but I know it's going to be so different with you. My whole body comes alive when I'm near you, but I'm scared he's always going to be in my head."

I hold her gaze, conflicted by what she's telling me. Hearing her say she wants me like I want her causes my heart to race, but knowing what her jerk of an ex has done to her makes me want to hurt him so badly. I want him to feel pain like she did, to know what it feels like to walk around with fractured ribs and a broken arm. That would never be enough though, and really, I want to lock him up so he never gets the chance to hurt Paisley or anyone else ever again.

"When you're ready, baby. Really ready, there'll be no one else in your head when we make love. It's just going to be me and you. I'm going to love you so fiercely, Paisley, you'll never have to question how I feel about you."

Tears slip down her cheeks, and I reach my hand to her face, wiping away her tears with my thumb.

"I wish I'd met you first."

"I wish that too, sweetheart."

She slides off my lap and sits next to me, pressing her body against mine. My arm winds around her, and she rests her head on my chest. As hard as it was to listen to her open up to me, I'm glad she has. I want her to be comfortable enough to tell me anything, and it feels like we're getting closer every day. I'm already all in with her, and I know she's it for me. I hope to God she ends up feeling the same way.

CHAPTER TWENTY-FIVE

Paisley

I brush my teeth with a spare toothbrush Nash has given me before staring at my reflection in the vanity mirror. It feels like the woman looking back is a completely different person to the one who arrived in Hope Creek a couple of months ago. I was so broken, and my only thought had been that somehow, I had to survive. The idea of meeting anyone and falling in love wasn't even on my radar. As nervous as it makes me, I can't deny that's exactly what's happened. When Nash said he was falling in love with me, saying the words back to him had been on the tip of my tongue. Despite knowing without a shadow of a doubt I love him too, I couldn't bring myself to say the words. I've only ever loved one other man and that love made me weak. Saying the words aloud makes it real, and I never want to feel that vulnerable again.

"Baby, are you okay? You've been a while," Nash says softly through the door.

His voice pulls me from my thoughts, and I push off the vanity unit and tug down the t-shirt he's lent me. It falls mid-thigh, and while I've kept my panties on underneath, I'm a little self-conscious going out there like this.

"I'll be right out," I shout, not wanting him to worry.

Taking a few deep breaths, I take one last look in the mirror before opening the bathroom door. Nash sits on the edge of the bed, wearing just a pair of sleep shorts, and he looks up when the door opens. His eyes track over me as he gets up and crosses the room to stand in front of me.

"You look good in my t-shirt, Paisley." His voice is husky and nerves swarm in my stomach as he takes my hand and leads me to his bed. He sits down and tugs me gently to stand in between his legs. He drops my hand, his fingers skating under my t-shirt before coming to rest on the bare skin of my waist. He drops his head onto my stomach and I tangle my fingers into his hair.

"Are you okay?" I ask quietly.

He looks up and smiles. "I'm more than okay, sweetheart. I love having you here." His hands fall from my waist and he scoots backwards. I climb onto the bed and sit a little stiffly on top of the comforter. I'm not sure what to do. He lies down and opens his arms. "Lie with me."

Lying down, I slide closer to him and drop my head on his chest. His arms wrap around me, and I finally relax. Being in his arms feels like home, and despite being nervous, I know he's not going to make me do anything I'm not comfortable with. We lie in silence for a few minutes, and I can't help my mind going back to how he'd made me feel on the sofa earlier. My body felt like it was burning from the inside out, and I want him to feel the same way. I push up onto my elbow, and he turns his head to look at me. Before he can say anything, I lean in and kiss him. I think I've surprised him as it takes him a second to respond, but when he does, his hand cups my neck and his tongue swipes across my bottom lip, seeking access. I open up to him, and he moans into my mouth as the kiss intensifies. I snake my leg over his, feeling his erection hot and hard against my thigh.

"God, Paisley. Feel free to kiss me like that whenever you want," he mutters against my lips as I pull out of the kiss. I brush my fingers down his sculptured chest, feeling him inhale sharply at my touch. When I reach the waistband of his sleep shorts, his hand comes over mine.

"You know you don't have to do this, don't you?" he says softly.

I look up into his worried eyes. "I want to, Nash. I want to make you feel good."

"You do make me feel good."

"I want to touch you."

"Okay, baby." He releases my hand, brushing his thumb against my cheek.

I slip my fingers under the waistband of his shorts and take him in my hand. He lets out a moan as I slide my hand up and down his length, circling the head of his cock with my thumb. Pumping his erection, I increase my pressure and his hips rise off the bed, pushing himself further into my hand.

"That feels so good," he groans, reaching his hand into my hair and pulling my lips to his. With my hand still working him over, he kisses me, pushing his tongue into my mouth. Heat pools in my stomach as he moans, and my clit pulses. I've never wanted someone to touch me as much as I want Nash to. Seeing him so turned on has my body aching for him. He pulls out of the kiss and drops his head back on the pillow, his hand that was tangled in my hair now fisting the comforter. My hand works up and down and his breathing increases, telling me he's close.

"I'm going to come, Paisley," he warns. I squeeze his cock and increase my speed, loving the soft moans escaping his lips. "Fuck," he cries as ropes of cum shoot all over my hand. His whole body shudders as he comes, and his breathing is erratic. I keep my hand on him until he comes down from his orgasm and his breathing levels out.

"Paisley, that was incredible." My cheeks heat and I drop my eyes from his. "Come here." He sits up and holds his hand out to me.

"I should clean up," I say softly.

"Kiss me first."

"Bossy." I laugh and move closer to him, pressing my lips to his. Pulling out of the kiss, I climb off the bed and quickly wash up so I can get back to him. When I'm done, I find him still lying on the bed, and he opens his arms to me. "Come here, baby." I go to him, pressing myself into his side. "Are you okay?"

"I'm good."

He smiles before kissing me. The familiar ache begins to build between my legs, and I moan into his mouth as his hand goes under my t-shirt and his fingers brush over my breast. My nipple pebbles under his touch, and I arch my back. He rolls my nipple between his fingers, and I'm so turned on I can barely breathe. His fingers move down toward my panties and he stops.

"Can I touch you, Paisley?"

"Yes," I mumble, raising my hips. He drags my panties down my legs and tosses them on the floor. He pulls my t-shirt over my head and I'm suddenly naked. Nash's eyes are all over me, and the heat from his stare makes me forget I'm naked in front of him for the first time.

"God, you are so beautiful, Paisley. I'm never letting you go." My eyes widen, and he smiles. "I mean that in a non-creepy way."

I giggle and reach for him. "Kiss me, Nash."

"Who's bossy now?" he jokes, his lips millimeters from mine.

He kisses me before brushing his lips across my jaw and down my neck. His body is over mine, but he's careful not to put his weight on me, and I know he must be conscious of me freaking out again. I'm not going to. I trust him and I want to feel his hands on me.

"Is this okay?" he asks against the hollow of my neck, and I nod.

"Yes. Don't stop." My voice is breathless, and my heart races as his lips trace over my collarbone. When he reaches my breast, he pulls my nipple into his mouth, circling it with his tongue. His hand comes up to my other breast and I arch my back.

"Nash," I moan, my hands going into his hair.

"I've got you, baby," he whispers, releasing my nipple and moving farther down my body. When I feel his hot breath on the inside of my thigh, I jump. Before I can overthink what's about to happen, his mouth is on my clit and all my apprehension disappears. His tongue continues its assault, and I moan when he pushes a finger inside me. He hits a spot inside me I thought only existed in books, and when he adds another finger, I raise my hips and he holds me down as his mouth continues to work me over. His fingers pump in and out of me and my body feels like it's going to explode.

"Oh, God," I whimper.

He must know I'm close and reaches a hand up, pinching my nipple. That pushes me over the edge, and I come hard, calling out his name. My legs trap him in place as I ride out my orgasm, his mouth and fingers pulling every last drop of pleasure from my body. When my legs finally relax, he kisses up my stomach and over my breasts before his lips find mine. I taste myself on him, and I snake my arms around his neck as he deepens the kiss. He pulls away before we both get worked up again.

"That felt so good, Nash," I say quietly. "No one's ever..." I trail off, embarrassed to voice what I was going to say.

He raises his eyebrows. "That was the first time?" I nod. "It won't be the last, baby. I love having my mouth on you." My cheeks heat, and he chuckles. "Let's get some sleep."

He rolls off me and leans over the side of the bed, picking up his t-shirt that he tossed on the floor. I sit up and he slips it over my head. "Thank you," I whisper. He smiles and brushes his lips softly against mine.

"I don't think I'll be able to keep my hands off you if I keep you naked." He winks, and despite feeling nervous about being with him, I find myself thinking I wouldn't mind if he couldn't keep his hands off me.

We both slide under the comforter and he pulls me into his arms.

"Are you okay? Things aren't moving too fast?"

I shake my head. "Things are perfect, Nash. Thank you for being so incredible."

"I always want you to tell me if you need us to slow down. I want you to be able to tell me anything."

"I'm not sure what I've done to deserve you, Nash Brookes." I reach up and cup his face, dragging my thumb over the stubble on his jawline. He's perfect. His hand covers mine, and he pulls my hand to his lips, pressing a kiss on my palm.

"It's the other way around, Paisley. I don't know what I've done to deserve *you*." I smile and press a kiss onto his chest.

"Should I let Sophie know I'm not coming back? I don't want her to worry," I ask after a few minutes.

"Yeah, maybe. Do you want to use my phone?"

"I'll grab mine. It's just in my purse."

I sit up and swing my legs to the side of the bed. Spotting my purse by the door, I pad across the room and bend down to grab it. Unlocking the screen, I see three missed calls and a text from Taylor. I pull up Sophie's name and send her a message, letting her know I'm staying with Nash. I'm sure I don't have to tell her where I am, but if I'm staying at her place, I don't want to be rude and not let her know.

Sitting on the edge of the bed, my finger hovers over Taylor's message. After speaking to her earlier in the week, I know her mom isn't doing great, and she's been spending a lot of time at the nursing home with her. I hope she's not messaging with bad news.

"Everything okay, baby?" Nash asks from across the bed.

"I've got some missed calls and a message from Taylor." I told him about my friendship with Taylor a couple of weeks ago. He knew she'd been the one to help me get away from Connor.

I open the message, frowning as I read it.

Taylor: Hey, Paisley. I didn't want to tell you in a message, but I can't get ahold of you. Connor's petitioning for divorce. He's insisting I know where you are and wants me to give him your address so the papers can be sent to you. He's getting pretty pissed with me. Can you call me?

"Fuck," I mutter, dropping my phone in my lap.

"Is it bad news?" Nash asks.

I sigh. After what we've just shared, I don't want to be thinking about Connor, but I know I have to if he's causing trouble for Taylor.

"Connor wants a divorce. He's shown up at Taylor's insisting she tell him where I am."

He sits up and takes my hand. "I'm sorry, baby. Does Taylor know where you are?"

I nod. "I told her I was in Hope Creek a few weeks ago. She wants me to call her, but it'll be the middle of the night in Pittsburgh now."

"You can call her in the morning. Are you okay?"

"I don't care that he wants a divorce. I want that too. I just don't want him to know where I am."

"We'll think of something. Maybe he can give the papers to Taylor and she can send them."

"Yeah, maybe." I pause and turn my head, my eyes meeting his. "I wonder if he's met someone else. I hope he's not hurting her."

"I hope not too, baby." He squeezes my hand. "Let's get some sleep."

He pulls me into his arms and under the comforter. He reaches across and turns the light off on the nightstand, plunging the room into darkness. I rest my head on his chest, my mind working overtime. I'm really not bothered about the divorce, or that he might have met someone else. I feel nothing for him anymore, but I can't bear the thought that he could be hurting someone. Maybe I should have gone to the police. All I could focus on was getting away, and now I can't help but wonder if I've made a mistake. If he hurts someone else, it'll be my fault.

CHAPTER TWENTY-SIX

Nash

Opening my eyes, I roll onto my side and smile as I look at Paisley asleep next to me. Her face is inches from mine, and her dark hair fans out on the pillow. She's beautiful, and I can't take my eyes off her. When I asked her to stay the night, I wasn't sure what her answer was going to be. I hope her saying yes means she's getting closer to fully opening up to me. If I had my way, she'd be with me all the time, but I know she's probably not ready for that.

As I gaze at her, my mind wanders back to her message from Taylor last night. Honestly, I'm glad her jackass husband wants a divorce. I want to make her mine. I was worried he'd met someone else though and could be hurting her like he hurt Paisley. As much as Paisley doesn't want to involve the police, it doesn't sit well with me as a cop that I'm not doing anything to lock this asshole up.

I'm pulled from my thoughts when Max bounds into the room and jumps on the bed, waking Paisley.

Sitting up, I grab his collar and pull him off her. "Max, off!" I chastise, tugging him off the bed. "I'm sorry, baby," I say, turning to Paisley. "That's not quite how I planned to wake you up."

She smiles shyly and yawns. "Really? What did you have in mind?"

I lean in closer and brush my lips with hers. "Well, it involved you moaning my name," I whisper, her cheeks flushing pink at my words.

"I like the sound of that," she admits, biting down on her bottom lip.

I kiss her again, and she moans into my mouth as I push my tongue against hers. My cock hardens in my sleep shorts as the kiss intensifies. A whining noise comes from the side of the bed and Paisley pulls out of the kiss and turns her head.

"Nash, look." She giggles, and I look to see Max standing at the side of the bed, his head resting on the mattress.

Max whines again, and I groan. "Cockblocked by my own dog!"

"Is he allowed on the bed?"

"You're a softy, you know that?" I tickle her side and she squeals, pushing my hands away. Max barks and jumps on the bed, trying to get between Paisley and me. I laugh and move my hands from her side. Max lies next to her and Paisley wraps her arms around him. "He's definitely forgotten our talk about sharing." I lean down and brush my lips with hers. "How about I make us some pancakes and I can make you moan my name later?"

215

"Okay," she agrees, heat flooding her face.

I chuckle. "I won't be long."

I climb out of bed and make my way downstairs. After putting the coffee machine on, I pull out the ingredients for pancakes and make quick work of making the batter. I'm halfway through cooking them when Max comes padding into the kitchen and waits by the back door. I open the door for him, and he goes into the backyard. I guess needing to go outside won over staying in bed with Paisley.

A few minutes later, I feel arms wind around my waist. "Do you need any help?" Placing my hand over hers, I lace our fingers together.

"I'm good, baby. Do you want some coffee?"

"Yeah. I'll make it. Do you want one?"

"Please. The cups are in there." I gesture to the cupboard above the coffee machine, and she releases her hold on me, pressing a kiss on my cheek.

I watch her moving around the kitchen like she's always been here, and I can't help but think how right this all feels. I love having her here, and I know I'm not going to want to take her back to Sophie's. Maybe she'll want to stay overnight again. I hope so.

An hour later, we've eaten breakfast in bed, and I've kept my promise to make her moan my name. I love watching her fall apart at my touch, and I know when we finally do make love, it's going to be explosive.

"What do you want to do today?" I ask, pulling her into my arms.

"This?" I smile. "What do you want to do?"

"I'm more than happy to keep you in my arms all day."

"Maybe we could walk Max later."

"Sounds perfect."

"Do you mind if I call Taylor back?"

"No, of course not. I'll shower while you call her."

"Thank you." She kisses me softly before I climb off the bed and cross the room to the bathroom.

Closing the door behind me, I drop my head back onto the wood. As much as I want to give her space to speak to her friend, I want to know what her ex has said. I shouldn't listen through the door, but I do anyway.

"Hi, Taylor, it's me... I'm okay. Sorry I missed your call. It was too late to call you back last night. I'm sorry Connor's hassling you." She goes quiet, and I'm assuming Taylor is talking. "I don't care about the divorce... I want to move on with my life... thank you for not telling him... I don't know. Could he give the papers to you and you mail them to me?" She falls silent again. "Okay. Is he dating someone?... I feel sorry for her. You'll just have to tell him where I am, then. I don't want him threatening you. I'll think of something."

I want to go out and tell her to give Taylor my address, but then she'll know I've been listening, so I hang back, hoping she'll tell me herself about the conversation. I'm about to turn on the shower when she carries on talking.

"I'm good, Tay. I've met someone..." She trails off and then laughs. "Nash. He's a cop. I actually met him on the flight from Pittsburgh. He was the one who told me about Hope Creek." She sighs loudly. "I didn't know when I met him. I never thought I'd be able to trust a guy again, and it took me a while. I pushed him away for a bit, but he never gave up on me... I've never felt this way, not even when I first met Connor. I love him, Taylor, and it freaks me out a bit..."

A smile erupts on my face and my stomach flips when I hear her tell Taylor she loves me.

She sighs again. "No, I haven't told him. I'm scared, Tay.

Love makes you vulnerable… I know, I know. He's nothing like Connor, but old habits die hard. I'm trying. I can't wait for you to meet him."

Realizing she's going to wonder why the shower isn't running, I cross the small space and turn on the hot water. I figure I've eavesdropped enough and kick off my shorts, climbing into the tub and under the spray. Despite grinning like an idiot knowing she loves me, I hate that her loving me scares her. I never want her to feel like that. She's everything to me, and I hope, in time, she knows that.

I make quick work of showering before climbing out of the tub and drying off. Wrapping the towel around my waist, I look up as the door opens.

"Hey, baby. You done on the phone?"

She nods. "Do you mind if I take a shower?"

"Of course not. If you'd have come in a few minutes earlier, I could have washed your back." I smile and color floods her cheeks. "Why are you blushing?" I ask, moving toward her and pulling her gently against me. "You know I've seen you naked, right? And had my mouth on *every* part of you?"

"Nash!" she gasps, dropping her head on my chest.

I chuckle. "It's true, baby." She lifts her head off my chest and her eyes meet mine. "When you're ready, I can't wait to make love to you in the shower," I whisper. "To have your legs wrapped around me and your back pressed against the tiles as I slide inside you."

Her eyes are wide and her breathing is shallow. She bites down on her bottom lip as she stares at me. My words have affected her, and I love that they have. I lean down and kiss her nose.

"I'll let you shower. I'll be right outside. Maybe we could walk Max when you're done?"

She nods, her eyes fixed on me as I walk backwards out of the bathroom.

"Holy fuck," I hear her mutter as I pull the door closed, and I smile as I pull on some boxers and a pair of jeans.

Twenty minutes later, I'm sitting on the edge of the bed when the bathroom door opens and Paisley emerges wrapped in just a towel. Her hair is wet and falls over her shoulders.

"Good shower?"

"Really good. Do you have a hairdryer?"

"No. Sorry."

"That's okay, I didn't think you would. I'll just braid my hair and let it dry."

She drops the towel and my eyes widen in surprise as they track over her naked body. Considering she was shy about me seeing her naked when we were in the bathroom, she doesn't seem shy now. She has no reason to be; she's the most beautiful woman I've ever seen, and my cock jumps as I take her in. I watch as she puts her bra on, followed by the dress she wore to Bree and Leo's yesterday.

"Where are your panties?" I ask, standing up and slipping my arms around her waist.

"I don't have any clean ones."

"Fuck. You'll have to keep some here for when you stay over."

"Why?"

"You're not wearing any panties, Paisley. How am I supposed to concentrate on *anything* knowing that?"

She laughs. "I think you'll manage."

"I'm not so sure!" I brush my lips against hers.

"What did Taylor say?" I ask. I know I heard most of the conversation, but she doesn't know that.

She sighs. "Connor's being an ass. He wants to know where I am so his lawyer can forward the divorce papers. I suggested he give them to Taylor and she'd pass them on, but she's already suggested that to him and he's refused." She shrugs. "I'm going to have to ask Sophie if I can give over the shelter's address, but it isn't ideal."

"Don't. Give him my address. I don't want him showing up at Sophie's when you're there."

"I don't think he'll come. Taylor says he's met someone."

"I'd rather not risk it, baby. Give him my address."

"Okay. Thank you."

"Stay with me again tonight?" I whisper against her mouth as I pull her in for a kiss.

She leans back and her eyes search mine before she nods. "Can I grab some clothes from Sophie's? I can go to work from here tomorrow, then, if that's okay?"

I grin. "Sure."

"Are you working tomorrow?"

"Yes."

"Hmm, I get to see you in your uniform, then," she says, winding her arms around my neck.

"You like my uniform?"

"I like *you* in your uniform. You look hot."

"I'll have to remember that."

I kiss her until we're both breathless, and my heart pounds in my chest. Pulling away, I reach for her hand.

"We should go for that walk, otherwise you'll be naked again."

She giggles and my heart slams in my chest. This is how I want my life to be. Lazy Sunday mornings, breakfast in bed, and Paisley in my arms. I thought my life before I met her was good, but now that she's here, I can hardly remember life without her. She's where she belongs, and I think she's slowly coming to realize that too. I hope so. I know I'll be devastated if she walks away.

CHAPTER TWENTY-SEVEN

Paisley

I've spent four nights this week at Nash's place. The only nights I don't sleep over are when he's working. He wants me to though. He wants me in his bed when he gets home, but I chose to stay at Sophie's. It feels strange to be there when he isn't. I love spending time with him though, and I find I never sleep as well when I'm not with him. He's become the most important person in my life. He consumes my thoughts, and I'm head over heels in love with him, but I still haven't told him. I want to, and despite knowing he's never going to make me feel like Connor did, fear still holds me back.

It's Saturday night, and I'm getting ready for my night out with Bree and Ashlyn. I'm staying at the shelter tonight. Nash is working tomorrow, and I don't want to disturb him if I'm out late. He's not too happy, but I don't want to wake him. I'm just deciding what to wear when my phone vibrates on the dresser. I smile when Nash's name flashes on the screen. He's been at work today and I've missed him.

"Hi," I say as I answer, putting the phone on loud speaker so I can carry on getting ready.

"Hey, sweetheart. I just finished work. Can I come and say hi?"

"Of course you can. You don't need to ask." The doorbell chimes, and I giggle. "Are you at the door?"

"Might be."

"I'll be right down."

I end the call and toss my phone on the bed. I'm only wearing my bra and panties, so I wrap a towel around myself and make my way downstairs, meeting Sophie in the entryway.

"It's Nash," I tell her, and she smiles.

"I'll let you get the door, then. I'm just making dinner. Say hi to him for me."

She turns and heads back to the kitchen. I swing the door open, and my eyes track over him as he stands on the porch in his uniform. He looks gorgeous with his blue shirt stretched tight across his chest. When my eyes meet his, I grab his hand and pull him inside, leading him upstairs. Neither of us has said a word, and as soon as my bedroom door is closed, I'm in his arms and he's kissing me. The towel falls from around me, landing in a heap on the floor, and his hands skate over my skin.

"Fuck, Paisley. You look incredible," he gasps as he pulls out of the kiss, looking down my body.

"So do you." I pull his mouth back to mine, and he picks me up, my legs going around his waist. He walks me backwards to my bed and climbs onto the mattress with me still in his arms. His mouth never leaves mine as he lays me down, his body coming over me. I can feel his erection, hot and hard against the thin material of my panties, and I roll my hips, trying to ease the ache that's building between my legs.

"You drive me crazy, baby," he mutters against my neck as he peppers kisses around my jaw and down my neck. I moan as his teeth nip at my skin before he soothes the sting with his tongue. I can't form any words to answer him as his mouth goes lower and his fingers pull down the material of my bra, revealing my nipple. He wastes no time circling the bud with his tongue, and I arch my back, moaning as my clit pulses.

"Can I touch you, Paisley?"

He asks me every time things get heated, and I love how considerate of my feelings he is.

"God, yes," I mumble, lost in a haze of lust.

His fingers go under the waistband of my lace panties, and his thumb circles my clit. He pushes two fingers inside me, and I cry out, his mouth coming over mine to swallow my cries. His fingers hit the spot inside that makes me see stars, and my hips rise off the bed as his fingers push in and out of me. His thumb never stops stroking my clit, and I can feel my orgasm building in the pit of my stomach. I fist the comforter with one hand and wind my other hand into his hair.

"I'm going to come, Nash," I moan, pulling out of his kiss.

"Let go, baby," he whispers against my lips.

My orgasm hits me like a freight train, and I shudder in his arms. Wave after wave of pleasure crashes over me, and Nash continues working me over with his fingers until the last of my orgasm dissipates. My breathing is labored and my heart is racing when he finally removes his fingers, and my body sinks into the comforter, completely spent.

"Wow... wow," I stutter, unable to form more of a sentence.

He chuckles and pulls me into his arms. "What time are you going out?" he asks after a few minutes.

"Eight. I'm meeting Bree and Ashlyn at Eden."

"I'll come back in a bit and walk you into town."

I lean up on my elbow. "You don't need to do that."

"I want to." His fingers brush across my cheek.

I smile. "Okay. Thank you." I love how he cares enough to want to walk me into town. I've never had that before.

"I guess I should go."

"I want to make you feel good too," I say quietly, but he shakes his head.

"I don't want you to think I came over just for that."

"I don't," I assure him.

"I just missed you today."

"I missed you too."

"I should go home and check on Max. I'll be back in an hour though."

"Okay." I stand up and adjust my bra and panties. Looking across at Nash, his eyes are heated, and he stares at me.

"You are so beautiful, Paisley." My cheeks flush with heat at his compliment, and I drop my eyes from his.

I cover the small space between us and wind my arms around his neck. His hands come to rest on the bare skin of my waist, and I press a kiss to his lips.

"You make me *feel* beautiful, Nash. I love the way you look at me. No man has ever looked at me like you do."

"You have to know how important you are to me and how I feel about you," he whispers, his fingers digging gently into my waist.

"I feel it every time we're together." Despite not being

brave enough to say the words to him, I hope he can feel my love for him too.

"I love you, Paisley."

Butterflies erupt in my stomach and my heart stutters as he lowers his head and kisses me softly. It's not a kiss that's going to lead anywhere, but it's a kiss that tells me his words are the truth, not that I doubted him. I want to tell him I love him too, but I don't. Instead, I pour everything I feel for him into the kiss, hoping and praying for now, that's enough. Pulling his lips away, he rests his forehead on mine.

"I'm sorry I can't say the words back," I whisper. "It's not because I don't feel them."

"I know, sweetheart. I feel it every time you kiss me. There's no rush to say the words."

I wish more than anything I could tell him how I feel. I hate that my insecurities are holding me back. I never want him to think he isn't everything to me.

"Stop overthinking it, baby. We're good."

"How is it you know me better than I know myself?"

He smiles. "I can see your mind working overtime." He kisses me again before taking a step back. "I really am going now or I'm never going to want to leave you, especially when you're only wearing that." His eyes track over my body again, and he gives a small shake of his head before walking backwards to the door. "I'll be back soon."

"Bye, Nash."

"Bye, baby."

I watch as he leaves and closes the door behind him. I flop down onto the bed, staring up at the white ceiling. I know he told me last weekend he was falling in love with me, and his actions show me he means it, but hearing him say those words again makes me so wish I could say them back. I want to more than anything. He's nothing like Connor, and I know he'd never hurt me like Connor did. I just wish my head would catch up with my heart.

Almost an hour later, I'm dressed and ready to go. I'm wearing a dark blue bodycon dress I brought a few weeks ago after I got my first week's pay. It fits me like a second skin, and I have to admit, I love how I look in it. I haven't worn anything like this in years, and I can't wait for Nash to see me. There is a low V at the front and back, and it hugs my boobs and ass, ending mid-thigh. It's short, but not uncomfortably short. I slip on a pair of nude heeled pumps and pick up my purse. I flick my curled hair over my shoulder and take one last look in the mirror before heading downstairs.

"Wow, Paisley. You look incredible," Sophie says from the living room.

"Thanks."

"A girls' night, isn't it?"

I nod. "I'm meeting Bree and Ashlyn at Eden. Nash is walking me into town."

She grins. "Oh, good! I'm going to get to witness Nash's reaction when he sees you wearing that dress."

I frown. "What do you mean?"

She laughs. "He's going to be picking his jaw up off the floor, Paisley."

Before I can answer her, the doorbell chimes. "I guess we'll find out," I say, smoothing down the material of my dress and making for the door.

I open it, and Nash's eyes widen when he sees me. As Sophie predicted, his mouth falls open. "Holy fuck, Paisley! You look stunning."

"Thank you."

He steps into the entryway and pulls me against him. "I

don't think I want to let you out of my sight wearing this dress." His hands drop to my ass and he squeezes gently. "You look so sexy."

His mouth finds mine, and he kisses me like he hasn't seen me in weeks, rather than the hour it's actually been. I kiss him back with the same intensity, and as he pulls me even closer to him, I can feel how turned on he is.

"We should go before I drag you back to my place and that dress ends up on my bedroom floor," he mumbles against my lips. He takes a deep breath, as if steeling himself, and reaches for my hand. I'm flustered and turned on after his kiss, and we're on the sidewalk before I realize I never said bye to Sophie.

"You make me forget my own name when you kiss me, Nash Brookes," I joke as we walk hand in hand to Eden.

He laughs. "As long as you remember my name."

We walk the rest of the way in comfortable silence, stopping when we reach Eden. "Are you coming in for a drink?"

"I don't want to crash your girls' night."

"I'm sure they won't mind you staying for one drink."

"Okay. If you're sure."

"I'm sure. Come on."

I push open the door to Eden and lead him inside. Even though it's early, it's already busy, and we fight our way through the crowds to the bar. Waiting to be served, Nash stands behind me, his arms circling my waist. He drops a kiss on my shoulder, and I shiver.

"Cold?" he whispers in my ear.

"No. You just give me goose bumps," I whisper back, and he increases his hold on me.

"You know, if you change your mind and want to sleep at

my place tonight, the offer still stands." His breath is hot on my bare skin, and I drop my head back onto his chest.

"I'll see how drunk I am. I don't want to wake you."

"I don't care if you do."

Before I can answer him, Seb appears in front of us.

"Hey, guys. What can I get you?"

"Bud for me, please. Paisley?"

"White wine, please, Seb."

"Coming right up."

He disappears, returning a few minutes later with a large glass of wine and a bottle of Bud. "Ash and Bree are at the booth in the corner. Are you crashing their girls' night, Nash?" he asks with a chuckle.

"No. I just walked Paisley here. I'm having one and then heading home."

"Probably a good thing. I'm sure Ash doesn't want both of us watching her on her night out. Catch you later." He waves as he moves on to serve someone else.

"Let's find the girls," I say, slipping my hand into his and heading to the corner booth. Bree stands when we get to the table and pulls me into a hug.

"You look amazing, Paisley," she says.

"Thanks. So do you."

"What are you doing here, Nash?" Ashlyn asks as she too stands and pulls me into a hug.

I chuckle. "He walked me here. I asked him to join us for a drink. I hope that's okay."

"Sure. Just one drink though. It's bad enough having Seb here, but at least he gives us free drinks," she teases. She goes past me and brushes a kiss on his cheek.

"It's so nice to be wanted!" Nash exclaims sarcastically.

I turn and go up on my tiptoes. "I want you," I whisper in his ear.

"Good. I want you too. Even more so when you're wearing that dress," he whispers back. He goes to kiss me when Ashlyn takes my hand and pulls me into the booth.

"That's enough of that! I don't need to watch my brother making out with his girlfriend."

I laugh, secretly loving it when she calls me Nash's girlfriend.

Nash slides into the booth next to me and places his hand on my bare thigh, his thumb stroking my skin. "What's Leo up to tonight, Bree?" he asks before taking a pull of his beer.

"He's on dad duty," she replies. "It's the first time I've left him with both of them, so I'm expecting a call before the night's out!"

"Nah! He'll be fine," I tell her, having no clue if he will be or not.

"Hope so, 'cause I'm not going back!" She laughs and takes a mouthful of her red wine. "I've even pumped, so I can have a drink."

"Sounds like it's going to be a messy night."

We chat easily for the next ten minutes, and when Nash has finished his beer, he stands up.

"I'm going to leave you to your girls' night. Have fun, ladies." I slide out of the booth and go to him. "Have a great night, baby." He takes me in his arms and brushes his lips with mine before waving to Bree and Ashlyn. Sliding back in the booth, I watch him disappear from view.

"How are things going with you two?" Ashlyn asks. "I've never seen Nash in love before." My cheeks flush with heat, and she grins. "You know he's in love with you, right?"

I nod. "Yeah, he told me."

"And you feel the same?"

"Yes, but…" I trail off, biting down on my lip. I can't help but feel a little uncomfortable talking to his sister about things I haven't fully shared with Nash yet.

"It's okay, Paisley. It must be strange talking to me about how you feel. I'm a good listener though, if you ever do need to talk."

"Thanks, Ash."

"He's a good guy."

"Yeah, he definitely is." I smile, thinking that's just how Seb described him to me, and Sophie too.

A few hours later, all three of us are drunk. Seb has kept the drinks flowing all night, and I can't remember the last time I drank so much wine or had such a good time with friends. We've talked, laughed, and danced, and I can't wait for another night out with them.

Deciding to call it a night, we say goodbye to Seb and head outside. Bree has a cab waiting for her, and after waving her off, Ash and I walk home. Ash lives not far from Sophie's place, so we walk some of the way together, and when I say walk, I mean stumble. We both giggle as we walk arm in arm, drifting from one side of the sidewalk to the other. The balls of my feet are burning, and I stop and bend down, removing my shoes.

"God, that feels better!"

Ashlyn laughs. "I can see Sophie's house. You're nearly home."

"I'm going to Nash's. I want to see him."

She wriggles her eyebrows at me and giggles. "Feeling a little needy after a night of drinking? God, I wish I had a guy to go home to!"

"Why haven't you? You're gorgeous, Ash."

She shrugs. "I guess I just haven't met the right guy." Her voice drops to a whisper. "Or maybe I have and he doesn't know I exist."

"Who?"

She shakes her head. "Ignore me. I'm drunk."

I pull her to a stop. "Ash, wait. I know I'm dating your brother, but I'd like to think we're friends too. If you ever need to talk, I'm here."

She wraps her arms around me in a hug. "We are friends, Paisley, and thank you. Maybe I'll take you up on that offer one day."

"I hope you do."

We walk for a few more minutes in silence. "I need to go this way," she says, gesturing in the opposite direction to Nash's place. "Go and wake my brother. I'm sure he can't wait to see you." She pulls me into another hug and kisses me on the cheek before walking away.

"See you soon," I shout after her, and she raises her hand in a wave.

Turning, I stumble along the sidewalk toward Nash's, nerves bubbling in my stomach. I know I said I didn't want to wake him, but I need to see him. Maybe I can let myself in without waking him up. I doubt it, but I'm hoping he won't mind. I want to fall asleep in his arms. I *always* want to fall asleep in his arms, and I'm loving that the idea of that doesn't scare me as much as it used to.

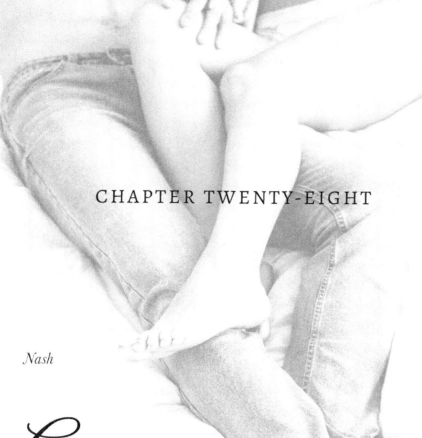

CHAPTER TWENTY-EIGHT

Nash

A loud crash startles me awake, and I sit up, reaching for my gun from the nightstand. Max barks from beside me, and I reach my hand out to calm him.

"Stay," I whisper, climbing out of bed. It's dark, but there's just enough light from the moon filtering through the drapes for me to cross the room without falling over anything. Opening my bedroom door, I keep my gun low as I silently pad along the hallway, slowly making my way down the stairs. I'm halfway down when I hear a voice.

"Shit. Shit. Shit."

I smile when I realize it's Paisley. "Baby, what are you doing?" I ask as I reach the bottom step and flick on the light. She looks up at me, her eyes wide.

"Oh, no! I woke you up." Her words are slurred and her

cheeks are flushed. Her wide eyes drop to the gun in my hand. "What's that for?"

"I thought someone was breaking in."

"Fuck! I'm sorry. I walked into the table and knocked the lamp over."

I chuckle. "Don't be sorry. I'm glad you're here. Let's get you to bed."

"Mmmmm, I like the sound of that."She tosses the shoes she's holding on the floor and crosses the room, winding her arms around my neck. "You look hot, Nash." I slide my free hand around her waist and pull her against my bare chest.

"So do you. Did you have a good time?"

She nods. "Yes, but I missed you. I wanted to see you. I hope that's okay?"

"It's more than okay. Come on. I want you in my bed." I drop my arm from around her waist and tangle her fingers with mine, guiding her upstairs.

"I think I might be a little bit drunk," she whispers from behind me.

I laugh. "I hadn't noticed, baby."

When we reach the bedroom, Max rushes to Paisley, jumping up her legs. She drops to her knees and pets him.

"Bed, Max." He skulks from the room, going to his bed in the kitchen. I close the door behind him and offer my hand to Paisley, pulling her up to stand. "Do you need some help with your dress?"

She nods and lifts her hands into the air. Her eyes are fixed on mine as I place my gun on the nightstand and reach for the bottom of her dress, pulling it up and over her head. All the air rushes from my lungs as she's left standing in a black lace bra and panties. The lace of her bra is see-through, and her nipples pebble and push against the barely there material as I stare at her.

"God, Paisley."

I reach around her back and undo her bra, knowing she won't want to sleep in it. As the material falls from her body, my cock jumps in my sleep shorts as I take her in. Her dark hair falls over her naked shoulders in waves, and her eyes are wide and full of heat. I wish she wasn't drunk. I need to touch her about as much as I need my next breath, but with what she's been through, I would never do anything when she's as drunk as she is.

Taking her hand, I guide her to the bed and lie down, pulling her into my arms. "We should sleep."

She lifts her head and pouts. "I don't want to sleep. I want to kiss you." She presses her lips to mine, and I kiss her back briefly before pulling away.

"I want that too, but you're drunk, and if I keep on kissing you, I don't know if I'll be able to stop."

"I wouldn't mind that," she whispers.

Her fingers, which were tracing patterns on my chest, reach under the waistband of my shorts, brushing against my hardening cock. I place my hand over hers, stopping her. Summoning up my last ounce of willpower, I move her hand away. I don't want to tell her no, but I don't want her to have any regrets.

"Sleep, Paisley."

She holds my gaze and frowns. "Okay." She gently pulls her hand from mine and rolls over and out of my arms. She drags the comforter over her, her back to me. "Night, Nash."

I close the distance between us and move her backwards so she's against my chest. "It's not because I don't want you, Paisley. I want you more than anything. I just don't want you to have regrets."

She sighs. "It's okay. Maybe I should have just gone back to Sophie's and left you to sleep."

I frown. "No, you shouldn't. I want you here. I *always* want you here."

"I want to be here too," she whispers. "Night, Nash."

I think I've upset her, but I'm hoping she'll understand in the morning when she's sobered up.

"Night, baby." I press a kiss on her shoulder, and with my arms still around her, I drop my head onto the pillow. Within minutes, her breathing has evened out and she's asleep. I tighten my hold on her just a little and let myself drift off to sleep, loving having her in my arms, even if she is a little annoyed at me.

My ALARM SOUNDS the next morning, and I reach over and silence it before it wakes Paisley. She's not asleep on me like she normally is when I wake up, and I pull her into my arms, wanting to hold her before I have to get up. I've never minded working weekends. It's always just been part of the job. I get downtime in the week, and that's always been fine, but knowing I could stay in bed with Paisley if I didn't have to work makes me wish I could be a cop nine to five, Monday to Friday. I don't want to leave her asleep in my bed on a weekend.

Knowing I have to, I press a kiss on her forehead before releasing her from my arms and climbing out of bed. She lets out a contented sigh as she hugs my pillow and stays asleep. Smiling, I cross the space to the bathroom, and after using the toilet, I have a quick shower. When I'm done, I wrap a towel around my waist and go back into the bedroom. Paisley's still asleep, and I make quick work of getting dressed. I'm not late, but I'm cutting it close after not getting straight up when the alarm sounded.

"Nash?" Paisley says, her voice full of sleep.

"Morning, baby." I sit on the edge of the bed and brush her tangled hair off her face. "How are you feeling?"

"Like I drank far more than I should have. I woke you up last night, didn't I?"

I smile. "It's fine. I'm glad you did."

"Are you going to work?"

I nod. "I wish I didn't have to and I could stay with you."

"I wish you could too, but I'm glad I woke up in time to see you in your uniform." She reaches her hand up and fists my shirt, pulling my mouth to hers. I smile against her lips as she kisses me. I pull away before it gets too heated. I know I definitely won't want to leave her if we carry on.

"Will you be here when I get back?"

"I can be. I need to go home and get a change of clothes. I'll have to do the walk of shame back to Sophie's." She giggles, and my cock jumps in my pants.

"I can give you a ride if you want to get up now."

"Okay. Have you had breakfast?"

"No, I didn't get up in time."

"Why don't you grab something quickly while I get ready?"

"I'd rather stay here and watch you get dressed."

"Pervert," she jokes, pushing the comforter off her and padding to the bathroom, naked apart from a tiny black lace thong. My eyes follow her across the room, and she wiggles her hips and laughs before disappearing into the bathroom.

Adjusting my hardening cock, I stand and jog downstairs, letting Max outside and putting down some food for him. When I go back upstairs, Paisley is dressed and is braiding her hair in the bathroom mirror. She frowns a little when she sees me watching her from the doorway.

"Did we argue last night? I feel like I need to apologize for something. I'm just not sure what."

"No. We didn't argue…"

"I feel like there's a but coming."

I sigh and drag my hand through my hair. "You wanted to do… stuff, but I said no because you were drunk."

Her eyes widen. "God, that's embarrassing." She lets out an awkward laugh.

"It was hot that you wanted me that much, and I *really* wanted to touch you, but not when you were so drunk."

She moves to the doorframe and wraps her arms around my neck. "Thank you, Nash. I know I probably wasn't very grateful last night, but I am this morning."

I breathe a sigh of relief. I knew last night I was doing the right thing, but hearing her agree makes me feel better for telling her no.

"I plan on making it up to you tonight, Paisley. I can't wait to get my hands and mouth on you," I say softly in her ear. She shivers in my arms, and I know my words are affecting her.

"Fuck," she mumbles, breathless.

"As much as I want to stay here with you, I really need to go. Are you ready?"

She nods, and I take her hand, leading her downstairs. Max comes to the entryway, and I leave her loving on him while I lock up the back door. When I'm done, I meet her back in the entryway, my eyes going to the large brown envelope on the table. I almost don't want to give it to her, but I know I have to. Reaching for it, I hold it out.

"This came while I was at work yesterday. I think it's the divorce papers." Her eyes drop to my outstretched hand, and she hesitates before taking it from me.

She sighs loudly. "Thanks."

"Are you okay?"

"I'm good. I'm going to sign them and mail them back so I can get on with my life."

I nod as I lead her outside to my truck and help her into the passenger seat. She's quiet on the short drive to Sophie's, and she insists I just drop her off at the curb when I pull up. I'd like to walk her to the door, but I'm late.

"Are you sure you're okay? You can tell me if you're not."

"I'm okay, Nash. I promise." I hold her gaze and she nods reassuringly.

I lean across the cab and capture her lips with mine. My hand cups her neck as I kiss her, and she moans into my mouth.

"I hope today goes fast," she says quietly as she pulls out of the kiss and opens the passenger door. "Be careful."

"I always am. See you later, baby."

She stands on the sidewalk, watching me as I drive away. I hope today goes fast too. I can't wait to get back to her. I really hope she is okay and she's not just putting a brave face on. She doesn't need to pretend with me. I can't imagine how it must feel to go through a divorce, regardless of the circumstances. No one gets married expecting the relationship to end.

Once I'm at the station, it seems like it's going to be a quiet day. There have been no more break-ins since the one at Mrs. Stone's bakery a few weeks ago, and the fingerprint that was pulled from the scene belonged to a teenager from a neighboring town, so case closed. As I sit at my computer, an alert flashes up on the screen. Looking up, my heart pounds in my chest when I see the name the alert is attached to. Connor Prescott.

Taking a deep breath, I open the alert. As my eyes scan the document, my stomach rolls. It seems he was arrested last night in Pittsburgh for battery and sexually assaulting a young woman by the name of Lyse Rhodes. I can't help but wonder if this is the new girlfriend I heard Taylor tell Paisley about. I hope he's thrown in jail and never let out. He might not serve time for what he's done to Paisley, but if he's locked away, at least he can't hurt anyone else.

In a split second, I decide not to tell Paisley. It's probably the wrong decision, but I'm hoping the news of his arrest will get to her via Taylor, and then she won't find out I filed a report or set an alert up for him. The last thing I want to do is lie to her, but I'm hoping a white lie when all I was doing was looking out for her is okay. I really hope so.

CHAPTER TWENTY-NINE

Paisley

I walk from Nash's place to the police station in town. After he dropped me off, I showered and changed before heading back to his place. I looked briefly at the divorce papers. I don't really understand them, but I can't afford an attorney to look over them. I signed where I needed to and I'll mail them back on Monday. I just want it over with. I know Nash was concerned about me this morning, but I really am okay. This is the last tie I have to Connor, and I can't wait for that tie to be severed forever.

Knowing Nash missed out on breakfast because of taking me back to Sophie's, I've made him a bacon sandwich and I'm taking it to him. I hope it's okay for me to just show up at the station. I haven't told him I'm coming. I want to surprise him.

Pushing open the door, I head to the reception desk. "Is Nash Brookes available, please?"

The woman behind the desk smiles kindly. "I can find out for you. Who shall I say is looking for him?"

"Paisley."

"Take a seat and I'll see if he's free." She gestures to a row of chairs behind me.

"Thanks."

Turning, I sit down, nervously bouncing my knee up and down. I only have to wait a few minutes before a door to the right of me opens.

"Paisley? Is everything okay?" he asks as he crosses the room and takes my hand, pulling me up to stand. His face is a picture of concern, and I feel stupid for not calling him first. I should have realized he would think something was wrong if I just showed up.

"I'm fine. Sorry, I didn't mean to worry you. I just brought you some breakfast." I hold up the wrapped bacon sandwich and he breathes a sigh of relief before his face erupts into a smile.

"Baby, you brought me breakfast?" I nod. "Thank you." He takes the sandwich out of my hand and lowers his head to brush his lips with mine. His eyes drop to what I'm wearing. "You look nice."

I look down at my shorts and tank. "Thanks."

"What are you going to do for the rest of the day?"

"I was going to spend the day with Max."

"Lucky Max." He smiles. "You'll still be there when I get home?"

"Yes. I've brought an overnight bag so I can go straight to work tomorrow," I say shyly. "I hope that's okay."

He slides his arms around my waist and pulls me against

his chest. "Paisley, if I had my way, I'd have you with me every night." My stomach dips at his words, and he drops a kiss on my head. He sighs. "I have to go. I'll walk you out." He drops his arms from around me and takes my hand, leading me outside. "I'll see you later." I go up on my tiptoes and kiss his cheek.

"Bye, Nash." I can feel his eyes on me as I walk away from the station, and I can't wait for him to get home. I think I'm ready to tell him I love him. I'm still nervous, but loving Nash is nothing like loving Connor. I don't feel vulnerable. I feel wanted and adored.

Deciding to make Nash Sunday dinner, I stop at the grocery store and buy everything I need. Once I'm back at his place, I spend some time in the backyard with Max before starting on the dinner. I'm not the best cook in the world, something Connor told me frequently, but I want to cook for him. An apology for the drunken state I was in last night.

A couple of hours later, I hear the front door open and close. Max must hear it too and he flies through the kitchen into the entryway. Laughing, I follow him.

"Hey, something smells good." He stops fussing over Max and comes to me, taking me in his arms.

"I wanted to cook you dinner."

"I could get used to this, you know? Having you here when I finish work and feeding me."

"You haven't tasted it yet," I tell him with a chuckle.

"I'm sure I'll love it, baby. Do I have time for a shower?"

"Sure. It's not quite ready yet." He kisses me softly before stepping out of the embrace.

"I'll be right back."

Ten minutes later, arms snake around my waist as I stand

at the stove. I bring my hand over his and tangle our fingers together.

"Hi," I whisper, squeezing his hand.

"Hi." He drops a kiss on my bare shoulder, and I lean my head back against his chest. "God, I missed you today."

"I missed you too."

"I love coming home and you being here." I smile, loving being in his space too.

"It's almost ready. Why don't you sit down and I'll dish up."

"I'll help you." He unlaces his fingers from mine and moves across the kitchen, taking out two plates from one of the cupboards. I watch him in surprise.

Connor never helped me in the kitchen, he just sat down and expected me to serve him. I should have known Nash wouldn't be the same. I stop staring before he notices.

When we sit down to eat, I can't help but hold my breath as I watch him take a mouthful. He looks up and sees me watching him.

"What's wrong?" he asks, looking from his plate to mine. "You look terrified."

"Is it okay?"

He frowns. "It's delicious, Paisley."

"Really?"

"Really. What's going on?"

I shake my head. "Nothing, it's just… Connor hated my cooking. He used to tell me I was useless. I want you to like it."

He puts his knife and fork down and reaches across the table for my hand. "No one other than my mom has ever cooked for me. You could have given me toast and it would have been the best meal I'd ever had because you cared enough to make it for me. Your ex is an ass, Paisley, and he never deserved you."

I give him a small smile, my heart exploding with love for him. I've no idea how he knows exactly what to say to make me feel like I'm the most important person in his life. He's the most important person in mine, and it's time he knows it.

"I love you, Nash."

A smile lights up his face, and I can't help but smile back. He stands from the table and comes to where I'm sitting, kneeling down beside me.

"You do?" I nod and cup his face with my hand. He turns his face and presses a kiss onto my palm. "I love you too, baby."

"I've wanted to tell you for a while… I just wasn't brave enough to say the words."

"What changed?"

"It's you. You make me feel like I'm your everything, and no matter what, I'm good enough."

He stands up and takes my hand, pulling me to stand with him. "Paisley, you *are* my everything. I've never felt this way about anyone before. You're all I can think about."

"You're all I can think about too, Nash."

I place my hands on his chest and go up on my tiptoes to kiss him. I moan into his mouth as his tongue collides with mine. My body ignites with his kiss, and my nipples pebble against my bra. His fingers dig into my waist, and I've never felt more alive than when I'm kissing him. Pulling out of the kiss, he tugs me against him and my hands slide over his shoulders and around his neck. We're both breathing heavily, and when we've caught our breath, he leans back slightly.

"As much as I want to carry on kissing you, the dinner you

made is going cold and I really want to eat it, so maybe we could finish this later?"

I smile. "Okay. That sounds good."

He goes back to his chair and grins at me as he loads his fork with food. "This is really good, Paisley," he says when he's swallowed down a mouthful. I pick up my fork and try what I've cooked for myself. He's right, it's good.

"I'm glad you like it. How was work?"

"It was quiet. Sundays tend to be."

When we've finished eating, Nash helps me to tidy up and loads the dishes in the dishwasher.

"Let's sit outside; it's still warm. Do you want a glass of wine?"

"Sure, if you are."

He sets down two glasses before pulling a bottle of white wine from the refrigerator. He fills them both and passes me one. I slide my free hand into his and we head outside to the decked seating area where a comfy corner sofa sits. Taking his drink from him, I place both glasses on the small table. I wait until he's sitting down and climb onto his lap. He smiles and wraps his arms around me.

"I thought we could finish what we started over dinner."

I don't let him answer, pressing my lips to his. He tangles his hand in my hair and pushes his tongue into my mouth. I moan as his tongue brushes against mine and I roll my hips, feeling just how turned on he is. A familiar ache begins to build as the kiss intensifies, and I can't seem to get close enough to him. His lips pepper kisses along my jaw and down my neck, and I lean my head to the side to give him better access. I roll my hips again, and he groans as I push against his erection.

"Fuck, Paisley. I want to touch you," he whispers against my neck.

"Take me inside, Nash," I mumble before my lips find his again.

He stands with me in his arms, and I wrap my legs around him. He breaks the kiss and carries me across the yard and into the house. My lips brush kisses against his neck and over his stubbled jaw. I'm aching to feel his hands and mouth on me, and I bury my face in his neck as he climbs the stairs, still holding on to me.

When we reach his bedroom, he kicks the door closed behind us and walks across the room to his bed. He lowers me gently onto the comforter and brings his body over mine. I reach up and tug his t-shirt over his head, tossing it onto the floor. My fingers go to the button on his jean shorts, undoing it before I pull them down his legs. He stands up and kicks them off, leaving him in just his underwear. His toned and tanned chest rises and falls as his breathing increases, and my eyes drop to his hard cock straining against his underwear.

"God, you're gorgeous," I mutter, holding out my hand to him.

He chuckles and stands next to where I'm lying on the bed. Taking my hand in his, he pulls me up to stand next to him. "So are you, but you're wearing too many clothes."

He lifts my tank up and over my head, throwing it on the floor next to his clothes. My eyes gaze into his as he makes quick work of removing my shorts, leaving me standing in front of him in just my white lace panties and bra. Despite him seeing me like this before, I feel a little self-conscious in just my underwear, but when I see the heat in his eyes, I know there's no need to be. He loves me. I can feel it every time he kisses me, and I'm ready to be with him. I've never wanted anyone like I want him.

I reach around my back and undo my bra, letting it fall to the floor. My hands then go to my panties, and I push them down my legs. Stepping out of them, I kick them to the side and wind my arms around his neck. "I want to be with you, Nash. I'm ready."

He pulls back slightly, his eyes finding mine. "Are you sure, baby? We can wait as long as you need."

"I'm sure. I love you and I know you love me."

"I do, Paisley. More than I ever thought possible." I smile and drop my arms from around his neck. Taking his hand, I pull him onto the bed with me. His mouth finds mine and I'm soon lost in him, his kisses working me up into a frenzy. When his lips leave mine, his teeth nip my neck before he soothes it with his tongue. He slowly makes his way to my chest, and I'm almost panting by the time he pulls my pebbled nipple into his mouth. I pull him up to my face and kiss him as I push him onto his back.

"Are you okay?"

I nod. "I want to touch you."

I kiss my way down his body, my tongue circling his nipple. His hand fists in my hair as my mouth goes lower, and he lets out a groan as my fingers go under the waistband of his boxer shorts. Taking his erection in my hand, I pump his shaft, eliciting a moan from him.

"God, Paisley, that feels incredible."

Lowering my head, I swipe my tongue around the head of his cock and he tugs gently on my hair, inhaling sharply. Using my free hand, I push his boxer shorts down and take him in my mouth. My head bobs up and down as I suck and lick up his length, feeling him rock hard in my mouth. I stop to circle my tongue around the head of his cock, and he gasps as my hand squeezes him. I drag my lips down his shaft, taking him to the back of my throat.

"Stop, baby," he moans, and I look up to see him watching me. His breathing is erratic and his eyes are full of heat. "I'm going to come if you carry on, and I want to be inside you."

His words make me press my thighs together, the ache between my legs almost unbearable. Despite that, I take my time with him and slowly lick up his cock as I pull my mouth away. Within seconds, he's kicked off his underwear and I'm on my back, his head between my legs. His tongue finds my clit, and I almost come off the bed as he sucks it into his mouth. My body was on fire before he even touched me, and I know it's not going to be long before I come. When he pushes two fingers inside me, I let out a long moan, my hand fisting the comforter at the side of me.

"Nash," I moan, my eyes closed as his mouth and fingers work me over. "I think I'm going to come."

He reaches a hand up, pinching and rolling my nipple between his fingers. That pushes me over the edge, and I cry out as my orgasm hits me. My legs tremble on either side of his head and his tongue never lets up, pulling every last drop of pleasure from my body. When my legs relax, he removes his fingers, and I open my eyes, biting down on my bottom lip as I watch him bring them to his mouth and lick them clean. He moves up my body and kisses me. As I open up to him and his tongue dances with mine, I can taste myself. Despite the mind-blowing orgasm I've just had, my clit pulses as I think about where his mouth has just been.

He drags his lips from mine, pressing kisses around my jaw and around to my ear. "Do you want me to make love to you, Paisley?" he whispers, his breath hot on my skin.

My body is aching for him, and I want nothing more than to feel him inside me. Despite that, nerves swirl in my stomach. Sex had become a weapon with Connor, and although I know it will be nothing like that with Nash, I don't want Connor in my head. I want it to be just me and Nash. Closing my eyes, I push Connor from my thoughts and wind my arms around Nash's neck.

"Yes," I whisper, opening my eyes and gazing into his.

CHAPTER THIRTY

Nash

"Do you want me to make love to you, Paisley?" I whisper against her neck. I hold my breath as I wait for her to answer. I can't even imagine how hard this is for her after what she's been through. I meant what I said earlier though. I'll wait forever for her to be ready. I know she's it for me. She was meant to catch that flight, and she was meant to sit next to me that day. Despite not knowing it at the time, I think I fell in love with her the second I saw her.

"Yes," she whispers.

I lift my head, my eyes searching hers for any doubt. I don't see any, just a heat that I'm sure mirrors mine.

"I love you, Nash."

A lump forms in my throat as I hear her tell me she loves me. I don't think I'll ever tire of hearing those words. I've loved her for weeks, but I knew she was worried about saying the words back, and my heart explodes as I gaze at her.

"I love you too, Paisley. Sometimes I can't believe how much I love you." She reaches her hand up and cups my face. I lean into her touch, our eyes fixed on one another.

"Thank you."

I raise my eyebrows. "What for?"

"For loving me." She smiles. "You said a while ago you were going to love me so fiercely I'd never have to question how you feel about me."

"I meant every word."

"I know. I can feel it, Nash."

I lower my head and kiss her, pouring everything I feel for her into that kiss. I remember saying those words a couple of weeks ago, and my heart swells knowing she believes them. As the kiss intensifies, I swipe my tongue along her bottom lip, and she opens up to me, moaning into my mouth. I'm rock hard, and I can't wait to sink inside her. Her body is so in tune with mine, I know making love to her is going to be explosive.

Dropping my lips to her neck, I reach down and circle her clit with my finger. She moans and arches her back as I continue to kiss down her neck and over her collarbone. When her breathing is labored, I sit up and reach across to the night-stand. Grabbing out a condom, she watches me in silence as I roll it down my length.

"You okay?" I ask quietly, and she nods, reaching for me. Settling between her legs, I kiss her softly before taking my cock and guiding it to her entrance. She gasps as I gently push inside her. She feels so tight, and her wet heat pulls me in. It takes everything in me not to thrust against her, but I want to take this slowly. Her eyes flutter closed, and I reach up my hand to cup her face.

"Look at me, baby," I say, my voice strained as I try to hold back. She opens her eyes and locks them with mine. I want her with me and not in her head.

"Please move, Nash," she whispers, and I smile. I don't need to be asked twice.

She gasps as I pull out and push gently back inside her. Her eyes hold mine as I move in and out of her.

I've never had sex like this. I've never wanted to look someone in the eye before, but I find I can't tear my gaze from hers, even if I wanted to. She brings her arms up and around my neck, pulling my mouth to hers.

"Harder, Nash. Please," she begs before her lips crash into mine.

Kissing her, I pull out and slam into her, my mouth swallowing her cries. Her nails dig into my shoulders as I thrust into her over and over again. She feels incredible, and after her mouth on me earlier, there's no way I'm going to last long, not with how her body's pulling me in and keeping me hostage.

"God, Paisley. You feel so good. I'm not going to last."

I can feel her walls fluttering around me, and I think she's close too. Sitting up slightly, her eyes lock with mine again, and I reach between us, my finger circling her clit.

"Nash," she moans. I increase the pressure on her clit and continue to pound into her. Suddenly, her eyes close, and her whole body shudders as she comes. I can feel her walls pulsing around my cock. Her orgasm triggers my own, and her name falls from my lips as the most powerful release I've ever felt consumes me. Breathing hard, I collapse onto her as I try to catch my breath. Her arms come around me, and we hold each other as our breathing evens out.

Lifting my weight off her, I kiss her softly. "Are you okay?" I ask, my eyes searching hers.

She nods. "I never knew it could be like that. It felt amazing. You felt amazing."

Relief floods my body knowing we haven't moved too fast. "You felt amazing too, Paisley. You should know it's *never* felt like that before. You take my breath away." She smiles shyly and she drops her eyes. I gently pull out of her and kiss her nose. "I'll just clean up. I'll be right back."

She nods and sits up on her elbows as she watches me scoot off the bed. I can feel her eyes on me as I cross the room to the bathroom. Looking over my shoulder, I smile as I see her watching me.

"What are you doing?" I ask.

"Just enjoying the view." I laugh and disappear into the bathroom. I quickly dispose of the condom, wanting to get back to her. When I come out of the bathroom, she's lying under the comforter, her arm over her eyes. Concern bubbles in my stomach as I cross the room and sit on the bed next to her.

"What are you thinking about, sweetheart?" I ask, stroking my fingers up and down her arm that isn't covering her eyes.

She moves her arm and grins. "I'm wondering when we can do that again."

I let out a breath I didn't realize I was holding and chuckle. "Anytime you want is good for me!"

"How about now? Or do you need some time to… recover? I know you're a little older than me, so…" She trails off and raises her eyebrows, a smile pulling on her lips.

"Hey!" I exclaim, reaching under the comforter to tickle her. "I'm thirty-two!" She giggles and tries to push my hands away. "I'm not an old man yet." My voice is laced with humor, and I know she hears it.

"I'm joking, babe. I think you're hot." She pulls me on top of her, her lips crashing against mine. Just as the kiss intensifies, the shrill sound of a ringtone fills the room.

"I think that's you, Paisley," I mutter against her lips.

"Urghhh," she groans, rolling from under me and reaching for her shorts on the floor. "I bet it's Taylor returning my call. I called her earlier but she didn't answer. She has shitty timing!"

My heart pounds in my chest, and I wonder if Taylor knows about Connor's arrest. An uneasy feeling settles in the pit of my stomach as I climb off the bed and pull on my boxer shorts.

"Hey, Taylor... No worries, I was just calling for a chat... Why? What's wrong?" She reaches for my t-shirt and slips it over her head, briefly pulling the phone from her ear. "What? When?" She turns to look at me and my heart breaks when I see tears swimming in her eyes.

"Paisley, what's wrong?" I ask, crossing the space to stand next to her. She shakes her head and sits down heavily on the bed.

"Who's the woman?" The hand that isn't holding her phone messes nervously with the edge of the t-shirt she's wearing. Reaching across, I take her hand in mine, lacing our fingers together. I rub my thumb over the back of her hand, trying to offer her some comfort. I know exactly what Taylor is telling her, and I hate that I knew before she did. I should have told her.

"His girlfriend. God, this is all my fault." She pulls her

hand from mine and stands up, pacing the room. "Is she okay?... I need to go, Tay. Can I call you back?" She continues to pace the room, and I want to take her in my arms and hold her. "I love you too. Bye."

She ends the call and bursts into tears. Going to her, I pull her against me and hold her while she cries. When her sobs subside, she looks up at me. "He's hurt someone else, Nash. It's all my fault. If I'd had the courage to go to the police, then he wouldn't have been able to hurt her. It's my fault. It's all my fault."

"No, Paisley. It's not your fault. This is all on Connor." I take her hand and have her sit down on the bed, dropping to my knees in front of her. "Look at me." She lifts her head, her bloodshot eyes meeting mine. "This is *not* your fault," I reiterate. "Okay?" She holds my gaze, but I know she doesn't believe me. "Say it, Paisley. This is not your fault. You had to leave to save yourself."

"But—"

"No buts. I'm not going to let you beat yourself up about this. You've been through enough."

She sighs heavily and slowly nods her head. "Okay," she whispers.

I'm not sure I believe her. I want to, but I don't think I've convinced her. I stand up and climb onto the bed with her.

"Come here." I open my arms and she doesn't hesitate in pressing her body to mine. After a few minutes of silence, she lifts her head.

"What will happen to him?"

I sigh and look down at her. "He'll be charged with battery, and unless he can post bail, he'll be kept locked up."

"Taylor said he raped the woman too."

I close my eyes and pull her against me. "If the court thinks he's too much of a threat, then he'll be held until it goes to trial. If he pleads guilty, then he'll be sentenced without a trial."

"I doubt he'll plead guilty."

I hold her tightly. "I'm sorry this is happening, Paisley. I wish I could make it all go away for you."

"I'm glad I was with you when Taylor called."

I gaze down at her. I want to ask her to move in with me. I know she's looking at moving out of the shelter, but even if she gets her own place, she'll probably spend at least half of the week here with me anyway. At least, I'd like to hope she would. I want her with me all the time though. I've no idea what her response will be, but I want to find out.

"Can I talk to you about something?"

She nods. "What's wrong?"

"Nothing's wrong, sweetheart." I sit up and she follows. She looks worried, so I take her hand in mine. "What do you think about moving in here with me?" Her eyes widen, and I can see by the look on her face she wasn't expecting me to ask her that. "I know you've been looking for an apartment to rent, but I'd love it if you moved in here."

"You don't think it's too soon?" She worries her bottom lip with her teeth. "We've only been together a few weeks."

"I know we're going to be together forever, Paisley. You are *it* for me. I've never felt this way about anyone before. I meant what I said this morning. If I had my way, I'd have you with me every night." I can see she's uncertain, and I squeeze her hand. "You don't have to decide now. Why don't you think about it?"

"Is that okay?"

"Of course it is. There's no rush to decide, baby. I'm not going anywhere."

I lower my head and brush my lips against hers. I know how much of a huge decision this is for her, and I don't want to pressure her into anything. I'll wait as long as it takes for her to be ready.

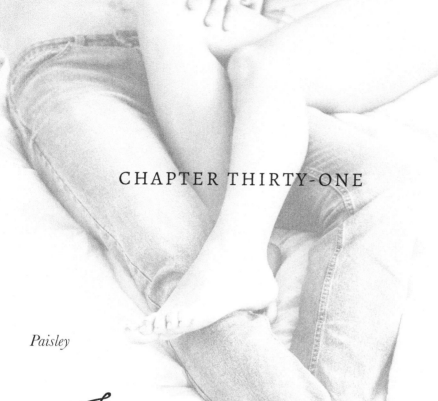

CHAPTER THIRTY-ONE

Paisley

I wake up the next morning nestled against Nash's chest. Despite loving being in his arms, between finding out about Connor's arrest and Nash asking me to move in with him, I've hardly slept. I couldn't turn my mind off enough to find sleep, and it wasn't until the early hours of the morning I finally dropped off. Nash isn't working today, and my shift doesn't start until lunchtime, so I'm grateful we didn't have to set the alarm.

"Morning, baby," Nash whispers, dropping a kiss on my head.

Lifting my head, I smile. "Morning."

He frowns. "You look tired. Didn't you sleep well?"

I chuckle. "What a compliment first thing in the morning," I joke, tickling his side.

259

He laughs and rolls me onto my back, his body pressing me into the mattress. "You know I think you're the most beautiful woman I've ever seen."

He kisses me before I can answer him, and within seconds, I'm lost in his kiss. His hand cups my neck as his tongue pushes into my mouth. He rolls his hips against mine, and I moan as his erection hits me right where I need him. He kisses around my neck, and his hand goes under the t-shirt I'm wearing, his fingers tugging and rolling my pebbled nipple. I arch my back and roll my hips, trying to ease the ache that's building between my legs. Before I know what's happening, the t-shirt I'm wearing is up and over my head, and his mouth is around my nipple.

"Fuck, Nash," I mutter as my fingers go into his hair, holding his mouth against me. As his lips move lower, he suddenly sits back on his heels and picks up one of my legs. With his eyes fixed on me, he brushes soft kisses from my ankle, up my calf, to my knee. By the time his lips are on the inside of my thigh, I'm practically panting, desperate for his touch. His mouth doesn't go where I need him though, and instead, he teases me, kissing everywhere but where I really want him to kiss me. When his head finally settles between my legs, he blows gently on my clit.

"Please, Nash," I beg as my legs twitch on either side of his head and my hand fists the comforter.

"What do you need, Paisley?" he asks, his breath hot on my clit.

"Touch me, please." I should be embarrassed I'm begging for his touch, but I'm too turned on to care. I hear him growl before his tongue swipes over my clit. My fingers find their way into his hair, and I hold him against me. His tongue is relentless, and I can feel my orgasm building. When he slides two fingers inside me, he hits a spot that makes me gasp.

He pulls his mouth off me and his eyes meet mine. "You're so ready for me, Paisley. I can't wait to sink inside you."

"Oh, God!" I mumble, his words turning me on even more. His mouth goes back to my clit, and his fingers continue to work me over. "I'm going to come." His name is a whisper on my lips as I fall apart, my body shuddering and my legs holding him hostage. His mouth and fingers continue their assault until I can't take anymore and I gently push his head away.

He makes his way up my body, and it feels like he kisses every inch of my skin before his lips reach mine. I push gently on his shoulder and roll him onto his back. Feeling brave, I wink at him as I lean over his body and search blindly in the nightstand drawer for a condom. Grabbing one, I sit back on my heels, my fingers going to the waistband of his sleep shorts.

"These need to go," I whisper, pulling his shorts down. He lifts his hips, and I tug them down his legs, tossing them onto the floor. His eyes are fixed on mine, and I smile shyly as I take his erection in my hand, pumping his length a few times before circling my thumb around the head. A groan escapes his lips as his eyes roll back in his head. Releasing him, I quickly open the condom and effortlessly slide it down his length. His heated eyes watch me the whole time, and I bite down on my bottom lip, suddenly feeling nervous. I want to take control, but it's been so long I hope I can make it feel good for him.

"If this doesn't feel good, we can try something else," I mutter as I straddle his hips. His hands go to my waist, and he moans as I grind over his cock.

"It feels incredible already, baby." His voice is breathless, and I can feel how turned on he is. It still amazes me I can make him feel like this.

I lean forward and kiss him, and he kisses me back like I'm the gravity that holds him to the earth. Feeling how much he wants me is a massive turn-on, and heat pools in my stomach as I kiss him, despite the mind-blowing orgasm he's just given me. Pulling out of the kiss, I lift my body slightly and sink down onto his length, gasping as he fills me.

"Do you realize how fucking sexy you look, Paisley?" His hands reach up, and he flicks and rolls my nipples between his fingers. I moan, dropping my head back and pushing my chest further into his hands. Suddenly, Nash sits up and moves us both backwards so he's sitting against the headboard. His mouth drops to my nipple, and his tongue circles my erect bud.

"Fuck," I moan as I move against him, loving how full of him I feel in this position. His fingers dig gently into my waist as he lifts my hips, increasing my movements. His mouth finds mine, and I lose myself in his kisses as we move against each other.

When Nash's thrusts increase, I know he must be close, and I'm right there with him. He pulls out of the kiss and I drop my forehead on his. His hand reaches between us and he strokes my clit with his thumb, sending me spiraling into an earth-shattering orgasm. I gasp and my body trembles in his arms as I drop my head into the crook of his neck. He lets out a cry as he comes, his breathing erratic as he increases his hold on me.

"I didn't think it could get any better," he mumbles after we've both caught our breath.

"I love you," I say against the hollow of his neck.

He sits me up and his eyes find mine. "I love you too, Paisley."

Before I can say anything, Max barks from the other side of the bedroom door, and I giggle. "I think we're wanted."

I gently climb off Nash and pull on his t-shirt as he crosses the room to the bathroom to get rid of the condom. I open the door to Max, and he goes crazy when he sees me, jumping up my bare legs. I've only stayed over a few times, and I guess he's not used to seeing me here all the time.

"Hey, boy," I say, dropping to my knees to pet him. "Do you want some breakfast?" He barks in response, and I laugh as I stand up.

"I'm just going to feed Max, babe," I shout to Nash, who is still in the bathroom.

"Okay," he shouts back. "I'll be down in a minute."

Making my way downstairs, Max races on ahead of me and he's waiting by the back door when I reach the kitchen. Opening the door, I watch as he rushes into the backyard. After putting down some food for him, I flick on the coffee machine just as Nash comes into the kitchen.

"Pancakes?" I ask him as I open the refrigerator and reach inside for the milk.

"I'll make them," he says, taking the milk from my hand. "You sit down."

"I don't mind," I assure him.

"I know." He drops a kiss on my nose. "I want to make you breakfast."

"Okay. Thank you." I sit at the breakfast bar and watch him as he busies himself making the pancake batter. It still surprises me that Nash wants to do things like making me breakfast. I've never had that, and I guess it will take some getting used to.

As Nash starts cooking the pancakes, my mind drifts back to last night when he asked me to move in with him. Nerves swirl in my stomach as I replay the conversation in my head. It was the last thing I expected him to say, and despite being head over heels in love with him, moving in together is a huge step. My head and heart are conflicted. My heart says yes, but my head is more reserved, and the fear of giving up my independence holds me back from saying yes. I know Nash is *nothing* like Connor, but I can't stop the niggling doubt that bubbles inside me when I think of moving in with him. If things don't work out, then everything around me will come crashing down again, and I'm not sure I'll survive that a second time.

* * *

WE'VE JUST FINISHED breakfast when the doorbell sounds.

"I'll go," Nash says, standing and heading out of the kitchen.

I hope it's not a visitor. I'm only wearing panties and one of Nash's t-shirts. I can hear voices, but I can't make out what's being said. A few minutes later, Nash walks back into the kitchen, holding a package.

"It's for you," he says with a frown, passing me the box.

"For me?" I ask in surprise. "Maybe it's something from Taylor." I look at the label, but it's typed and not handwritten. It has to be her, though. The only other person who knows this address is Connor. An uneasy feeling settles in my stomach as I pull off the packaging. Taking a deep breath, I open the box.

"Oh my God!" I cry, pushing the box holding a dead bird away from me. My shaking hand comes over my mouth, and within a second, Nash is by my side.

"What is it?" he asks, reaching for the box.

I turn away as he looks inside. "Holy fuck!" He lifts me into his arms and carries me upstairs. When we reach his bedroom, he lies down with me on his chest.

"Why would Connor send me that?" I ask quietly.

"I don't know, baby. He's a sick bastard."

"I'm happy he's locked up," I whisper. "I hope he never gets out."

He increases his hold on me and drops a kiss on my head. "Are you okay?"

I nod. "I'm glad you're here."

"There's nowhere else I want to be, Paisley." We're both silent as we hold each other. After a few minutes, he sits up. "I'll go and get rid of it."

"Thank you."

He kisses me softly before climbing off the bed and heading downstairs. I close my eyes, an image of the dead bird engrained in my mind. I knew giving over Nash's address for the divorce papers was dangerous. A huge part of me was worried he would show up, but naively, I thought if he wanted to end the marriage, he was ready to move on and let me go. The mail delivery today tells me otherwise.

When we've both showered, Nash walks me to work. He wants me to call in sick, but I can keep busy at work and not think about it. He stays for a drink when we arrive and takes a seat in one of the booths. The bar's fairly quiet with only a couple of the tables occupied. I take a food order and disappear into the kitchen, handing the order over to the chef. Just as I'm leaving the kitchen, my phone vibrates in my back pocket and I pull it out, frowning when I see a Pittsburgh number flashing on the screen. After what happened this morning, fear grips my heart thinking Connor has somehow gotten my number. I want to ignore it, but I know if it is Connor, he'll only keep calling. Taking a deep breath, I answer the call.

"Hello,"

"Hello, is that Paisley Prescott?" I breathe a sigh of relief when I hear it isn't Connor.

"Yes, speaking."

"Hi, Paisley. My name is Detective Everest, and I'm calling from the Pittsburgh Police Department."

I stop walking and lean heavily against the wall. "Is it my parents?" I ask, my voice breaking.

"Erm… no. I'm sure your parents are fine. I'm calling about your husband, Connor Prescott."

The fear's back, and it swirls in my stomach, making me feel like I'm going to throw up. "What about him? We've split up. I haven't seen him in months."

"He's been arrested—"

"Yes. I know. My friend told me. I'm not sure what it has to do with me."

"Do you know why he was arrested?"

"Yes."

"Paisley, a report was filed a few weeks ago detailing injuries you sustained at the hands of Connor Prescott." He pauses, and I hear some papers rustling. "A broken wrist and cracked ribs sustained on April twentieth. It states you were treated at Hope Creek Hospital where you suffered a miscarriage as a result of the attack. Is that right?"

I can hear what he's saying, but I can't process the words. Has he somehow gained access to my medical records, or did someone from the hospital file a report? I remember how insistent the doctor had been the morning I was waiting to be discharged. Maybe it was him. I'm so confused, and a million questions swarm in my mind, but I can't pull myself together enough to ask them.

"Paisley, are you still there?" Detective Everest asks.

"Ye-yes. I'm still here."

"The report also states that this incident wasn't the first time Connor had assaulted you. Is that right?"

"Yes," I whisper, tears filing my eyes.

"Paisley," he says gently. "We're going to charge Connor with the attack on you. If he pleads not guilty, we'll need you to testify at the trial."

My eyes widen and panic swirls in my stomach. "What? No! I can't do that. I don't want him charged."

"I'm sorry if I've upset you, Paisley. This was really just a courtesy call to let you know about the charges. I'm sure this has come as a shock, and I can appreciate how hard this is for you, but men like Connor Prescott need to be locked up."

"I don't want to see him ever again. Who filed the report?"

"Let me check." I can hear more papers rustling, and he must be looking for a name. "It was a… Nash Brookes."

"What?" I gasp. "That can't be right. When?"

"About four weeks ago."

"I have to go," I whisper, pulling the phone from my ear and ending the call. Sliding down the wall, I sit on the floor as my mind works overtime.

He must have it wrong. There's no way Nash would do that to me, not when he knows I didn't want the police involved.

"Paisley, what's wrong?" Nash asks as he rounds the corner and sees me sitting on the floor. "I was trying to find you to check you were okay before I left." He drops to his knees in front of me and reaches for my hand.

I eye him warily and stand up, pulling my hand from his.

"Did you file a report on Connor after I opened up to you a few weeks ago?"

The color drains from his face and he's answered my question without uttering a word. Tears sting my eyes and my hand comes up to cover my mouth. "How could you do that?" I ask from behind my fingers.

"Paisley." He reaches for me, but I take a step back.

"Don't. Don't touch me." My voice breaks as the tears that were threatening to fall streak down my cheeks. "I trusted you," I whisper through my tears. "I told you all of that in confidence."

"Paisley, please. Let me explain." I can hear the devastation in his voice, but the sound of my own heart breaking drowns him out.

I shake my head. "No. What is there to say? You knew how hard it was for me to open myself up to someone after what Connor did, and you threw it in my face. I have to go."

I push past him and run into the bar. "Go where?" he shouts, following me.

"Away from you," I bite back.

"Paisley, what's wrong?" Seb asks, his face clouded with concern as he sees the tears running down my face.

"Ask Nash. I'm sorry, Seb, but I can't work my shift. I need to go." I untie the apron I'm wearing and push it into his hands. "I'm sorry," I say again as I run across the bar.

"What the hell is going on?" I hear Seb ask Nash as I run out onto the sidewalk. I don't wait to hear the reply or look back. I just want to get as far away from everyone as possible. My heart feels like it's breaking in two. Have I put my trust in the wrong person again? How could he go behind my back and do that? He knew I didn't want the police involved, and now his report means I'm going to have to face Connor in court, dragging up everything I've just put behind me. Despite that, the pain I'm feeling now from Nash's betrayal hurts more than any broken arm or cracked rib ever did, only this time, it's my heart that's shattered and not my body.

CHAPTER THIRTY-TWO

Nash

"*D*id you file a report on Connor after I opened up to you a few weeks ago?"

My eyes widen and my heart pounds in my chest. My silence must give her my answer and her hand comes up to cover her mouth.

"How could you do that?" she asks from behind her shaking hand.

"Paisley." I reach for her, but she takes a step back and my arm falls to my side.

"Don't. Don't touch me." Her voice cracks and my heart breaks as tears fall down her cheeks. "I trusted you," she whispers. "I told you all of that in confidence."

"Paisley, please. Let me explain."

She shakes her head. "No. What is there to say? You

knew how hard it was for me to open myself up to someone after what Connor did, and you threw it in my face. I have to go."

She pushes past me and out of view. "Go where?" I shout, running after her.

"Away from you."

"Paisley, what's wrong?" Seb asks, his eyes going from Paisley to me.

"Ask Nash. I'm sorry, Seb, but I can't work my shift. I need to go." She pulls off the apron she's wearing and gives it to Seb. Before I can stop her, she's run out of the bar and is on the sidewalk.

"What the hell is going on?" Seb asks me. Ignoring him, I start to follow Paisley. "Nash, stop!" His hand goes around my arm, stopping me in my tracks.

"Let me go, Seb."

"Look, I don't know what's going on with you, but she looked devastated. Just give her a minute."

"No!" I shout, pushing him off me. "I need to go after her. I need to make her understand."

"Understand what?" he asks, following me across the bar and out onto the sidewalk. "What have you done?"

I sigh and drop my head into my hands. "I filed a police report on her ex and what he'd done to her. I didn't tell her, and now he's been arrested. I'm guessing the arresting officer has seen my report and called her about it."

"Fuck, Nash. Come back in and give her some time to cool down."

"No. I have to go to her now. I can't lose her, Seb. What if she runs from me like she did her ex?"

"She loves you, Nash. Anyone can see that. She's not going to run from you."

I shake my head. "I can't take that risk. I have to go after her."

"Okay. I can't stop you. You know her better than I do. Good luck." He pulls me into a hug, and I slap his back before pulling out of the embrace. Leaving him on the sidewalk, I run in the direction of Sophie's place. I've no idea if that's where she's gone, but I've got to start somewhere.

I'm breathing hard by the time I race up the porch steps at Sophie house, and I bend over as I catch my breath. When I stand up, I knock on the door, nervously moving from foot to foot. The door opens, and before I can say anything, Sophie beats me to it.

"She doesn't want to see you, Nash."

"Please, Sophie. I have to explain."

"I'm sorry, but I can't let you in."

"Sophie, please." I don't care that I'm begging. I'd get down on my knees if I thought it would help. I go to push past her, desperate to get to Paisley, but she puts her hand on my chest.

"Nash! No! Don't make me call the cops."

"I am the fucking cops!"

She pushes me out of the doorway and steps out onto the porch, closing the door behind her. There's a coded lock on the door, and there's no way I can get in with the door closed.

"Please, Nash. Take a breath. This is a women's shelter. You can't just show up, demanding to come in. If Paisley doesn't want to see you, then her feelings come first." She puts her hand on my arm and my eyes meet hers. "Just give her some time," she says softly.

I drop down heavily on the porch swing next to the front door and drop my head in my hands. "Have I lost her?" I whisper.

Sophie kneels down in front of me and waits until I look up. "I haven't spoken to her for long. We were talking, but then you showed up. She's hurt, Nash. Really hurt, but she loves you."

"I never meant to hurt her. I wanted her ex to pay for what he did. Knowing how badly he hurt her, I just couldn't do nothing about that."

"I get it. You're a cop. You're going to want to protect the people you love. I think she'll realize that when she's had a chance to think it through."

"God, I hope so. You should go back inside. I don't want her to be on her own if she's upset."

"You'll be okay?"

I shrug. "I don't care about me. I just want Paisley to be okay."

She gives me a small smile before heading inside and closing the door. I sit for a few more minutes, desperately hoping Paisley will come out to me, but knowing deep down she won't. Eventually, I stand up and leave, looking over my shoulder and up to the window of her bedroom. There are blinds at the window, but they're closed, so there's no way I can see inside. Sighing, I walk home slowly, feeling like I've lost the best thing to ever happen to me. I have to make this right. Anything else just isn't an option.

Paisley

MY BEDROOM WINDOW IS OPEN, and I can hear every word of Sophie and Nash's conversation. Despite feeling like the bottom has just dropped out of my world, I still love him. I can't just switch off my feelings, and I listen eagerly to what he has to say. He sounds devastated, and I know his intentions were good. I just can't get past the complete and utter betrayal I feel. I've never opened up to *anyone* about what Connor did to me, not even Taylor. He's the first person I've ever told, and to know he then documented everything I said in a police report makes me feel like he was only listening so he could get as much information as possible. I fought with myself for so long over my feelings for him. I was terrified to give myself to him, and to make myself vulnerable again. I let my guard down, truly believing Nash would never hurt me, but here I am, crying over a guy again.

When the conversation falls silent, I climb off my bed and go to the window. The blinds are closed, but I open them slightly, allowing me to see out but knowing no one can see me. Nash is walking slowly away from the house when, suddenly, he turns and looks up at my window. Even though I know he can't see me, I take a small step back. His face is clouded with worry and my heart squeezes in my chest. I know he loves me, but what if that isn't enough?

"He's gone," Sophie says from the doorway. "Are you okay?"

I turn from the window and wipe my tearstained face. "No. Not really." I bite down on my bottom lip. "Am I over-reacting?"

She walks in and sits on the edge of my bed. "Whatever your feelings are, Paisley, they're valid. No one can say if you're overreacting. Your feelings are your feelings."

"He looked upset."

"He was. He loves you."

"I love him too." Fresh tears track down my cheeks, and

she stands and pulls me into her arms. "He promised he'd never hurt me," I say, wetting her tank with my tears.

"No one can promise that, Paisley. We're all human and we all make mistakes. You just have to decide if Nash's mistake is something you can forgive." She pauses and lets out a sigh. "Sometimes we hurt the people we love because we think we're doing the best for them. Some mistakes are made out of love, even if it doesn't seem that way to the other person."

I step out of her embrace, my eyes searching her tear-filled ones. "It sounds like you're speaking from experience," I say softly.

"I guess I am."

"Cade?" She nods. "I'm sorry."

"Me too." She takes a shaky breath and gives me a small smile. "Enough about me. What are you going to do?"

"I don't know. I wish I did."

"Take your time to think it through. Maybe you should sit down with Nash and hear him out."

"Yeah, maybe. I should message Seb and check I still have a job."

"I'm sure your job is safe."

"I hope so. I can't afford to lose that."

There's a knock on the front door, and I go to the window, seeing Nash on the porch with Max.

"I'll go and see who that is."

"It's Nash again," I tell her. "He's got Max with him."

She leaves my room, and I hear the front door open.

"I brought Max round for Paisley. I know how much she loves him, and I can't bear to think of her upset and alone. He can stay as long as she needs him."

"I'll take him up. I'm sure she'll love to have him here."

"Will you tell her I love her?" he says, and my heart breaks as I hear the pain in his voice.

"I'll tell her," Sophie promises him. "Bye, Nash."

The front door closes, and I hear Sophie and Max making their way upstairs. My door is open, and I drop to my knees as Max rushes toward me. Fresh tears track down my cheeks, and I bury my face in his soft coat.

"I guess you heard what he said?" I nod. "I'll give you some space. You know where I am if you need me," Sophie says softly before she closes the door behind me.

When I finally lift my head from Max, I frown as I notice a rolled-up piece of paper attached to his collar.

"What's this, boy?" I ask, slipping the paper from its hiding place. Climbing on the bed, Max settles next to me, his body pressed against my side. Opening the paper, I read the words Nash has written.

Paisley,

I am so sorry, baby. I know you're mad at me and don't want to talk, but I couldn't bear it knowing you're alone and upset. I've sent Max to keep you company. I hope he's as good a listener as he was the last time you were upset. It breaks my heart to know I'm the reason for your tears. I never meant to hurt you. I thought I was protecting you. I know I've broken your trust. I will do ANYTHING to gain that trust back again, starting with giving you some space. Whenever you're ready to talk (and I pray that happens), I'll be waiting.
I love you so much, Paisley.
Nx

My heart hurts as I read his words over and over again, and I'm torn. Part of me wants to run to him, but a larger part is guarding my heart. I can't help but wonder if I can allow myself to be with a man who has the power to crush me. I worried before about falling in love and making myself that vulnerable again, but I'd convinced myself Nash's love could never make me feel like that. Only I *do* feel that way. Maybe that was the nature of love, and when emotions are involved, nothing is guaranteed. Love is a risk, but am I willing to take that risk again? I wish I had the answer.

CHAPTER THIRTY-THREE

Nash

It's been five days since I've seen Paisley. It feels like five years, and I've picked up my phone countless times to text or call her. I promised to give her space in the note I sent, though, and I'm trying to keep that promise. I've kept in touch with Sophie, who assures me Paisley is okay, but I'm worried about her. With the dead bird in the mail, finding out about Connor's arrest, and then what I've done, it's enough to push anyone over the edge. I know from Seb she hasn't been back to work yet. I'm guessing she's worried she'll bump into me. I've stayed away from Eden on purpose. I don't want to make things difficult for her, but I can't deny I'm desperate to see her.

I park on the driveway at home after finishing work and

drag my tired body from the truck. I'm not sleeping, and I'm exhausted. The house feels so empty without Paisley and Max, and I almost don't want to go inside. When I open the front door, I'm surprised to be greeted by an excited Max. Hope erupts in my chest, and I wonder if Paisley is here too.

"Paisley?" I shout as I rush through the entryway and into the kitchen. "Paisley?" I'm met with silence, and a wave of sadness washes over me as I realize she isn't here. She must have just brought Max back. He follows me into the kitchen, and I drop to my knees next to him, burying my head in his fur. As ridiculous as it sounds, he smells of Paisley, and I hold him against me, knowing he's as close to her as I can get at the moment. Despite saying I'd give her some space, the need to know she's okay wins out, and I reach for my phone to send her a message.

Me: Thanks for bringing Max back. Nx

I stare at the screen, praying for a reply. When nothing comes, I sigh and climb the stairs to my bedroom, flopping down on the bed. Tears sting my eyes, and I rub my hands across the crushing pain in my chest. I never knew heartbreak was a physical pain, but it actually feels like someone is crushing my heart with their bare hands. I miss Paisley so much. I wish I knew what to do to make everything right.

After a quick shower, I head to my parents' place. Thursday roast has been moved to Saturday this week, and as much as I want to stay and wallow in my own self-pity, I know my mom won't let me. I'd spoken to her earlier in the week, telling her how I'd messed up with Paisley. She listened, never once judging. She knows better than anyone how hard it is for

Paisley to trust someone, but even knowing that, she didn't call me out on what I'd done. I think she knows it came from a place of love, however misguided.

I'm almost surprised when I park in my parents' driveway, having no recollection of the journey at all. My mind is consumed with thoughts of Paisley, and it's a good thing the roads to my parents' place are quiet. As I climb out of the truck, it looks like Seb, Ashlyn, and Cade are already inside, their cars and Seb's motorcycle parked in a line.

"Hey, Nash," Ashlyn says as I walk into the kitchen. She crosses the space and pulls me in for a hug. "How you doing?" she asks as I hug her back fiercely.

"I've been better."

"Have you spoken to her?"

I pull out of her embrace and shake my head. "No. I'm trying to give her some space."

"She looks like you. Like she hasn't slept in days."

"You've seen her?"

"Yeah. Yesterday."

"How was she?" I ask, desperate for any bit of news on her, however small.

"She's a mess, Nash."

"Fuck," I mutter, dragging my hand down my face.

"She misses you."

My eyes widen and hope erupts in my chest. "She does?"

"Of course she does. She loves you, you idiot. You need to fight for her."

"I agree," Seb says as he walks into the kitchen and pulls me into a one-armed guy hug.

"She won't see me. I texted her earlier and she didn't reply."

"She's working tonight, and it's busy. If she's got her phone with her, she probably hasn't had time to check it."

"I guess that explains why she brought Max back. Have you seen her?"

He nods. "Yeah, she stopped by Eden yesterday to apologize for missing her shifts."

"Did she say anything about me?" I know I sound like a pussy, but I'm floundering. I have no idea how to make things right.

"No, but then she's not going to talk to me about you. You need to make things right, Nash. She looked like…" He trails off and sighs.

"She looked like what?" I ask when he doesn't finish his sentence.

"Like she'd been crying for days," he says reluctantly. "I'm sorry, man. I'm not saying that to try and make you feel bad. Maybe she's had enough space and now she needs to know how much you love her."

My heart squeezes in my chest hearing she's being crying. Have I waited too long? Should I have gone to her earlier? I thought giving her time was what she wanted. Does she think she's not worth fighting for? I drop down heavily onto the stool at the breakfast bar stool and hold my head in my hands.

"I have no idea what I'm doing," I admit. "I've fucked everything up."

"No, Nash. You haven't," my mom says, who up until now has stayed silent. "You made a mistake. Everyone makes mistakes. You need to talk to her. Explain why you did what you did, and when she's heard you out, she has to decide if together you can move on from it."

"And if she decides we can't?"

She sighs. "Then you let her walk away."

I close my eyes and bite the inside of my cheek to stop myself from falling apart in my parents' kitchen. I can't comprehend her walking away. She *has* to know how much I love her and how sorry I am. I have to make her see. I can't lose her. I just can't.

Paisley

EDEN IS PACKED, and despite being exhausted, I'm glad to be busy. It stops my mind going to Nash and what he's doing. He's all I can think about. He consumes my every waking moment, and when I do manage to sleep, my dreams are full of him too. I'm still upset about him filing the report behind my back, but I miss him so much it hurts. He's become my everything these past few weeks, and as scared as I am to admit it, I feel lost without him. I might not have wanted to become so emotionally dependent on someone after everything that happened with Connor, but spending time away from him has made me realize I've done exactly that.

"Table four, Paisley," Ryder says, pulling me from my thoughts. Looking up he gestures to the tray he's slid in front of me. "Are you sure you're okay? You're a million miles away," he says, his voice laced with concern.

"I'm okay, Ryder. Thanks." It's about the third time in an hour he's asked me if I'm okay. I'm clearly not putting on much of a brave face.

I pick up the tray and fight my way through the crowds, handing out the drinks to a rowdy table of guys.

"Are you on the menu, sweetheart?" one of the guys asks as I load the tray up with empty glasses. The rest of his friends hoot and holler, and I roll my eyes. The guy reaches out his hand and swats my ass before I can stop him.

"Don't!" I warn, and the whole table erupts into laughter. Ignoring them, I make my way back to the bar. When I get there, Ryder frowns at me.

"I saw that. Do you want me to get them to leave? Seb would have them out on their asses if he were here."

"I'd have who out on their assess?" Seb asks, appearing behind me.

"There's a table of assholes hitting on Paisley. I was just asking her if she wanted me to ask them to leave."

"It's fine, Seb. I can handle them," I assure him. "I don't want to cause any trouble."

"What are they doing?"

"One of them smacked my ass, that's all."

"I'll have a word with them. I'm not having them touching you."

I put my hand on his arm. "Seb, it's fine."

"It's not. Nash would kill me if he knew."

I drop my eyes from his, and my fingers play with the edge of my apron.

"Shit," he mutters. "I'm sorry, Paisley. I didn't mean to bring him up."

"It's okay," I say quietly. Looking up, I meet his gaze. "Was he at dinner?"

"Yeah."

"How is he?" I ask, biting down on my bottom lip.

"Honestly?" I nod. "He looks like shit, Paisley. He misses you."

"I miss him too," I whisper.

I'm surprised when Seb reaches for me and pulls me into his arms. When he releases me, he smiles sheepishly. "You looked like you could do with a hug."

"Thank you," I tell him, going up on my tiptoes to brush a kiss on his cheek. "I should get back to work. Leave those guys. I can handle them."

"I'll be taking their next round of drinks. Let's see if they want to smack my ass!"

I laugh as I unload the tray of empty glasses on the bar.

"Why don't you take your break now that I'm back? Ryder and I can manage."

"Okay. Thanks. I'll be in the back, then."

Leaving the noise of the bar behind me, I head for the staff room, turning on the coffee machine before flopping down on the worn leather sofa. I've got another couple of hours left, and if I'm going to make it through without falling asleep, I'm going to need a large cup of coffee. Pulling my phone from my back pocket, my heart stutters as I see a message from Nash. In the letter he sent with Max, he said he was giving me some space, and he's kept to his word. This is the first time I've heard from him. That hasn't stopped me checking my phone every five minutes over the past few days though, hoping for a message from him.

I'm so confused about my feelings. I know I'm pushing him away, but a huge part of me wants him to push back. It makes no sense, but I'm beginning to realize love *doesn't* make any sense. Taking a deep breath, I open his message, seeing he sent it hours ago.

Nash: Thanks for bringing Max back. Nx

It's late and I don't know if I should reply or not. I don't want to wake him up. My need to hear from him wins over though, and I type out a reply.

Me: That's okay. I thought you might be missing him.

I leave my phone on the sofa and stand up, crossing the small room to pour myself a cup of coffee. Just as I'm adding the milk, my phone chirps with an incoming message, and nerves swirl in my stomach. Making my way back to the sofa, I put my coffee on the small side table and pick up my phone.

Nash: I was, but not as much as I'm missing you. Nx

Tears fill my eyes as I read his message. I miss him too, more than I ever thought possible. An overwhelming need to see him washes over me, and I have to speak to him. I have to see if we can get past this. I need to hear his reasons for doing what he did and see if I can open myself up to him again. Despite only being together a short time, I feel more devastated at the thought of losing him than I did at my five-year marriage ending.

Me: I miss you too. Are you working tomorrow?

I don't have to wait long for a reply.

Nash: Yes, until six. Nx

Me: Can we talk when you've finished work? I could come to your place?

Nash: Yes! Shall I pick you up? Nx

Me: Okay. Night, Nash.

Nash: Night, baby. Nx

The tears that were threatening to fall streak down my cheeks when I read his last message, and I push my phone back in my pocket as I wipe my eyes and try to pull myself together before my break ends.

Thankfully, the last couple of hours go by quickly, and I put the last of the empty glasses on the bar.

"Get yourself home, Paisley. I'll see you next week, if not before," Seb says as he loads the glasses into the dishwasher.

"Night, guys," I call over my shoulder as I head for the door.

I step out onto the sidewalk and gasp as I see Nash sitting on the bench directly opposite the entrance. He stands when he sees me and holds his hands up.

"I just want to make sure you get home okay. We don't have to talk. We don't even have to walk together. I'll walk behind you." His words tumble out in a rush, and I stare at him. He looks how I feel. Exhausted. He's clearly not sleeping either.

"You should be in bed if you're working tomorrow," I tell him.

He shrugs. "I wouldn't be able to sleep knowing you'd be walking home alone."

"How did you know I was working?" I ask, knowing it was probably Seb who told him.

"Seb mentioned it at dinner."

I nod. "Thank you." He gives me a sad smile, and my heart twists as I see how dejected he looks. Sighing deeply, I turn and walk in the direction of Sophie's place. It feels weird for him to be walking behind me, and I stop and wait for him to catch up. "We can walk together," I tell him quietly, and he nods.

It's only a five-minute walk to Sophie's place, but an

awkward tension hangs in the air as we walk side by side. I don't want to walk in silence, but I don't know what to say. I don't want to talk about what happened, I'm too exhausted, but making small talk doesn't seem right either.

"Thank you for letting me keep Max for a few days," I say when the silence gets too much.

"That's okay. I know how much you love him."

He sounds nervous, and I've never seen him like this. He's always been so confident and sure of himself.

"How have you been?" he asks, and I turn my head to look at him, my eyebrows raised in surprise. "Sorry, that was a stupid question. I'm guessing shit."

"Yeah, you could say that. You?"

"Same."

Silence descends again, and I almost breathe a sigh of relief as the house comes into view. I hope tomorrow's conversation won't be as awkward, and that it's just because we're both trying our best not to mention why things are so strained. When I reach the end of the driveway, I stop.

"Thank you for coming and walking me home, Nash."

"It's okay."

"I'll see you tomorrow?"

He nods. "Night, Paisley."

"Night, Nash."

I turn and walk up the driveway, looking over my shoulder to see him watching me as I climb the porch steps. I key in the numbers to the coded lock, silently pushing open the door. He's still standing at the bottom of the driveway, watching me. Raising my hand in a small wave, I slowly close the door and drop to a heap on the floor as big, ugly tears track down my cheeks. I so desperately want to get back to how we were before this, but the fear that kept me away from him when I first came to Hope Creek is back, and I don't know if I have the strength to fight that fear again.

CHAPTER THIRTY-FOUR

Paisley

It had taken me longer than normal to fall asleep last night after seeing Nash. He consumed my thoughts, and when I did finally fall asleep, he played a starring role in my dreams too.

When I wake the following morning, it's almost midday. Climbing out of bed, I wince as I catch sight of my reflection in the free-standing mirror. I look awful. My eyes are red and bloodshot from where I cried myself to sleep last night, and the dark circles under my eyes tell everyone I'm not sleeping. My hair looks like a bird's nest, and I'm guessing I must have tossed and turned all night to have it looking like it does.

Padding across the room, I go into the bathroom and turn the shower on. I use the toilet and brush my teeth as the water warms up. When steam fills the bathroom, I climb into the tub, taking my time washing my hair and body. The hot water has a soothing effect on my tired and aching body, and I dry off, feeling a little more human. I've just braided my wet hair and pulled a tank and some shorts on when a knock sounds on my door.

"Come in," I call out.

"Hey, Paisley. Do you feel like having lunch at Eden? It's too hot to cook."

"Sure. I could do with getting out of the house." I need something to take my mind off meeting up with Nash later, and lunch with Sophie sounds like the ideal distraction. "Do I need to get changed?" I ask, seeing she's wearing a pale blue sundress.

"No," she says, her eyes sweeping over me. "You look great."

I grab my purse and phone and follow her downstairs and out of the house.

"Nash is picking me up after he's finished work. I'm going to his place so we can talk," I say quietly as we walk toward town.

"That's great, Paisley. I hope you can work things out."

"Me too. I miss him so much."

"How are things with you and Cade?"

She looks across at me in surprise. "What do you mean?"

I smile sheepishly. "Nash and I saw you kissing that night a few weeks ago in Eden." Her cheeks flush pink. "Have you talked to him about it?"

She sighs. "He won't return my calls. Nash gave me his number a couple of weeks ago, but… nothing."

"What happened with you two? Nash said you were inseparable when Cade was in medical school."

She goes to say something but stops herself. "I can't talk

about it, I'm sorry. I'm scared you'll hate me if I do, and having Cade hate me is bad enough. I can't deal with you and the whole Brookes family not speaking to me."

I frown at her and reach for her hand, pulling her to a stop on the sidewalk. "I could never hate you, Sophie, and I can't believe you would ever do something bad enough to make Cade hate you either. It definitely didn't look like he hated you when he had you pushed up against the wall in Eden."

"There's a fine line between love and hate, Paisley. I'm more convinced than ever that the night in Eden was a massive mistake on Cade's part. He might have loved me once, but I know for sure he hates me now."

"You still love him?" She nods as a single tear tracks down her cheek. She takes a deep breath and wipes it away before I've got a chance to react to it.

"I'd do anything to change what I did, but I can't." She starts walking again, looking over her shoulder at me. "Come on. I'm starving."

I take her abrupt change of topic to mean that the conversation is over. I hope she knows I'm here for her if she does ever what to talk about it.

Walking into Eden, Seb raises his hand in a wave, and we both head to the bar.

"Afternoon, ladies. What can I get you?" he asks, smiling at us.

"White wine, please, Seb," Sophie says.

"Same for me, please."

I look around the bar as I wait for Seb to make our drinks. It's quiet, but then Sunday lunchtimes usually are. There's only us in here. They've not been open long though, and Sunday evenings usually see a few more people coming in for a drink.

"First one's on me," Seb says, sliding the wineglasses across the bar to us.

"Thanks, Seb," we say in unison, and he laughs.

We pick up our drinks, then cross the bar and take a seat at one of the high tables. I pass a menu to Sophie, and we're both quiet as we look at what we want to order. Suddenly, a succession of three loud bangs sound out, and my head flies up from the menu.

"Was that gunshots?" I ask Sophie.

Before she can answer, Seb shouts. "Paisley! Sophie! Behind the bar, now! Ryder, tell the kitchen staff to stay in the back and lock the doors."

I grab Sophie's hand as I scramble off the chair, and we run toward the bar together. Seb passes us, going in the opposite direction, and I look over my shoulder to see him quickly close and lock the doors before making his way back. He flicks the lights off on the back wall and drops down on the floor with us. My heart's pounding, and my whole body shakes as we sit behind the bar, wondering what the hell is going on.

"I've called the cops," Ryder says quietly as he comes through from the kitchen and sits on the floor with us. Panic rolls through me knowing Nash is working today. When my phone rings in my back pocket, I let out a yelp, startled by the noise. Reaching for it, I rush to answer when I see Nash's name flashing up on the screen.

"Nash," I say as I answer.

"Paisley. I don't have long to talk. There are reports of a gunman in town. Stay at home and I'll call you when I can."

"I'm at Eden," I whisper, and the line goes quiet.

"Fuck!"

"I'm okay. Seb has us behind the bar. He's locked the doors."

"Stay out of sight, baby. I'll come for you when I know what's happening."

"Okay," I whisper. "Please be careful. I love you." Despite what's happened between us in the past few days, I do love him, and he needs to know that. Especially now.

"I love you too, Paisley. I have to go."

The line goes dead, and I drop my phone as my hand comes over my mouth to stifle a sob. Seb reaches for my hand.

"Nash is a great cop, Paisley. He'll be okay."

"God, I hope so," I whisper around my hand, tears falling down my cheeks.

Our argument seems so insignificant in this moment, and I know without a shadow of a doubt I want to be with him. I can't even comprehend something happening to him. I've been such a mess this past week. I don't want to live a life he's not part of.

It feels like we've been sitting huddled on the floor for hours, but checking the time on my phone, only minutes have passed since I spoke to Nash. I can hear sirens in the distance, and I wonder if it's him. Suddenly, the sound of something being tapped on the window fills the silent room.

"What's that?" Ryder whispers.

"I don't know," Seb mutters, going up on his knees to peer over the bar.

"Don't!" I whisper shout, pulling back on his arm.

"It might be the cops," he says.

"Nash would call. Please, Seb. Please don't go."

"Okay." He drops to the floor and entwines his fingers with mine.

A voice from the sidewalk breaks the silence, and I squeeze Seb's hand when I realize it's Nash.

"Drop the weapon and get on the floor! Drop the—"

Nash is cut off mid-sentence by a hail of gunfire and the terrifying sound of breaking glass. Seb's arms go around me and Sophie, and he holds us close. More gunshots sound out, and I reach for Sophie's hand, tears streaking down my face. I can feel Sophie shaking, and I'm sure I'm doing the same. Now that the window has been shot out, there's nothing between us and the gunman, and any second now, I'm expecting to come face-to-face with him.

"Paisley!" Nash shouts, and relief floods my body knowing he's okay.

"Nash!" Scrambling to my feet, I stand up, my wide eyes finding his worried ones over the bar.

"Oh, thank God," he says, and I run around the bar and into his arms. My hands cling to his shirt as he holds me against him. "You're shaking," he whispers against my hair.

"Are you hurt?" I ask, leaning back slightly so I can see his face. "I was so worried knowing you were out there."

"I'm fine. Better now that I know you're okay."

"What happened?"

I look past him, seeing someone lying on the sidewalk in a pool of blood.

"Don't look, baby."

"Is he dead?"

He nods. "I had no choice. When I saw him shoot into Eden, I knew you were inside. There was no way I was letting him get in here." He drops a kiss on my head and pulls me closer against him. "Is everyone else okay?"

Turning, I see Seb with his arm around Sophie, tears running down her face. Leaving Nash, I go to her. "It's okay. It's over," I tell her, pulling her into my arms. She holds on to me tightly, and I watch as Seb and Nash embrace.

"Do we know who the guy is?" Seb asks, and Nash shakes his head.

"No idea. I don't recognize him, and he's not carrying any ID."

"Just a fucking whack job, then!"

"More than likely."

By the time we leave Eden, the street is swarming with police and EMTs. A sheet has been placed over the body on the street, and with Nash's arm tightly around my shoulder, I try not to look as we walk past. The sheet doesn't cover all of the man though, and I stop dead in my tracks when my eyes are drawn to a clock and rose tattoo on his forearm.

"Paisley, what's wrong?" Nash asks as I move closer to the body.

"Can you lift the sheet?" I ask, my voice sounding calmer than I feel.

"What? Why?"

"Please, Nash. I need to see." His eyes hold mine for a second before he kneels down and pulls the sheet back, revealing what I already knew when I saw the tattoo. Gasping, I stumble backwards, Seb catching me before I hit the sidewalk.

"Paisley!" Nash shouts, coming over and taking me from Seb.

Noise rushes through my ears, and all I can hear is the pounding of my heart. I'm sure Nash is still speaking to me, but I've no idea what he's saying. His voice is muffled, and it sounds like he's underwater. My hands begin to tingle and my breathing becomes erratic as I feel someone take my hands in theirs. Their fingers rub circles over my skin, and eventually, I can hear again.

"Breathe, Paisley. Look at me." Somehow, the soothing

tone of Nash's voice pulls me from the edge of a panic attack, and as his fingers stroke my skin, I feel myself calming down.

"Is she okay?" I hear Sophie ask.

"I think so," Nash says, as my eyes finally find his. "Paisley, what happened?"

I look past him to the guy lying on the sidewalk. Someone has covered him back over with the sheet, and an officer stands over his body.

"The guy," I say, gesturing with my head. "It's my husband."

CHAPTER THIRTY-FIVE

Nash

"What?" I heard what she said, but my mind won't comprehend the words.

"I recognized the tattoo on his arm."

She bursts into tears, and I pull her into my arms. "Fuck!" I mutter into her hair. He must have made bail. A little heads-up would have been nice. I close my eyes as the reality of what's just happened hits me. I've just shot dead her husband.

"I need to get out of here," she says suddenly, pulling herself out of my arms. "Sophie, can we go home?"

"Of course." Sophie looks at me and I nod.

"Paisley, I have to finish up here, but I'll come over when I'm done."

"Okay." She won't look at me, and I can't help but wonder if I really have lost her now.

She walks away with Sophie, and all I can do is watch her go. When she rounds the corner and disappears from view, I sit down heavily on the sidewalk and drop my head in my hands.

"Nash, are you okay?" Seb asks as he sits down next to me.

I shake my head. "I'm not sure. I've just shot and killed my girlfriend's husband."

"You had no choice."

"Maybe."

"There's no maybe about it. Do you think he was coming for her?"

"Yeah, I think so. He sent her a dead bird in the mail last week." I look across at the body that's still lying on the sidewalk.

"That's fucked up."

"I should go and let the chief know who he was."

Standing up, Seb stands with me. "You saved her life, Nash. Hell, you saved all our lives." He pulls me into a hug, and I hug him back tightly. I know he's right, and I'd do it all over again if I had to. I just hope this doesn't cost me my relationship with Paisley. How is she going to want to be with me now, knowing I killed her husband? He might have been an asshole, but when the person you're in a relationship with shoots your ex-husband dead, that's messed up.

After hours of debriefs, I'm allowed to go home. There'll be an internal investigation into the incident, and I'll be off work until the outcome. It's standard procedure, and despite knowing it was Connor Prescott I shot, after discussing what happened countless times, I'm sure I did nothing wrong. He was heading into Eden with a loaded gun. Regardless of whether Paisley was in there or not, I'd have shot him anyway.

I decide to drive home and take a quick shower before

going to Paisley. It's been a hell of a day, and I want nothing more than to get out of my uniform. I've checked my phone a few times over the course of the day, but I've heard nothing from her. Our relationship was in trouble before all this happened, and I've no idea where we stand now.

When I walk in the entryway, I'm surprised not to be greeted by Max. Assuming he's asleep upstairs, I kick off my shoes and drag my tired body up to my bedroom. My heart squeezes in my chest as I push open the door and see Paisley curled up on my bed with Max, fast asleep. She's stripped out of her clothes and is wearing one of my t-shirts. Her face is red and puffy, and it breaks my heart to know she's been crying on her own. Despite that, she's still the most beautiful woman I've ever seen. I wish I could have gotten back here sooner. I hate that she's been here upset with only Max for company.

Not wanting to wake her, I pad silently to the bathroom and shower in record time. When I walk back into the bedroom, she's still asleep. I slip on my sleep shorts and stand awkwardly next to the bed. I really want to climb in beside her and wrap her in my arms, but I'm conscious we haven't talked things through yet. I don't want to assume anything, but the optimistic side of me hopes she wouldn't be here, asleep in my bed, if she didn't want to work things out. I pray to God I'm right.

"Nash," she whispers, her eyes fluttering open and meeting mine. Her face is soft with sleep and she's never looked more perfect.

"Hey," I say softly, sitting on the bed next to her. She reaches her hand out and tangles her fingers with mine.

"Are you okay?" she asks. "I've been worried about you."

My eyes widen in surprise. "Worried about me?"

She nods. "You shot a man, Nash. I don't know how you even begin to deal with that?"

I sigh and drop my head. "I shot your husband, Paisley. I'm more worried about you right now."

"You saved my life. You saved all our lives. He'd come looking for me, hadn't he?"

"I think so, sweetheart, but it's my fault. If I hadn't filed that stupid report, he wouldn't have come. I put you in danger."

She pulls her hand from mine and sits up before kneeling in front of me. "You don't know that. It was probably nothing to do with the police report. Giving over your address for the divorce papers told him exactly where I was. The dead bird was proof of that. He must have been watching me. It's a small town. It wouldn't take much to find me."

"Maybe. I can't believe he made bail."

"Is it wrong I'm glad he's dead?" Her voice is quiet and I look up, cupping her face with my free hand.

"No, Paisley. He hurt you so badly. It's not wrong." She nods, but I'm not sure she believes me. "I'm so sorry I filed that report without talking to you. There's really no excuse, but I want to try and explain if you'll let me."

"Okay," she whispers.

Nerves swirl in my stomach as she looks at me. This is it. I hope I don't fuck it up. Taking a deep breath, I entwine her fingers with mine.

"I felt so helpless after you opened up to me. As your boyfriend, I wanted to hurt him like he'd hurt you. I wanted nothing more than to make him suffer. Knowing what he did to you made me so angry, but the cop in me wanted to lock him up and throw away the key. I knew you didn't want to bring charges, but I thought if I filed a report and he was ever arrested for something similar, they'd know it wasn't the first time he'd done it. I never thought he'd be charged with your attack as well. I'm so sorry, baby," I rush out. "I know I betrayed your trust, and that's the last thing I wanted to do. I know how hard it was for you to trust me." She's silent when I finish talking, and I almost hold my breath as I wait for her to say something.

"I can't go back to being in a relationship where the other person makes my decisions for me. I can't be controlled like that again."

Fear creeps up my spine and a wave of nausea washes over me as I drop my eyes from hers.

"But I know you did what you did because you love me. If you'd talked to me about it, I might even have agreed with you." My eyes fly up to hers, and I reach for her when I see tears falling down her cheeks, my heart breaking to see her cry again. "I felt so guilty when I found out he'd hurt someone else. If I'd been brave enough to go to the police when it happened, I might have been able to stop that woman being attacked."

I hold her against me while she sobs. "None of this is your fault, Paisley. You did what you had to do to survive. I'll be forever grateful you chose to get on that flight to Phoenix. We were meant to meet that day. It was fate that you were sitting next to me."

She wipes her eyes and sits up. "I've missed you so much this past week, Nash. I might have been scared to open myself up to someone when we first met, but loving you was so easy. I'm not going to lie, I thought my heart was breaking when I found out about the police report. I didn't care that you'd filed the report. I just felt so betrayed that you'd done it behind my back, but sitting huddled behind that bar today, knowing you were out there while gunshots rang out put everything into perspective. I knew I wanted to try and sort things out when you showed up at work last night, and I wish now we'd just talked then. If anything had happened to you today and you didn't know how much I love you…" She trails off, her hand going over her mouth to stifle a sob.

"I know how much you love me, Paisley. I can see it every time you look at me."

"Are we going to be okay?" she asks, her voice unsure.

I nod. "We're going to be more than okay, Paisley. I can't wait to start a life with you. The life you've always deserved. I want it all with you, sweetheart. Marriage, babies, the works. You are everything to me, and I'm never going to make you doubt my love for you again."

Her hands cup my face and her eyes hold mine. "Everything you've ever done for me was out of love, Nash. It just took me a while to realize that. I've never had a guy have my back before, but I know you always will."

I take her in my arms and kiss her. I will always have her back, and I'll always be her biggest supporter. I truly believe we were meant to meet on that flight all those weeks ago. I didn't realize it at the time, but from the moment I helped her fix her seat belt, I was done for. She was always in my thoughts, and it wasn't long before she was in my heart too. I know without a shadow of a doubt we're exactly where we need to be, and I can't wait to see what our future holds.

EPILOGUE

Paisley
4 Months later

I lay out the last of the food on the breakfast bar and head outside to the backyard, where Nash has the grill on. Walking over to him, I go up on my tiptoes and brush a kiss on his cheek.

"Hey, roomie," he says, turning and wrapping me in his arms. I look up at him and smile widely. Four months after he asked me, I'm finally moving in with him. In reality, we've never spent a night apart since we worked things out, but this weekend, we're making it official. We've already moved over the small amount of things I had at Sophie's place, and to celebrate, Nash's family is coming over for a barbecue.

I'm looking forward to seeing everyone. I see Seb all the time, working at Eden, and I've become even closer to Ash in the last couple of months, but it's been a while since the whole Brookes family has been together in one place. Even Wyatt has managed to get a few hours off to join us. They've quickly become the family I've never had, and they've all welcomed me with open arms.

Nash had been cleared from any wrongdoing after he shot Connor outside Eden, and he's been back at work for a couple of months now. Initially, he'd been worried about how I'd feel, knowing he'd been the one to pull the trigger, but I was relieved it was over and Connor was finally out of my life. Our relationship is stronger than ever and I've never been happier.

"Hey, you," I whisper as he lowers his head and kisses me. My stomach dips, and I think I'm more in love with him now than I've ever been. Nash is my everything, and I know he feels the same way about me. He shows me how much I mean to him every day.

"Put her down!" Seb shouts from behind us.

"Leave them alone. They're in love," Ashlyn says.

Nash takes no notice and continues to kiss me. I smile against his lips and pull out of the kiss, dropping my head on his chest, embarrassed to be caught making out. He chuckles and holds me closely against him.

"Paisley's not at work now, Seb! I can kiss her whenever I want," he shouts back.

"You kiss her whenever you want when she *is* at work!" He laughs and I step out of Nash's embrace, my cheeks heated.

"It's not my fault I can't keep my hands off her."

"Okay. Who wants a drink?" I ask, wanting to change the subject seeing that it's not only Seb and Ashlyn that have arrived, but their parents, Sophie, Wyatt, and Cade too.

Chuckling, Nash swats my ass as I head into the kitchen, Ash and Tessa following me.

"Is there anything you need any help with, sweetheart?" Tessa asks as I reach in the refrigerator for a bottle of wine.

"No, it's all done, but thanks. I want everyone to relax and have a good time."

"We will, don't worry," Ash says with a grin as she takes the unopened bottle of wine from my hand and picks up a glass from the side.

Laughing, I grab some beers and follow her outside. When everyone has a drink, I sit on the outdoor sofa, chatting with Ash, Sophie, and Tessa. Nash keeps looking over, and he smiles whenever our eyes meet. I also see him checking his watch a couple of times and I can't help wondering why.

When Max starts to bark and rushes into the house, I realize there must be someone at the front door. I've no idea who when everyone is here. Nash notices too, and as I stand up to go and answer it, he waves for me to sit down.

"I'll get it, babe."

I nod and go back to chatting to Ash.

"Paisley, there's someone here to see you," he calls out a few minutes later.

I look up, and as he moves to one side, tears fill my eyes as I see Taylor standing behind him. My hand flies up to my mouth, and I run across the backyard to her, throwing my arms around her neck.

"Oh my God," I sob, holding on to her tightly. "What are you doing here?"

She laughs and squeezes me tightly. "Nash contacted me and arranged for me to come and surprise you. I've missed you so much, Paisley."

"I've missed you too."

Her voice breaks, and I can't hold her close enough.

After years of caring for her mom, she'd recently had to

say goodbye to her, and I know how hard it had been on her own back in Pittsburgh.

She pulls out of my embrace and her eyes track over me. "Love looks good on you, Paisley. You look so happy."

"I am happy. The happiest I've ever been." She smiles. "Come and meet everyone."

After a round of introductions, I slip away while Taylor and Ashlyn are talking. Nash is alone at the grill, and I wind my arms around his waist, pressing my chest to his back.

"Thank you. You're incredible, you know that?"

He turns around and tangles his hands with mine. "I know how much you miss her, and after everything you've both been through, you deserve to spend some time together."

"Did everyone know she was coming?"

He nods. "They were sworn to secrecy."

"Do you know how happy you make me?"

"I always want to make you happy, Paisley. You mean everything to me."

"I love you."

"I love you too."

Coming to Hope Creek was undoubtedly the best decision I ever made. Nash and the whole Brookes family have made me feel like I belong, something I struggled with for so long. I met them at the lowest point in my life, but they built me up, and I couldn't be happier. I can't wait to see what the future holds. I'm going to enjoy every second.

THE END

COMING SOON

Echoes of Love, book 2 in the Hope Creek Series.
Coming early 2022.

Is it a second chance at happily ever after—or merely an echo of the love they once had and lost?

Sophie Greene thought she was doing the right thing when she left Hope Creek at eighteen. She knew it would break Cade Brookes's heart...and her own. But at the time, she was certain she'd made the right choice. Now, back in the small town after her mom died, she's far from sure.

Cade's spent the last twelve years trying—and failing—to forget Sophie. And now that she's home, she wants a chance to explain why she ruined everything they had. Part of him wants to hear what she has to say. And part of him isn't sure he can ever let her into his heart. Not again, anyway.

But the truth can't stay hidden forever. And when Sophie's secrets are revealed, Cade will need to decide if the possibility of a future with Sophie is worth the risk—or if their love should remain firmly in the past forever…

ALSO BY LAURA FARR

SOCIAL MEDIA LINKS

Facebook Profile: https://www.facebook.com/laura.farr.547

Facebook Page: https://www.facebook.com/Laura-Farr-Author-191769224641474/

Facebook Reader Group: https://www.facebook.com/groups/1046607692516891

Instagram: https://www.instagram.com/laurafarr_author/

Twitter: @laurafarr4

ACKNOWLEDGMENTS

Thank you to my beta readers, Anne Dawson, Layla Rathbone, Tracey Jukes and Tracy Wood. I couldn't publish without you.

To James, Charlie and Isla, my biggest fans. Love you millions.

Printed in Great Britain
by Amazon

81567553R00181